Ma

MEMO

To: Matthias Barton
From: Kendall Scarborough
Re: My Resignation

Following up on our earlier conversation, I am hereby submitting my resignation. While I have enjoyed my five years as your personal assistant, I feel it is time for me to move on to an opportunity where my qualifications can be used to their fullest. I am sure you will find someone who can programme your BlackBerry, make your coffee and organise your office to your liking.

Please rest assured that my resignation is solely for professional purposes and has nothing to do with your engagement, your unengagement or any other personal matters. The timing is strictly coincidental.

Married to His Business

by Elizabeth Beverly

Six-Month Mistress
by Katherine Garbera

ᗝᎧᏞᏸᏄ

"I have a dress for you," he declared.

"I'd prefer to wear my own clothes," she told him.

"And I'd prefer you to wear the dress I selected."

"I think we're at a stalemate," she said.

"No, we're not."

"We're not?" she asked. She shook her head. "I know you think you're going to get your way, but—"

"I don't think it, Bella. I *know* it. Because as my mistress, you'll put my preferences first."

Married to His Business
ELIZABETH BEVARLY

Six-Month Mistress
KATHERINE GARBERA

⊚™ MILLS & BOON®
Pure reading pleasure™

First published in Great Britain 2008
by Harlequin Mills & Boon Limited,
Eton House, 18-24 Paradise Road, Richmond, Surrey TW9 1SR

The publisher acknowledges the copyright holders of the
individual works as follows:

Married to His Business © Elizabeth Bevarly 2007
Six-Month Mistress © Katherine Garbera 2007

ISBN: 978 0 263 85906 5

51-0708

Printed and bound in Spain
by Litografia Rosés S.A., Barcelona

MARRIED TO HIS BUSINESS

by
Elizabeth Bevarly

Dear Reader,

Whenever you get a group of writers together, something interesting always develops. Something like, oh…I don't know, a romance series. That's what happened with the book you're reading now. When some of us gathered in a hotel room at a romance writers' conference and called another writer on the phone, we somehow ended up brainstorming this six-book MILLIONAIRE OF THE MONTH series.

We came home from the conference and immediately formed an e-mail loop, and little by little, the series took shape. One of us even located a magazine featuring log homes that included the perfect lodge for the Seven Samurai to occupy in the stories.

I had so much fun working with the other writers on this series, and I loved how it all turned out. Here's hoping you enjoy our millionaires, as well.

Happy reading!

Elizabeth Bevarly

ELIZABETH BEVARLY

is a *New York Times* bestselling, award-winning author of more than fifty novels and eight novellas. Her books have been published in nineteen languages and more than two dozen countries, and have been included in launches in Russia, China and the Spanish-speaking North American market. There are more than eight million copies of her books in print worldwide.

Although she has claimed as residences Washington, DC; Virginia; New Jersey and Puerto Rico, she now lives back in her native Kentucky with her husband and son, where she fully intends to remain.

For all my Desire™ readers over the years.
Thanks for joining me on the ride.

One

As Kendall Scarborough watched her boss close his cell phone, stride to the northernmost window of his office and push it open, then hurl the apparatus into the wild blue yonder, she found herself thinking that maybe, just maybe, this wasn't a good day to tender her resignation. Again. But she would. Again. And this time she would make it stick.

And how fitting that one of her last tasks for Matthias Barton would be ordering him a new phone. Again. At least phones were easier to program and format to his liking than were PDAs and MP3 players, a number of which also lay at the bottom of the reflecting pool in the courtyard of Barton Limited—which just so happened to be situated directly below the northernmost window of Matthias's office. In fact, there were at least five years' worth of PDAs and MP3 players and other small apparatuses…apparati…little gizmos…in the pool, Kendall knew. Matthias Barton was, without question, one of the finest minds working in big business today. But when it came to itty-bitty pieces of machinery, he was reduced to, well…throwing a lot of stuff out the window.

She straightened her little black-framed glasses and plucked out the pen that was perpetually tucked into the tidy, dark blond bun knotted at the back of her head. Then she withdrew a small notepad from the pocket of the charcoal pin-striped, man-style trousers she'd paired with a tailored white, man-style shirt. All of her work clothes were man-style, because she was convinced they gave her petite, five-foot-four-inch frame a more imposing presence in the male-dominated society of big business. After scribbling a few notes—not the least of which was *New phone for Matthias*—she flipped the notepad closed and stuffed it back into her pocket.

"Kendall," he began as he closed the window and latched it, then turned to make his way back to his desk.

"Got it covered, sir," she told him before he said another word. "We'll go with VeraWave this time. I'm sure that service will suit you much better than the last one."

To herself, she added, *And the one before that. And the one before that. And the one before that.* It was just a good thing Barton Limited was headquartered in a city like San Francisco where new phone services sprang up every day. The year wasn't even half over, and Kendall had already been forced to change cellular companies three times.

"Thank you," Matthias told her as he seated himself behind his big mahogany desk and reached for the small stack of letters she'd typed up that morning, which were now awaiting his signature.

His attire was, of course, man-style, too, but she didn't

think that was what gave him such an imposing presence—though certainly the espresso-colored suit and dark gold dress shirt and tie, coupled with his dark hair and even darker eyes, didn't diminish it. Matthias himself was just larger than life, be it sitting at the head of the massive table that bisected the boardroom of Barton Limited, or slamming a squash ball into the wall at his athletic club, or charming some bastion of society into a major investment at a dinner party. Kendall had seen him in each of those situations—and dozens of others—and she couldn't think of a single moment when Matthias *hadn't* been imposing.

He'd intimidated the hell out of her when she'd first come to work for him straight out of graduate school, even though, back then, he'd barely been out of grad school himself. In spite of his youth, he'd already made millions, several times over. Kendall had been awed that someone only five years older than she—Matthias had only recently turned thirty-two—was already light-years ahead of her on the corporate ladder. She'd wanted to observe his habits and policies and procedures and mimic them, thinking she could achieve the same rapid rise and level of success through emulation.

It hadn't taken long, however, for her to realize she would never be in Matthias's league. He was too focused, too intense, too driven. His work was his life. He needed it to survive as much as he did oxygen or food. Over time, she'd gotten used to his ruthless single-mindedness when it came to achieving success, even if she'd never been able to understand it. And not just any old run-of-the-mill success, either. No, Matthias Barton had to be the absolute, no-close-seconds, unparalleled *best* at everything he set out to do.

Not that it mattered now, Kendall told herself, since she

wasn't going to be a part of his pursuit—or his success—much longer. She had a pursuit—and success—of her own to accomplish, and she should have started years ago. With her MBA from Stanford, she'd been overqualified for the position of personal assistant when she'd taken the job with Matthias. But she'd known that working for someone like him for a couple of years, even as a personal assistant, would offer her *entrée* into an echelon of big business that most recent grads never saw. She'd learn from a legend and make contacts up the wazoo, swimming with the proverbial sharks. But "a couple of years" had become five, and Kendall was savvy enough around the sharks now to be able to grill them up with a nice wasabi sauce.

It was time to go.

"Okay, where were we?" Matthias asked.

"Well, sir," she began, "you'd just, um, concluded your call with Elliot Donovan at The Springhurst Corporation, and I—" She inhaled a deep breath, steeled herself for battle, and said, in a surprisingly sturdy voice, "I was about to give you my two weeks' notice." To herself, she added silently, *And this time, I'm going through with it, no matter how hard you try to change my mind.*

His head snapped up at her announcement, and his bittersweet chocolate eyes went flinty. "Kendall, I thought we'd already talked about this."

"We have, sir, several times," she agreed. "Which is why it shouldn't come as a surprise. Now that your wedding to Miss Conover is off—"

"Look, just because Lauren and I canceled our plans," Matthias interrupted, "that doesn't mean I don't still need you to take care of things."

His now-defunct wedding to Lauren Conover had just

been the most recent reason he'd used for why Kendall couldn't leave his employ yet, but she was still surprised he would try to use it again. Technically, the wedding hadn't been canceled. There had just been a change of date and venue. Oh, and also a change of groom, since Lauren was now planning to marry Matthias's twin brother, Luke.

"Anything left to do will be taken care of by Miss Conover and her family," Kendall pointed out. "If there's anything left to do."

And she doubted there was. Matthias hadn't spoken much about his broken engagement, but Kendall hadn't been surprised when she'd heard the news. Well, maybe the part about Lauren's falling in love with Luke Barton had been a little surprising. Okay, a lot surprising. But even without Luke's intervention, the marriage, as far as Kendall was concerned, would have been a huge mistake. Matthias had proposed to Lauren Conover only because he'd wanted to merge his business with her father's, and Lauren Conover had accepted the proposal only because…

Well, frankly, Kendall was still trying to figure that one out. She'd met Lauren only a few times, but she'd never gotten the impression that Lauren was in love with Matthias—or even in like with him. Obviously she hadn't been in love, because she wouldn't have fallen for his brother, identical twin or not, if she had been. Personality-wise, Luke and Matthias Barton couldn't be more different from each other—save the fact that Luke was as driven professionally as his brother was. At least, that was what the office scuttlebutt said. Kendall had never met the other man in person.

There was no question that the match between Luke and Lauren was indeed a love match. With Matthias, however, any life he'd envisioned building with Lauren had been more about business than pleasure, more about ambition than affection. There were times when Kendall wondered if the man could care about anything *but* building his business.

Matthias said nothing for a moment, only met Kendall's gaze levelly. "But there are other things I'm going to need you to—"

"There is nothing," she quickly, but firmly, interjected, before he had a chance to create and/or fabricate a host of obligations that anyone could see to. "We're coming up on the slowest time of the year for Barton Limited," she reminded him. "I have you up to speed on everything for the next month. Now that the Stuttgart trip is out of the way, you don't have any international travel scheduled until the fall. No conferences until September. Nothing pressing that whoever you hire to take my place won't have plenty of time to prepare for. And since you'll be spending the entire month of July at your friend's lodge, anyway, that makes this the perfect time for me to—"

"I'll need you more than ever at Hunter's lodge," Matthias interrupted. "Even with all the preparation I've done—"

You mean *I've* done, Kendall thought to herself, since it had been she, not Matthias, who'd made all the arrangements.

"—it's still going to be difficult, being away from the office for that length of time. It's essential that I take someone with me who knows what's going on."

"Then I'd suggest you take Douglas Morton," Kendall said, naming one of Barton Limited's newest VPs.

"Morton needs to be here," Matthias said. "*You* need to be with me."

So now he was going to use the mysterious month at the

mysterious lodge to keep her on her leash, Kendall thought. She knew his upcoming trip to his friend's lodge on Lake Tahoe was much more than a trip to his friend's lodge on Lake Tahoe, even if she had no idea exactly why. All she knew was that, in January, he'd received a letter out of the blue from some law office representing the estate of a friend of his from college. The man had passed away, but before going had imparted a dying wish he wanted fulfilled by his old friends. They were each to spend one month in a lodge he owned on the lake.

Why? Kendall had no idea. But Matthias had driven her crazy for weeks, trying to rearrange his spring schedule so that he could spend his assigned month of April in Lake Tahoe. Then, when he'd been unable to reschedule a trip to Germany in April, he'd driven her even crazier rearranging everything she'd spent weeks rearranging so that he could switch months with his brother Luke—whom he hadn't even spoken to in years at that point—who had been assigned July.

There were seven friends in all, Kendall knew, dating back to Matthias's time at Harvard, all of whom had gradually lost touch with one another after graduating. Matthias hadn't wanted to talk about it in detail, and Kendall had respected his wishes. She'd also managed the impossible, reworking his schedule and obligations—twice—so that he could abide by his friend's last wishes and spend his month in Lake Tahoe.

It would have been so much better if he'd been able to stick with the original plan. Not only because she would have saved herself a lot of trouble, but because Lake Tahoe was where Kendall would be going to complete the necessary training for her new job—starting the first week of

July. She was dreading the possibility—however remote—
that she might run into Matthias there so soon after
severing ties with him. He was bound to be unhappy about
her leaving. Even more so once he discovered who her new
employer was.

"I can't be with you, sir," she reiterated. Inhaling a deep
breath, she told him the rest. "I've been offered a position
elsewhere that I've already accepted. They want me to take
part in a week-long training seminar that starts the first of
July—two weeks from today," she added for emphasis.
"And I'll report for work at the company immediately after
completing my orientation."

Matthias said nothing for several moments, only leaned
back in his chair and crossed his arms over his expansive
chest. Then he looked at her in a way that made Kendall feel
like her backbone was dissolving. Fast. Finally, he said,
"You've already accepted a position somewhere else?"

She nodded. And she hoped she sounded more confident than she suddenly felt when she told him, "Um, yes?"

Oh, yeah. That sounded totally confident. There was
nothing like punctuating a statement with a question mark
to really hammer home one's point. Provided one was a
four-year-old child.

"Mind telling me where?" he asked.

Kendall braced herself for his reaction, reminding
herself to be forceful and assertive and end her sentences
with a period. Maybe even an exclamation point where
necessary. By golly. Or, rather, By Golly! "With, um,
OmniTech Solutions?" she said. Asked. Whatever. Oh,
hell. "I'm going to be their new VP? In charge of Public
Relations?" When she realized she was still speaking in the
inquisitive tense, Kendall closed her eyes and mentally

willed her age back up to twenty-seven-and-a-half. If she kept this up, Matthias wouldn't let her have her milk and cookies for snack later.

When she opened her eyes again, she saw that his dark brows had shot up even farther at her declaration. Question. Whatever. Oh, hell.

"OmniTech?" he asked. Using the proper punctuation, Kendall couldn't help noticing. Unlike *some* people. "Who the hell recruited you to work for OmniTech?"

Strange that he would assume she was recruited, she thought, and that she hadn't gone looking for the position on her own. Even if, you know, she had been recruited for the position and hadn't gone looking for it on her own. "Stephen DeGallo," she told him. And she applauded herself for finally grasping the proper rules of punctuation. Now if she could just do something about the sudden drop in volume her voice had taken....

Although she wouldn't have thought it possible, Matthias's eyebrows arched even higher. "The CEO of the company recruited you to come work for him?" he asked with obvious disbelief. "As a vice president?"

Kendall didn't see what was so unbelievable about that. She was perfectly qualified for the job. Tamping down her irritation, she repeated, "Yes, sir."

Matthias narrowed his eyes at her. "Stephen DeGallo never hires from outside the company. He always promotes from within. He doesn't trust outsiders. He likes to surround himself with people he's trained to think like he does. You know. Suck-ups."

Kendall ignored the comment. Mostly because she couldn't help thinking that, after five years of working for Matthias, she was even better qualified for the job of suck-up than she was vice president in charge of public relations. "Stephen said—"

"Stephen?" Matthias echoed, this time punctuating the comment with an incredulous expulsion of air. "You're already calling him by his first name?"

"He insisted. Sir," Kendall added meaningfully, since Matthias had never extended her the invitation to address him so informally, even after being his right-hand woman for five years. Before he could comment further, she hurried on, "Stephen said I had impeccable credentials. And I do," she couldn't help adding. "In case you've forgotten, I have an MBA from Stanford, and I graduated with highest honors."

Matthias actually smiled at that. "Oh, yeah, I'll just bet DeGallo's impressed with your…credentials." He leaned back in his chair even more, folding his arms now to cradle his head in his hands. It was a position Kendall knew well, one that was meant to lull the observer into a false sense of security before Matthias struck with the velocity and toxicity of a cobra.

"You realize," he said, "that the only reason DeGallo offered you the job is because he's competing with Barton Limited for the Perkins contract, and he's going to expect you to tell him everything you know about the work we've done so far to win it."

The barb hit home, just as she knew Matthias had meant for it to. Instead of reacting to it, however, Kendall only replied calmly, "That would be highly unethical, sir. Possibly even criminal. Not only could Stephen *not* be expecting me to provide him with any such information, but he must know I'd never betray you that way."

"Wouldn't you?" Matthias asked easily.

Kendall gaped at him. Now that was a reaction she *hadn't* expected. "Of course I wouldn't. How can you even ask me something like that?"

She realized then how right she'd been to accept the new position. If Matthias could suspect she was capable of turning on him so completely, so readily, then he truly didn't view her any differently than he did the phones he tossed out the window. He'd also implied she wasn't qualified for her new job, even after the countless times she'd proved how valuable an employee she was.

Clearly, it was time to go.

"Fine, then," he said, dropping his arms and sitting up straight again. "But, Kendall, haven't you learned anything from me in the time you've been at Barton Limited? Big business isn't the gentleman's game it was a generation ago. No one's going to do you any favors. Why should you do any favors for them? For me? When it comes to business, you think of yourself first, others not at all. Feel free to report to OmniTech tomorrow if you want. Since you'll be going to work for one of my competitors, I can't risk having you around the office any longer and potentially compromising the work we're doing here. Your two weeks' notice won't be necessary. You're fired. Clear out your desk immediately. I'll have Sarah call security and they can escort you out of the building. You have ten minutes."

And with that, he turned his attention back to the stack of papers requiring his signature and began to sign each without another glance in her direction.

Kendall had no idea what to say. She hadn't expected this from Matthias at all. She'd thought he would react the way he'd reacted every other time she'd tried to resign, with a seemingly endless list of reasons why she couldn't go, none of which was in any way legitimate. Never in a million years would she have thought he would fire her, even if she was going to work for one of his competitors. Barton Limited had scores of competitors. She would have been hard-pressed to find a position with a company that *didn't* compete with Matthias in some way. She'd thought he would view her acceptance of a new job the same way she did: as business. Instead, he seemed to have taken it…

Personally, she marveled.

Immediately, she told herself that was impossible. Matthias Barton didn't get personal. About anything. He was just reacting this way because he was worried she would compromise his pursuit of the Perkins contract. That, she thought, *wasn't* surprising. That he would think of his business first, and others…well, as he'd said, not at all. She just wished he had enough faith in her to realize that she would never do anything to sabotage him or his work.

Clearly, it was *so* time to go.

With a briskly muttered "Yes, sir," Kendall spun on her heel and exited Matthias's office, giving him the same courtesy he'd extended to her and not looking back once. She wasn't the kind of person to look backward. Only forward. That was the reason she'd come to work for Matthias in the first place, because she'd been thinking ahead, to a better future. Now that future was the present. It was time to start thinking forward again. And that meant never giving another thought to…

Well. She could barely remember Matthias Thaddeus Barton's name. Or how his espresso eyes flashed gold when he was angry. Or how that one unruly lock of dark hair fell forward whenever he had his head bent in concentration. Or how one side of his mouth turned up more than another whenever he smiled that arrogant smile...

Matthias looked at the closed door through which Kendall had just exited and silently cursed it for ruining the view. Not that there was anything especially scenic about Kendall Scarborough. With her librarian glasses and those mannish, colorless clothes hiding what was doubt-less a curve-free body, anyway, and with her hair always bound tightly to her head, she wasn't likely to be showing up as a trifold with staples taped inside the locker of a dock-worker. Of course, that had been the first thing to grab his attention during her interview five years ago, because the last thing he'd wanted or needed in a personal assistant was someone he might want to get personal with.

Not that *personal* to Matthias was all that personal, but the risk for screwing up was always there, since he had, in the past, been swayed by beauty, with disastrous results. He was understandably wary around beautiful things and beautiful women. But he'd never been able to resist either.

He'd thought he'd solved his problem by arranging a marriage with Lauren Conover that would have provided him with not just a suitable wife for a man in his position, but a beneficial merger with her father's company, as well. Lauren was beautiful, smart, accomplished and chic, but there hadn't been a spark of any inconvenient passion between them. The two of them could have lived in a beau-tiful home, had beautiful children and a beautiful life, without Matthias ever having to get too deeply involved with any of it. It had been so perfect. Until his brother, Luke, had come along and, as had been a habit with Lunkhead since their childhood, screwed up a perfectly good thing.

But it wasn't Lunkhead Luke who had screwed up things with Kendall, Matthias reminded himself. Kendall, who was exactly what Matthias *did* want and need in a personal assistant: pragmatic and professional, enterprising and efficient. In the five years she'd worked for him, she'd been his calendar, his clock, his coordinator. His bartender, his astrologer, his conscience. His butcher, his baker, his candlestick maker. His tinker, his tailor, his spy.

That last word hit Matthias hard, since it was precisely what he'd just accused Kendall of being for someone else. Even though he knew she wouldn't. Even though he knew she couldn't. Although there was no question that Stephen DeGallo's motive in hiring her had been driven by his hope—hell, his certainty—that he could persuade her to share information about both Matthias and Barton Limited that would work to his benefit, Matthias couldn't honestly see her turning on him that way. He'd just been so surprised by her announcement that she'd already accepted a job somewhere else—and with his biggest competitor—that he hadn't known what to say.

Whenever she'd tried to tender her resignation before, Matthias had always been able to talk her out of it. And he'd always talked her out of it because he'd needed her here. Hell, he knew she was overqualified for her position. That was why he'd given her so many raises over the years that she was now making almost twice what her predecessors had made. Yeah, okay, maybe she could be doing more with her degree and her savvy, he conceded reluctantly. But she didn't have to do it for OmniTech.

There was no way Stephen DeGallo had recruited

Kendall for her résumé. He didn't see her the way Matthias did—pragmatic and professional, enterprising and efficient. She was just an opportunity to mine the practices and policies of Barton Limited. Nothing more.

He expelled a disgruntled breath of air as he continued to look at the closed door. Well, he'd just have to get along without her, wouldn't he? He'd just hire another personal assistant, that was all. Someone else who was pragmatic and professional, enterprising and efficient. Someone else who would be his calendar, clock and conscience. That shouldn't be so hard, right? He'd put Kendall on it right away.

His finger was actually on the buzzer to call her in before he realized what he'd been about to do. Ask Kendall, the woman he'd just fired—not to mention insulted—to hire a replacement for herself. He shook his head and chuckled at himself for the gaffe, even if he couldn't find anything especially funny about it. Man. If he didn't know better, he'd almost think he couldn't do *anything* without Kendall. And that, he knew, was nuts.

He was a captain of industry. He had made his first million less than a year after graduating from college, and he'd multiplied it dozens of times over since. He headed a Fortune 500 Company that employed thousands of people all over the world.

So he'd lost his personal assistant, he thought. So what? Personal assistants were as easy to find as cheap champagne on New Year's Eve. He'd hire another one tomorrow. Have the person trained well enough by the time he left for Tahoe that they would at least have the basics down. Actually, the timing, as Kendall had said, was perfect. He could use the month in Tahoe with his new assistant to mold him or her to his liking.

Matthias would get along just fine without Kendall Scarborough. Hell, yes, he would.

Hell, yes.

Two

Kendall made the trip to Tahoe courtesy of OmniTech, enjoying the brief flight in first class. A rental car awaited her on arrival, a luxury sedan that was quite the posh way to travel, compared to her little economy car at home. Maybe on her new salary, she could ultimately buy something like this, she thought as she settled into the leather seat and pushed the button to open the sunroof. As the balmy summer air tumbled into the car, she donned her sunglasses, fastened her seat belt over her white oxford shirt and khaki trousers and tuned the radio to the jazz station. Then, feeling like a corporate executive for the first time in her life, she pulled out of the rental lot at the airport basking in contentment.

Until she thought about Matthias Barton. Then her contentment fled. And what she'd hoped would be a peaceful, introspective drive that was filled with planning for her future at OmniTech suddenly turned into a grueling marathon of disgruntlement instead.

But then, thoughts of Matthias—never mind disgruntlement—had been regular companions over the two weeks that had passed since she'd last seen him. So as she merged onto the highway, Kendall did her best to think of something—anything—else. How she needed to replace the hardware on her kitchen cabinets. The fact that women's shoe manufacturers still hadn't figured out how to wed style with comfort. Why the sky was blue and the grass was green. The atomic weight of boron. Where the contestants of *Survivor* should go next—though, admittedly, it probably wasn't polite for her to say aloud where *she* thought they should go. Whatever it took to keep from hearing again those two little words she'd never thought she'd hear Matthias say to her.

You're fired.

She still couldn't believe he'd done it. After giving him five years of her life, years she could have spent building her own career instead of bolstering his, he'd cut her loose in the most insulting way possible. She'd seen him fire plenty of people during the time she'd worked for him, but they were people who'd deserved the boot. Employees who had been, at best, ineffective, and at worst, dishonest. People who had cheated him, or lied to him, or stolen from him. Now Kendall, who had never missed a day on the job, and whose work ethic had been irreproachable, had been relegated to their ranks.

But even that wasn't what bothered her the most. What bothered her the most was her own reaction to having been fired. She told herself she should be angry with Matthias for the way he'd dismissed her. She should be resentful.

She should be outraged. She should be reporting him to the Equal Opportunity Commission. Instead, what she felt was hurt. Hurt in the same way a little girl feels hurt when she's always picked last for kickball. And hurt feelings were *not* something a consummate professional like Kendall should feel.

Matthias was right about one thing. She hadn't learned as much from him as she'd thought she would when she accepted the position, if she couldn't be the focused, unflinching businesswoman she'd envisioned becoming. She could be as ruthless and determined as Matthias was, she told herself. She *could*. And she would be, too. Starting the moment she passed through the doors of the Timber Lake Inn.

That must be a new hotel in Tahoe, Kendall thought as she exited onto the road that would take her to her final destination. She'd never heard of it before. It was kind of an odd name for a conference hotel, too. They must be trying to make business travel sound less businessy or something.

She glanced at the numbers on a shop window to get her bearings and calculated that the hotel was another eight blocks down, toward the lake. She hadn't been to Tahoe since college, she realized as she drove, smiling at the shops boasting kites and artwork and jewelry and clothes. In the winter, there would be skis lined up everywhere, but during the summer, there were water toys and rafts instead. People dotted the streets in their bright summer colors and sunglasses, lolling at café tables and sauntering in and out of stores. The weather was perfect for being outdoors, the air kissed with just a hint of the cool breeze gliding off the lake, the sky a faultless blue streaked with gauzy clouds.

Kendall smiled at the promise inherent in the day. It was a good omen. She had been right to leave Matthias's employ. Stephen DeGallo's offer couldn't have come at a better time. Funny how things just worked out perfectly sometimes. She had a full week to spend in one of the most beautiful places on earth, learning about a new career that, she hoped, would be hers for the rest of her life. Her future at OmniTech was wide-open. If she worked hard and did everything right—who knew?—she might even become the CEO of the company herself someday. Stephen DeGallo was a confirmed bachelor in his late forties with no family he was bringing up through the ranks, and he was known for rewarding his workers with generous benefits and bonuses. Even if he never groomed Kendall for his own position at the company, there was every reason to believe he might someday install her as the head of one of the scores of businesses he owned. Unlike Matthias, who had never offered any indication that he would ever consider Kendall for anything more than his assist—

Dammit. She was thinking about him again.

She pushed Matthias out of her brain—again—and looked for another street number. Two more blocks.

When she braked for a red light, she used the opportunity to get her bearings. A glance at her watch told her it was just coming up on three o'clock, precisely the time she'd anticipated arriving, knowing her room would be ready by then. She was supposed to meet Stephen and the other trainees at six for an informal dinner, so they could all get to know one another, and training officially began at eight in the morning. Dress would be casual, but Kendall had packed a couple of suits in with her trousers and shirts, just in case. She was, after all, a consummate professional.

Of course, she was in Lake Tahoe, too, so she'd also included blue jeans and T-shirts and shorts and sandals, her preferred attire for relaxing. She wasn't such a workaholic that she didn't take advantage of her off time. Unlike Matthias, who—

Dammit, she was doing it again.

The light changed green, so she banished thoughts of Matthias—*again*—and urged the accelerator down lightly, taking the last two blocks slowly. The lake was in view now, but she didn't see any hotels large enough to qualify for corporate lodgings up ahead. She took her eyes off the road long enough to glance down at the passenger seat, where she'd laid the directions and a map, to confirm she had the address right. Maybe she'd written it down wrong, she thought. Because this block and the one beyond it was nothing but more quaint shops and cafés and cozy B and Bs.

Just as she neared the end of the last block and began to look for a place to turn around, she saw a sign with an arrow pointing to the right that read Parking for Timber Lake Inn. Braking quickly, she was able to make the turn just in time.

But the drive led to the entrance of a tidy, cheerful little bed-and-breakfast. Kendall frowned, wondering where she'd gone wrong, then noted a sign above the door that identified it as the very hotel she'd been looking for. Huh. That was odd. The place looked more like a honeymoon hotel than it did a corporate facility. Stephen DeGallo must like to use places like this to make his new hires feel more comfortable. Yet another way in which he differed from Matthias, who, Kendall was sure, would have scheduled an orientation for…

Well, actually, Matthias would have trained people in the buildings where they would be working, she thought. Or rather, he'd have *other* people training his new employees in the buildings where they would be working. It would be more professional that way. More businesslike. God forbid he should ever want anyone to feel any other way.

When Kendall realized she was thinking about Matthias *again,* she shoved the thought away *again*—harder this time—and pushed open the car door. By now a bellman had emerged from the hotel and was descending the stairs to help her with her bag. Instead of the liveried uniform he might have worn at a larger hotel, however, he was dressed in khaki shorts and a polo bearing the logo of the Timber Lake Inn stitched on the breast pocket. Coupled with his shaggy blond hair and ruddy complexion, he looked as if he should be standing at the edge of the ocean toting a surfboard instead of lugging bags for a lakeside hotel.

"Dude," he greeted her with a smile, reinforcing the image. "Welcome to the Timber Lake Inn. I'm Sean. I'll get your bags."

"Thanks," Kendall replied with a smile of her own as she reached into the car to pop the trunk open. "I'm Kendall Scarborough. I'm here for the OmniTech orientation session."

Sean nodded. "Well, wherever that's going on, you can probably get there by walking. We're pretty centrally located here."

The comment puzzled Kendall. "It's going on here," she said. "At the hotel."

Sean's eyebrows shot up at that. "Whoa. First I've heard about it. But then, I was on vacation last week and just got back today. All I knew about going on this week was the Tyson-Gerhart wedding and the Truckee Ski Club reunion. Those have got us booked to full capacity."

Kendall looked at the hotel again. It didn't look big enough to host those functions and a training session. Not that she'd expected the OmniTech orientation to be a huge event, but since it would run for a week, and since Stephen DeGallo himself would be part of it, she'd just assumed the company would be training quite a few people. A business that size employed hundreds in San Francisco alone, and Kendall had been under the impression that this session would include new hires from all over the Northwest. There must be more to the hotel than the two stories she could see.

Sean collected her bags and she followed him into the lobby, which immediately made her feel comfortable. It was everything a place called the Timber Lake Inn should be, from its knotty pine walls to the huge creek stone fireplace on the opposite side of the room. The hardwood floors were covered here and there by woven rugs in Native American geometrics, and wrought iron fixtures hung from the exposed log ceiling. A wide staircase to the right of the reception desk led up to a line of rooms on the second floor, but none of them seemed to be meeting rooms. As if to illustrate that, one of the doors opened and a couple exited, looping their arms around each other and cuddling like newlyweds.

Nothing about the place suggested it was used for business events. In fact, the place looked…well, cozy. That was the only word that came to Kendall's mind.

The word returned when she entered her room…until she discovered it was actually a suite appointed with more pine walls and more exposed ceiling beams and more Native American rugs. In the main room, French doors opened onto a spacious balcony that offered a glorious view of the lake, which was picked up again in the bedroom by a broad picture window. The bathroom boasted a jacuzzi and small television, and there was a wet bar tucked into the far side of the living room. An enormous basket of fresh fruit and wine sat at the center of the dining table, and a massive bouquet of flowers, fragrant and splashy, was perched on the desk. Envelopes bearing her name—her *first* name—were tucked into each.

"Still think DeGallo wants you only for your MBA and your business savvy?"

Kendall spun around with a start at the question to find Matthias leaning in the still-open door to her room. Her lips parted in surprise, but not entirely because of his unexpected arrival. He looked…different. And not just because he was casually dressed in clay-colored trousers and a navy-blue polo, where she was more accustomed to seeing him in suits. She'd seen him dressed for non-business-related functions before, everything from rugby in the park to black-tie opening nights. It wasn't Matthias's clothing that looked off today. It was Matthias.

His clothes were a little wrinkled, his hair was a little shaggy, and his eyes were a little shadowed, as if he wasn't getting quite enough sleep. In fact, his whole face looked a little shadowed, a little leaner, a little rougher. And Matthias had never been "a little" anything. He was an all-or-nothing kind of man, emphasis on the *all,* especially where his physical appearance went.

She ignored the little pang of concern that pinched her at seeing him in his less-tidy-than-usual state. It was none of her business if he was working too much. None of her business if whoever he'd hired to take her place wasn't keeping him on track the way she had. She wasn't her boss's keeper. Especially since Matthias wasn't even her boss anymore.

"What are you doing here?" she asked by way of a

greeting, congratulating herself on keeping her voice steady, clear and indifferent. "I mean, I know why you're in Tahoe. But what are you doing *here?* At my hotel?"

He raised a shoulder and let it drop, then pushed himself away from the doorjamb. As he strode into the room, he told her, "I made better time driving from San Francisco than I thought I would, so I'm a little ahead of schedule. I don't have to meet the caretaker for another hour, so I thought I'd drop in and say hello."

Kendall eyed him suspiciously. It wasn't like Matthias to "drop in" on anyone, for any reason. And he must have gone to some lengths to find out where she would be staying and when she would be arriving, because she hadn't shared any of that information with him. Not to mention they hadn't exactly parted on the best of terms. They hadn't spoken to or seen each other since he'd had her escorted out of the building like a common thief. If he was here now, it had to be because he wanted something.

So she asked him, "What do you want?"

Matthias looked at Kendall and wondered which of dozens of answers to that question he should give her. He wanted a lot of things, actually. He wanted the Perkins contract. He wanted the Barton Limited stock to go through the roof. He wanted to be worth a billion dollars by the time he was forty. Hell, he even wanted world peace, since it would create so many new business-friendly governments. And, okay, he wanted a new personal assistant, too, since, so far, everyone he'd interviewed had been, at best, unqualified and, at worst, a lobotomy gone tragically wrong.

Mostly, though, he wanted Kendall to open her eyes and see what was so obvious to him. Talk about a lobotomy. What had happened to the pragmatic, professional, enterprising, efficient woman he'd hired? Looking at Kendall now…

Well, actually, looking at Kendall now, Matthias wondered what she'd done to herself. The dark blond hair she normally had twisted up out of her way hung loose, cascading past her shoulders in a thick, silky mass. Wow, it was a lot longer than he'd thought—not that he'd ever thought much about Kendall's hair. But it was long. Thick. Silky. Had he mentioned silky? And long? And thick? Her glasses were gone, too, and he noted with some surprise that her eyes were huge without them. And green. He'd never noticed that Kendall had green eyes. Really green eyes. Pale green. Like bottle glass. And every bit as clear.

"What do you want, Mr. Barton?" she asked again, bringing his thoughts back to where they needed to be.

It was a good question, he thought. He wished he had a good answer to go with it. But the fact was, he still wasn't sure why he was here. Yeah, her hotel was on his way, but even if it hadn't been, he would have driven the extra miles to see her. He'd done a little checking this week—okay, he'd done a lot of snooping—to find out where Kendall would be staying and the particulars of this "week-long orientation." But his mole at OmniTech—yes, Matthias had one there, just as he was sure DeGallo had one at Barton Limited—hadn't been able to uncover much about it.

Which had just hammered home to Matthias that the guy was up to no good. Had there been a legitimate orientation seminar going on, it would have been a matter of company record. As far as Matthias could tell, however, Kendall was the only new hire of any consequence that Stephen DeGallo had made recently. As he'd told her two weeks ago, the guy didn't hire outside the company for the kind of position he'd offered her. And any alleged orientation there might have been for her position should have taken place on-site—not in a cozy, romantic little hotel overlooking Lake Tahoe.

"I've come to offer you your job back," he said, surprising himself as much as he'd obviously surprised Kendall. He really hadn't been intending to do that at all when he drove into town. He'd just been planning to…

Okay, he wasn't exactly sure what he'd been planning to do. But now that he thought more about it, offering Kendall her job back made sense. No one he'd interviewed had come close to matching her qualifications. Matthias was confident that if he made her the right offer, she'd come back on board. Everyone had their price. Kendall was no exception. She'd just been feeling unappreciated, he told himself. He hadn't emphasized enough how valuable she was to Barton Limited. Oh, sure, he'd given her raises and more benefits. But any good employee needed ego stroking, too. Just because Kendall had never seemed like the kind of person who wanted that kind of thing didn't mean it wasn't important to her.

He didn't know why he hadn't thought about that before. At least not consciously. Evidently his brain *had* been considering it *sub*consciously, to have thrown out the offer to hire her back. That was probably what had been behind Matthias's driving into town to find her in the first place. He'd been planning—subconsciously—to renegotiate the terms of her employment and invite her back.

Yeah, that was it. It had to be. Why else would he have come?

Kendall, however, didn't seem to be as open to the idea of her return to Barton Limited as Matthias was, because she didn't answer him right away. In fact, she was looking at him as if she was kind of indignant.

No, it must be grateful, he told himself immediately. Indignity, gratitude…those got mixed up all the time. They had a lot of the same letters in common. After all, why would she feel indignant?

"I have a job," she said tersely.

Or maybe she'd said it sweetly. Those got mixed up a lot, too. Matthias was sure of it. The letter thing again.

"And I'm very excited about it," she added.

No, definitely terse, he thought. And not a little shirty.

Instead of replying, he strode across the room to the broad panoramic windows that looked out over the crystalline blue water of the lake and the bright blue sky above it. The day was glorious, the view crisp and clean, the dark green mountains on the other side of the water streaked with purple shadows from the forests of trees, the sun dappling the water as if it were scattering diamonds. This place was as far removed from the skyscrapers and concrete of San Francisco as it could be, and the last thing anyone should think about here was work. Which was why Matthias so seldom visited places like this. And which was why—one of many *whys*—he knew Stephen DeGallo was up to no good.

He sensed more than heard Kendall as she came up behind him, and was unprepared for the feeling that washed over him when she came to a halt behind him. He'd been edgy since leaving San Francisco, as he always was when he traveled. Travel was such a waste of time, and Matthias was always impatient getting from point A to point B so he could get on with business. This time, however, the feeling hadn't lessened once he'd arrived at his destination.

He'd still been feeling anxious when he entered Kendall's room. But when she stood beside him then, he was suddenly overcome by a feeling of calmness. Peacefulness. A strange sense of well-being that he hadn't felt for…

Well, a couple of weeks, anyway.

She said nothing as she gazed out the window, only studied the same view Matthias was considering himself. But he knew there must be some part of her brain that was questioning DeGallo's motives by now. She was a smart woman. She had good instincts. It was what made her so good at what she did.

"Look at that view," he said anyway, trivializing with a cliché what was a staggeringly beautiful piece of work. "You don't see views like that in the city." He turned to face Kendall before adding meaningfully, "Where most job orientations take place."

She slumped a little at the comment, expelling a tired-sounding sigh. But she said nothing to deny his more-than-obvious allegation.

"And look at this room," he said further, turning again and sweeping both arms open. "Who gets a place like this when they're undergoing orientation for a new job?"

Kendall sighed again, still sounding weary, but turned her body in the same direction as his. "New vice presidents for the company," she told him. "That's who. Stephen just wants to make a good impression, that's all."

Matthias dipped his head in concession, however small, to that. Then he strode to the table where there sat a bouquet of flowers more massive than *any* man *any*where had ever sent to *any* woman for *any* reason—be it declaring his love or groveling for forgiveness. He plucked the card from a particularly luscious-looking bloom and began to open it.

"Matthias, don't—" Kendall began.

He halted, snapping his head up at that, not because she had told him to stop, but because she had addressed him by his first name. Never, not once, during the five years she'd worked for him had she called him Matthias. Because never, not once, had he given her the okay to do it. And the fact that she had stepped over that line now so thoroughly, without his permission...

Hmm. Actually, now that he'd heard her call him Matthias, he realized he kind of liked the way his name sounded coming from her lips. In fact, he kind of liked the way her lips looked right now, having just said his name. Parted softly in surprise, and maybe embarrassment, as if she hadn't intended to call him Matthias, and now she wasn't sure what to do to take it back, or if she even wanted to take it back. What was strange was that Matthias didn't want her to take it back. In fact, he wanted her to say it again. Even more surprising, he realized the context in which he wanted to hear her say his name had nothing to do with her job, and everything to do with, well, other reasons people came to Lake Tahoe.

"Don't," she said again, more softly this time. Omitting the use of his name.

This time, too, she extended her hand toward the small envelope he still held tucked between his index and middle fingers. Not sure why he did it, Matthias pulled his hand toward himself, out of her reach. She took another step forward, bringing her body to within touching distance of his, then hesitated. But she didn't drop her hand, and for a moment, he thought—hoped—she would trail her hand after his to retrieve the card. He even found himself looking forward to her fingers tangling with his as they vied for possession. And although it was clear she was grappling with the possibility of that very thing herself—or maybe because she was grappling with it—she dropped her hand to her side again, ceding to him with clear reluctance.

The victory was strangely hollow, but Matthias shouldered it anyway. Opening the envelope, he withdrew the card, then scanned the sentiment upon it. He wasn't sure if it was DeGallo's writing, but it was masculine and forceful, and he suspected DeGallo himself had indeed penned the words. The task hadn't been left to an assistant to complete, which was what Matthias would have done in the same situation.

Then again, Matthias would never have been in this situation. Oh, he might have wooed someone away from one of his competitors specifically to learn more about that competitor's practices, but he would have been straightforward about it. He wouldn't have set up the new hire in a honeymoon suite with a breathtaking view of a romantic environment and called it orientation. And he wouldn't have sent flowers—with *any*one's signature.

He shook his head as he read aloud the sentiment DeGallo had written. "Kendall," he said, "Can't wait to have you navigating our PR waters. Welcome aboard!" He looked up at Kendall then, but she was staring at the wall. "Navigating our PR waters?" he repeated. "Was that the best he could do?"

Now Kendall turned to look at Matthias, her huge, clear green eyes penetrating deep enough to heat something in his chest. "Well, there *is* a lake out there," she said lamely. "Besides, what would *you* have said to welcome a new employee?"

"I would have said, 'Get to work,'" he replied. "And I would have said it to that new employee's face. I wouldn't go through all this ridiculous pretense to make her feel like she was more important than she actually is."

Two bright spots of color flared on Kendall's cheeks at that. She nodded brusquely. "Of course you wouldn't," she said. "Because no one is important to you. You think the success of Barton Limited is because of you and you alone. You have no appreciation for how many people it takes to make a company prosper, and you have no clue how to take care of the ones who are doing the best work. And if you're not careful, then—"

She halted abruptly, her eyes widening in what he could only guess was horror that she'd just leaped like a gazelle across the line she had previously only overstepped. Matthias narrowed his eyes at her, his own lips parting now in surprise. Kendall had never challenged him like this before. Hell, challenged? he asked himself. Compared to her usual self-containment, she'd just read him the riot act. With a bullhorn. Sure, she'd taken exception in the past to some of his decisions—okay, edicts—but she'd always pointed out her concerns with discretion. And deference. But this reaction was completely unlike her. Totally unexpected. And extremely...

Matthias stopped himself before allowing the impression to fully form. Because the impression had nothing to do with his reaction to Kendall as an employee, and everything to do with his reaction to her as a...a person.

"Is that what you really think?" he asked, deciding to focus on that instead of...the other thing.

She hesitated only a second, then nodded. And then, a little less forcefully than she'd spoken before, she added, "Yes. Sir." And then, a little more forcefully, she altered her response to, "Yes. Matthias."

There it was again, he marveled. That ripple of heat that should have been disapproval of her familiarity by using his first name, but which was instead…something else. Something he told himself to try to figure out later, because he really needed to respond to Kendall's allegation that he was so self-centered. But because of the way she was looking at him, all clear-green-eyed and hot-pink-cheeked and tumbling-silky-haired, all he could manage in response was, "Oh, really?"

A moment passed in which neither of them spoke, or moved, or even breathed. Then Kendall's lips turned up almost imperceptibly, into a smile with what only someone who had the vast experience Matthias had with the emotion could identify.

Victory.

Kendall Scarborough had it in her head that she'd just won whatever the two of them had been engaged in. Now if Matthias could just figure out what the two of them had just engaged in, maybe he'd know what to do next.

Kendall, however, didn't seem to be having the same problem he had. Because she settled her hands on her hips in a way that was at once relaxed and challenging, and she asked again, "Was there some reason you came here this afternoon, Matthias? Is there something you wanted?"

He honestly had no idea how to answer her. Because for the first time in his life, Matthias didn't know what he wanted. He was too off-kilter looking at Kendall and thinking about Kendall and listening to Kendall saying his name and marveling at how Kendall had thrown him so off-kilter.

But he didn't want to look foolish, either—that would have been another first he would have just as soon done without. So he reached into his trouser pocket and removed a small gadget he'd purchased for himself the day after she'd left his employ. Something called a... Well, he couldn't remember what it was called now, but it was supposed to be even better than the... Whatever that other thing was he used to use for keeping track of his appointments and obligations.

Then he held it out to Kendall and replied, "Yeah. Do you have any idea how this thing works? I keep getting e-mail from some deposed prince in Nigeria who needs my help freeing up some frozen assets he's trying to get out of the country, and I'd really like to help him out, because he promised me a more than generous share once he's fluid again. Plus, this woman named Trixie just got a new Web cam she wants to show me, and I'm thinking it might be technology I'd like to invest in."

He looked at Kendall, who was looking back at him as if he'd just grown a second head. "What?" he said.

She crossed the room in a half-dozen long strides and opened the door. Then she pointed to the hallway beyond with one finger. "Out," she said. "Now."

His mouth dropped open in surprise. "What, you're not going to help me?"

"I'm not your assistant anymore, Matthias."

Oh, as if he needed reminding of *that*. "But—"

"Out," she repeated. "Now."

He shook his head in disbelief. But he did as she asked him to. Told him to. Demanded he do. The door was slamming shut behind him before he'd even cleared it, missing his backside by *that* much. He spun around, and went so far as to lift a fist to pound on it again. But he stopped himself before completing the action.

There was a better way to go about this, he told himself.

He just had to figure out what it was. Because Kendall *was* making a mistake, thinking OmniTech was the place she needed to be. Where she needed to be was with him. Or, rather, with Barton Limited, he quickly corrected himself. Now all he had to do was figure out a way to make her realize that, too.

Three

Kendall leaned back against the door through which Matthias had just exited and tried to get a handle on everything that had just happened.

She'd thrown him out, she marveled. She'd looked at the BlackBerry in his hand, incredulous that, just when they were starting to have an exchange that felt evenly matched, he would ask her to program the little gizmo the way she had so many others when he was paying her to be his underling, and then she'd asked—no, *told*—him to leave. Even more stunning than that was the fact that Matthias had done as she asked—no, *told*—him to and had left. Without a word of argument. Without a word of exception. Without a word of reproach.

Okay, and without a word of farewell, either.

The point was that Kendall had taken charge of a situation with Matthias and she had mastered it. Eventually. Just because there had been a few moments in between that had been filled with strange bits of weirdness didn't diminish the enormity of that achievement.

But just *what,* exactly, had that weirdness been about? she asked herself now. There had been times during their conversation when Matthias had looked at her almost as if he were seeing someone else, someone he didn't quite know, someone with whom he wasn't entirely comfortable. Someone he wasn't sure he liked. It had been…weird. And her response had been weird, too. She'd suddenly been aware of him in a way she hadn't been when she'd worked for him. Or, at least, in a way she hadn't allowed herself to think about when she worked for him.

She let herself think about it now.

The day Matthias had announced his engagement to Lauren Conover, Kendall had experienced a reaction that had surprised her. A lot. And she'd realized that day that her feelings for her boss might perhaps, possibly, conceivably go a little beyond professional. Because where she had never minded the other women who came and went in Matthias's life—because they always came and went—when he'd made a move to join himself permanently to someone else, Kendall had felt a little…

Well, weird.

At first, she'd told herself it was just disappointment that such a smart man would do something as stupid as arrange a marriage of convenience for himself. Then she'd told herself what she felt was annoyance that, because of his engagement, he wanted her to arrange so many events for him that had nothing to do with work. In fact, she'd run through a veritable grocery list of feelings in response to

Matthias's announced nuptials: denial, then anger, then bargaining, then depression…

Hang on a minute, Kendall thought now. Those were the stages of grief. And no way had she felt *that*. No way had she been *that* far gone on her boss.

Ultimately, however, she had been forced to admit the truth. That maybe, perhaps, possibly, conceivably, she had developed…feelings… for her employer. Feelings of attachment. Feelings of allegiance. Feelings of… She closed her eyes tight and made herself admit it. Feelings of…affection.

The recognition that she had begun to feel things for her boss that she had no business feeling—even her allegiance wasn't for things that related to work—was what had cemented her conviction that she would, once and for all, tender her resignation. Even after his engagement to Lauren was canceled, she'd known she had to go. She couldn't risk falling for Matthias, because he would never care for her in any way other than the professional. He didn't care about anyone in any way other than the professional. That the offer from Stephen DeGallo had come on the heels of the cancellation of Matthias's wedding had just been an exclamation point to punctuate the obvious. She had done the right thing by leaving Matthias. Or, rather, she hastily corrected herself, by leaving Matthias's employ.

She just hoped taking the job with Stephen DeGallo had been the right thing to do, too.

Some lodge, Matthias thought as he pulled into the drive of what looked more like a boutique hotel than a private residence. Had it not been for the fact that he'd been here once before—three months ago, when his brother, Luke, was in residence—he wouldn't have been sure he was in the right place. He turned off the ignition and exited the car, hauled his leather weekender out of the backseat and made his way to the entrance where the caretaker was waiting for him.

The woman was dressed in a pale yellow straight skirt and a white sleeveless top, a canvas gimme cap decorated with a logo he didn't recognize pulled low on her forehead. Coupled with her sunglasses, it was hard to tell what she looked like, but what he could see was pretty, in a whole-some kind of way. The ponytail hanging out of the cap's opening was streaked dark blond, and she had some decent curves, so it wasn't surprising that Matthias found himself comparing her to Kendall…and thinking how nice it would be if it was Kendall who was here to greet him instead. Not because he wanted to spend a month here with Kendall, of course, but because if Kendall was here, he could get a lot more work done, that was all.

"I assume you're Mary?" he asked the woman by way of a greeting. "I'm sorry I'm late."

She seemed to deflate a little when she got a good look at him, and only then did he realize she had seemed kind of expectant as he strode up the walk. Maybe she'd thought he was someone else, since his own appearance probably wasn't easy to discern, either, thanks to his own sunglasses.

She nodded. "I'm the caretaker." Without further ado, she extended a key that dangled from a rather elaborate key chain and added, "Here's the key. Just leave it on the kitchen table at the end of the month. I've stocked the re-frigerator and cabinets, and there's some carryout from a local takeaway gourmet. But if it's not to your taste or you'd like something specific, there are menus for some restaurants in Hunter's Landing on top of the fridge. I can recommend Clearwater's and the Lakeside Diner for sure. Or if you do the cooking thing, there's a market just east of where you turned off to find the lodge."

Her voice was soft but dispassionate, and she spoke as if she were reading from a script. And not very dramatically, at that. "Tahoe City is about a half hour north, the Nevada state line about twenty minutes east. If you want to gamble," she added, as if wanting to clarify.

"Not like that," Matthias told her. When he gambled, he liked for the stakes to be much higher than mere cash.

Mary nodded. "Would you like for me to show you around the place? Explain how everything works?"

"I assume it's all pretty standard," he replied. Not to mention he had no intention of seeing how anything worked. That way lay madness.

"Standard, yes," Mary told him. "But there are quite a few amenities. Hot tub, Jacuzzi, gourmet kitchen, plasma TV…"

He held up a hand to stop her. He wasn't the type to indulge in any of those things. He had too much work to do. "It won't be necessary," he told her. "Thanks, anyway."

"Then, if you won't be needing anything else?" she asked.

Well, there was nothing he needed that she could provide, anyway, he thought. So he told her, "Nothing, thanks."

"Emergency numbers are on the fridge, too," she said. "Including mine. Hopefully you won't need them, either."

She hesitated before leaving, studying Matthias's face for a moment as if she were looking for something. Then, suddenly, she said, "Goodbye," and turned to walk down the front steps. For the merest, most nebulous second, she seemed a little familiar somehow. He didn't know if it was her walk, her voice, the way she carried herself or what, but there was…something about her that reminded him so much of someone else. He just couldn't quite put his finger on who.

And then the impression was gone, as quickly as it had materialized. Mary was gone, too, having climbed back into her car and backed it out of the driveway. Matthias jingled the key in his hand absently, shrugged off his odd ruminations and turned to unlock the front door, closing it behind himself once he was inside. Out of habit, he tossed his battered leather weekender—the one he'd traveled with since college—onto the nearest piece of furniture. No small feat, that, since the place was huge, with a foyer the size of a Giants dugout, and the nearest piece of furniture was half a stadium away. He didn't care if he knocked something over in the process. He was still pissed off at Hunter for making all of them rearrange their lives for a month to come here and do whatever the hell it was they were supposed to do.

But then, he was still pissed off at Hunter for dying, too.

Of course, if he were honest with himself, Matthias would have to admit that he was more pissed off at himself than anyone else. He hadn't meant to lose touch with the Seven Samurai over the years. It had just…happened. Time happened. Distance happened. Work happened. Life happened. People grew up. They grew apart. They went their separate ways. Happened all the time. He and Hunter and the rest of them had all been kids when they'd made pacts and promises to stay friends forever. Hell, Matthias hadn't even kept in touch with his own brother. Then again, when your brother did things like accusing you of cheating him in business and stealing your fiancée, it was understandable why you'd allow for some distance.

As soon as the thought formed in his head, Matthias pushed it away. He was being unfair to Luke. Really unfair this time, and not the phony-baloney unfairness of which his brother had always accused him. Their father hadn't exactly been a proponent of fairness, anyway. He had pitted the two of them against each other from the day the twins were old enough to compete. Which, to the old man's way of thinking, had been within seconds of their emerging from the womb. If there had been some way to make the boys vie for something against each other, Samuel Sullivan Barton found a way to do it. Who could win the most merit badges in Cub Scouts. Who could sell the most wrapping paper for the school fund-raiser. Who could score the most baskets, make the most touchdowns, pitch the best game. As children, they'd been more like rivals than brothers.

It had only gotten worse after their father's death and the terms of his will had been made public. Samuel had decreed that whichever of the boys made a million dollars first, the estate would go to him in its entirety. Matthias had won. Though winning had been relative. Luke had accused him, unjustly, of cheating and hadn't spoken to him for years. It hadn't been until recently that the two men had shared anything. And then what they'd shared was Lauren Conover, the woman who'd agreed to be Matthias's wife. It had been the ultimate competition for Luke…until he'd fallen in love with the prize. And although Matthias had come to terms with what had happened, things between him and his brother still weren't exactly smooth. Or simple. Or settled.

Man, what was it about peoples' last wills and testaments that they always sent Matthias's life in a new direction?

He sighed as he leaned against the front door and drove

his gaze around the lodge. In college, they'd said they wanted to build a cabin. But "cabin" evoked an image of a rustic, no-frills, crowded little shack in the woods with few amenities and even fewer comforts. This place was like something from *Citizen Kane,* had the movie been filmed in Technicolor. The great room ceiling soared up two stories, with expansive windows running the entire length of one wall, offering an incredible view of the lake. The pine paneling was polished to a honeyed sheen, the wide planked floors buffed to a satin finish. At one end of the room was a fireplace big enough to host the United Arab Emirates, a sofa and chairs clustered before it that, ironically, invited an intimate gathering of friends.

The place was exactly the sort of retreat Matthias would have expected Hunter to have. Handsomely furnished. Blissfully quiet. Generously outfitted. And yet there was something missing that prevented it from being completely comfortable. Something that Hunter had obviously forgotten to include, but Matthias couldn't quite put his finger on what.

He pushed himself away from the door and made his way to where his weekender had landed—just shy of actually hitting the nearest piece of furniture he'd been aiming for. His footsteps echoed hollowly on the hardwood floor as he went, an auditory reminder of just how alone he would be while he was here. Matthias wasn't used to traveling alone. Kendall had always come with him on business trips, and even though they'd naturally had separate quarters, he'd seen her virtually from sunup to sundown. Of course, this wasn't, technically, a business trip. But he would have brought Kendall along, had she still been in his employ, because he would be working while he was here. And Kendall had been a big part of his work for five years.

Five years, he thought as he grabbed his bag and strode toward the stairs that led up to the second floor. In the scheme of things, it wasn't such a long time. But it comprised the entirety of Kendall's work life. He was the only employer she'd had since graduating. He'd been her first. Her only. He'd been the one who had introduced her to the ways of business, the one who'd taught her how to achieve the most satisfaction in what she did, the one who'd shown her which positions to take on things that would yield the most pleasurable results. And now, after he'd been the one to initiate her in all the intricacies of the working relationship, another employer had wooed her away.

"Oh, for God's sake, Barton," he muttered to himself as he climbed the stairs. "You're talking about her like she's an old lover."

He waited for the laughter that was bound to come from entertaining a thought like that, but for some reason, it didn't come. Instead, he was overcome by a strange kind of fatigue that made him want to blow off work for the rest of the day and instead go do something more—

The thought made him stop dead in his tracks, halfway up the stairs. Blow off work? Since when had he *ever* blown off work? For any reason? And how could anything be *more* than work? Work was everything. Talk about something that should have made him erupt into laughter.

But he didn't laugh at that, either. Instead, he realized he'd left his laptop out in the trunk of the car. Worse, he realized that, even if he'd remembered to bring it in with him, he wasn't completely sure how to get to all the files he needed to get to. That had always been Kendall's job. Knowing how to pull up whatever needed pulling up and pulling it up for him. Hell, half the time, she'd taken care of whatever needed pulling and then pushed it back down again.

He was going to have to hire a temp for now, he told himself. Surely there was a temp agency close by. Tahoe City maybe. Too bad Kendall wasn't here. She would have found just the right person, and she would have had the person here five minutes ago. But how hard could it be? he asked himself. He just needed to find the phone book, and he'd be good to go.

So where did people keep their phone books, anyway…

By the time she entered the bar of the Timber Lake Inn that evening, Kendall had accepted the fact that it, like everything else in the establishment, would be cozy. Sure enough, it was. Like the rest of the hotel, it was pine-paneled with hardwood floors and Native American rugs, but the lighting was lower than in the other public rooms, softer and more golden, and very… Well, there was just no way around it. Romantic.

Matthias was right. This wasn't the sort of hotel any businessman in his right mind would use for business functions. Nevertheless, she was confident Stephen DeGallo had his reasons for using it. *Besides* trying to lull Kendall into a false sense of security, which Matthias had implied— hah—was the case. Or to lull her into anything else, either. For all she knew, the Timber Lake Inn was the only hotel in Lake Tahoe that had had any openings when Stephen scheduled the orientation. And the fact that Lake Tahoe itself was such a cozy, romantic destination that was kind of an odd choice for a business orientation had nothing to do with anything. It was centrally located, that was all.

She shook the thought almost literally out of her head

and smoothed her hand one final time over the chocolate-brown trousers and cream-colored shirt she'd donned for the evening. Stephen had said the evening would be casual, and what she had on was casual attire. It *was*. Even if it was the same kind of thing she'd worn to work every day when she was with Matthias. Ah, *working for* Matthias, she quickly corrected herself. And the reason she'd wound her hair up into its usual workplace bun and put on her usual workplace glasses wasn't because she was trying to overcompensate for the cozy, romantic environment. It *wasn't*. It was because she just hadn't felt like going to any trouble. She had low-maintenance hair. So sue her. And even though she didn't need her glasses all the time, what with the low lighting and everything, she figured she'd need them.

So there.

She scanned the bar for a group of people who looked as if they were training for new careers, but saw only couples at a handful of tables here and there. Cozy couples. Romantic couples. In fact, one couple was being *so* romantic Kendall wanted to yell, "Jeez, people, get a room!" Glancing down at her watch, she realized she was a little early, so maybe she was the first member of the OmniTech orientation group to arrive. Then a movement in the corner of the room—the *farthest* corner—and the *darkest* corner, she couldn't help noticing—caught her eye, and she realized it was Stephen DeGallo, waving at her.

She lifted a hand in return and made her way in that direction, picking her way through the tables as she looked around for anyone else who might be joining him. And somehow, she refrained from muttering, *Jeez, people, get a room* as she passed by the overly demonstrative couple.

Nor did she toss a glass of ice water over them, which was another thought she hadn't quite been able to quell.

"Kendall," Stephen said warmly when she was within earshot. "Great to see you again. Glad you made it in one piece."

"It's great to be here, Stephen," she said as she extended her hand in greeting. "Thanks again for giving me this opportunity. I'm very excited about working for OmniTech."

He grasped her hand in both of his, not really shaking it, per se, just holding it for perhaps a moment longer than was necessary, something that made her think about Matthias's warning again. Which she immediately pushed out of her brain. Stephen was just being friendly. And she was just being overly sensitive, thanks to Matthias's ridiculous ideas about Stephen only wanting her because of her ties to Barton Limited. This was what happened when you were employed by a workaholic for so many years. You forgot that normal people could be casual and friendly, even in professional situations.

And Stephen's smile did put Kendall immediately at ease. Although he wasn't a handsome man, he was by no means unattractive. He was slim and fit, and was dressed according to his own edict—casually—in a pair of softly faded blue jeans and a white polo shirt. His blue eyes held intelligence and good humor, and his dark blond hair was just beginning to go gray, threaded here and there with bits of silver. What he lacked in handsomeness, he more than made up for in charisma. He was just one of those people who had a gift for taking charge of a situation without being overbearing, and making people feel better that he had.

Kendall had done her homework after his offer of employment, so she knew quite a bit about him. In many ways, he was as devoted to his company as Matthias was to Barton Limited, but where Matthias's extracurricular and social activities all still seemed to involve his work, Stephen DeGallo was a man who enjoyed his leisure time. He was a champion yachtsman and active in a charitable foundation he had started ten years ago that mentored gifted, but underprivileged high school students.

He was not just a good businessman, but a good guy, Kendall had discovered. And her admiration of him was due to both.

She seated herself in the chair he held out for her, folding her elbows on the table and weaving her fingers lightly together. Then she gave him her most businesslike smile. "Am I the first to arrive?" she asked, even though the answer was obvious.

"Actually," Stephen said as he folded himself into the chair opposite hers, "right now, you're the *only* one who's here."

Kendall told herself she just imagined the note of vague discomfort she thought she heard in his voice. More of Matthias's influence on her nerves, she was sure. Still, it was odd that no one else had arrived yet.

"Don't tell me I'm the only one who got here on time," she said.

"No, of course not," he told her. "The others just aren't scheduled to arrive until Wednesday."

Wednesday? Kendall thought. That was two whole days away. "Oh," she said, the word sounding more disappointed than she'd intended.

"The others are training for management positions," he said by way of an explanation. "You're the only VP candidate this time around. So I thought it would be nice if the two of us could have a couple of days where I could go over some of the policies and procedures that won't be pertinent to everyone else's training."

That made sense, Kendall thought.

"But first, a drink," he said, motioning to a waiter who had been hovering within range. "What would you like? I discovered a wonderful California pinot noir recently that's absolutely delightful."

"Thanks," Kendall told him, "but I'll just have a bottle of sparkling water."

He threw her a look of mock effrontery. "But we're celebrating your joining the OmniTech team," he objected.

"Which is why I ordered *sparkling* water," she said with a smile.

He smiled back, dipping his head forward in acknowledgment. "Then I'll have the same," he told the waiter. "Now then," he added as their server departed, "I thought we could spend much of tonight talking about how—"

"Stephen DeGallo!"

Kendall flinched at the sound of the booming, all-too-familiar voice, but managed to otherwise keep her irritation in check. Well, enough that no one would notice it, anyway. Though she had to admit that Stephen didn't look any happier about the interruption than she was. Nevertheless, good businessman—and guy—that he was, he smiled as he rose to greet Matthias. Kendall turned in her chair to acknowledge her former employer, but remained seated, hoping that small act of discourtesy would illustrate her pique in a way that wasn't quite as impolite as other actions might have been. Actions like, oh…Kendall didn't know. Tripping him as he strode past her to shake Stephen's hand. Calling him a big poophead. Stuff like that.

She noticed Stephen didn't grasp Matthias's hand in

both of his the way he had hers—in fact, he gave Matthias's one, two, three firm, manly shakes and released it. Then again, Matthias was a rival, so naturally, Stephen's greeting to him wouldn't be as familiar as his to Kendall had been. Similarly, it was understandable why Stephen's posture, too, with Matthias would be more assertive, more straight-forward, more businesslike, than it had been with Kendall. Wouldn't it?

Yeah. Sure. Of course.

"Matthias Barton," Stephen greeted him. "Long time, no see. What have you been up to?"

"Besides competing with you for the Perkins contract?" Matthias replied. "Not much."

Well, he'd recently lost his personal assistant of five years, Kendall thought irritably. Or so she'd heard. That was kind of major.

As if he'd read her mind, Matthias turned to her then and feigned tremendous surprise—though, Kendall thought, not very well.

"Why, Kendall Scarborough," he said with overblown amazement. "What are you doing here? I haven't seen you since…" He pretended to search his memory banks—again, not exactly an Academy Award-winning performance—then snapped his fingers. "Since you gave me your two weeks' notice to go work for some fly-by-night company."

She sighed wearily. "Well, except for this afternoon in my room, when you offered me my job back."

Now Stephen was the one to look surprised, Kendall noted. Only his was obviously genuine. Then he smiled, and looked at Matthias again. "Really?" he asked the other man.

Matthias looked a little uncomfortable now, and this time, he wasn't pretending. "It was just a formality," he said. "I always offer my exes the chance to come back, once they come to their senses and realize what a mistake they made, leaving Barton Limited."

Kendall couldn't prevent the snort of laughter that escaped her at that. Yeah, right. Matthias had the longest memory of anyone she'd ever met, and he never forgot a slight—real *or* imagined. If someone elected to leave the company for any reason, he had that person's personnel file expunged within the hour, as if they never existed. And he certainly never went looking for that person to offer them an opportunity to return.

Not until this afternoon, anyway, she reminded herself.

But the only reason he'd come looking for her, she further told herself, was because he hadn't known how to program his new BlackBerry. The offer to take her back had obviously been off-the-cuff, and had doubtless been extended for the same reason. He thought she was the only one who knew how to program one of those things. He didn't realize anyone could do it for him. Well, anyone except Matthias Barton.

"Well, Barton," Stephen said now, "had you appreciated Kendall's possibilities, the way I do, then maybe you wouldn't have lost her in the first place."

Kendall started to smile at that, then stopped. Something about the way Stephen had said it made it sound kind of unprofessional. Just what had he meant by *possibilities?* That was kind of a strange word to use. Why not *abilities?* Or *talents?* Or *expertise? Possibilities* made it sound as though he considered her a blank slate or unformed mass that he could turn into whatever he wanted.

"I assure you, DeGallo," Matthias replied, "that Kendall was one of my most prized possessions at Barton Limited. I hope you realize what an asset she'll be to OmniTech."

All right, Kendall thought. That did it. Forget about blank slates and unformed masses. Matthias had just made her sound like a new computer system. Possession? Asset? Just who did he think he was?

"Prized possession?" she echoed indignantly.

Matthias looked down at her and must have realized immediately from both her voice and her expression—and, most likely, the quick drop in temperature among the small group—what a colossal gaffe he'd just made. "Uh..." he began eloquently.

"If that's the case," she continued while he was still off balance, "then you better go over my operating instructions while you're here. I wouldn't want Stephen to think he acquired a defective machine."

The look Matthias gave her then was almost convincingly distressed. Almost. "Kendall, that's not—"

This time his words were cut off by Stephen's light, good-natured laughter. "Sounds to me like she works just fine," he said. "In fact, this particular model is promising to work better than I initially hoped."

Matthias's lips thinned at that. "Yeah, she's a piece of work, all right," he muttered.

She smiled sweetly. "And now I'm working for someone else."

Matthias opened his mouth to respond, but this time was prevented by the arrival of their server, who placed tall sweaty glasses of mineral water in front of Kendall and Stephen. Then the waiter looked at Matthias and asked, "Will you be joining this party?"

Even Matthias, Kendall thought, wouldn't be crass enough to crash her meeting with Stephen. And he didn't. Instead, he told their server that no, he was on his own and didn't want to interrupt anyone's dinner, so would just take a seat at a table by himself. Then, even though there were at least a dozen empty tables in the restaurant, he pulled out a chair from the table immediately beside Kendall's and Stephen's, and seated himself without a care.

Unbelievable, Kendall thought. Evidently, Matthias was that crass, after all. If not in blatantly joining them, then certainly in doing his best to destroy any chance the two of them might have for speaking freely about her new obligations as vice president. There was no way Stephen would discuss the policies of his company in the presence of one of his competitors, even superficially. He confirmed that by shrugging philosophically when Kendall looked at him—not that she needed any confirmation.

So instead of talking about her new job over the course of dinner, Kendall and Stephen instead discussed superficialities like the weather, books, current events and a favorite TV show they had in common…with Matthias throwing in his own commentaries here and there, completely uninvited.

It was going to be a long orientation.

Four

The temp Matthias ordered from a Tahoe City agency—once he found the phone book after thirty minutes of looking for it—arrived promptly at eight o'clock the morning after his arrival. Unfortunately, he'd done something wrong when he tried to set his alarm clock the night before—no, the alarm clock was defective, that was the problem—because it was the ringing of the front doorbell that alerted him to the arrival of his early-morning appointment. Not Kendall, who would have normally alerted Matthias to that. Kendall, too, would have been infinitely less intrusive about her reminder than the doorbell was.

Damn, he thought as he looked groggily at the clock and realized it had stopped working completely. He lifted his watch from the nightstand and grimaced when he saw the time. He never slept this late. And he'd never been unprepared for an appointment. Shoving off the covers, he jackknifed into a sitting position and scrubbed both hands briskly over his face to rouse himself. He grabbed a plain white T-shirt from the bag he hadn't even begun to unpack, shook it out quickly and thrust it over his head as he descended the stairs. And he thought dryly how lucky he was that it matched his sweatpants so well, otherwise he might have to be embarrassed about his attire. It was only as he was reaching for the doorknob that he realized he'd forgotten to put on shoes, so would be greeting his temporary employee barefoot. Somehow, though, he couldn't quite rouse the wherewithal to care.

The young man on the other side of the door looked surprised by Matthias's sudden appearance—and, doubtless, by his slovenly appearance—but quickly schooled his features into indifference. He obviously hadn't overslept, because he was well-groomed and dressed impeccably in a pale gray suit and white dress shirt, his necktie the only spot of color on his person—if you could consider pale yellow a color. He was young, early twenties at most, his blond hair cut short, his gray eyes nearly the same color as his suit. He looked to Matthias like something from a middle school poster advertising Junior Achievement.

"Mr. Barton?" he said.

Matthias ran a quick hand through his dark hair to tame it as best he could. "Yeah, that's me," he replied. Quickly, he amended, "I mean, yes. I'm Matthias Barton."

"William Denton," he said, extending his hand. "From DayTimers. I'm your new temp."

"Whoa, whoa, whoa," Matthias said, holding up a hand. "I haven't hired you yet."

This was clearly news to young William. "But they said

you need an assistant for the month you'll be spending here in Hunter's Landing," he said.

"I do need an assistant for the month," Matthias told him. "But I'm not going to take any Tom, Dick or William they send my way. I need to make sure you have all the qualifications I need for an assistant."

Young William smiled confidently. "No worries there, Mr. Barton. Temping is just my summer job. I earned my BS from the Haas School of Business at UC Berkeley in May, and I'll be returning in the fall to start work on my MBA. I'm more than qualified to take on this position."

Matthias's back went up at the kid's presumption. "Are you?" he asked coolly.

William Denton's confidence seemed to waver a bit. Nevertheless, he replied, "Yes. I am." As an afterthought, he added, "Sir."

Matthias nodded, settling his hands on his hips in challenge. They'd just see about that. Without even inviting William Denton into the lodge, he barked, "What are the major managerial and organizational challenges posed by electronic commerce?"

William Denton blinked as if a too-bright flash had gone off right in front of his eyes. "I…what?"

Matthias shook his head, sighed with much gusto, and asked, "All right, if that one's too tough, then how about this. True or false. In the simple Ricardian model, trade between similar economies is unlikely to generate large gains from that trade."

William Denton's lips parted in response to that one, but no words emerged to answer the question. Until, finally, he said, "I…what?"

Man, Matthias thought, this guy was never going to

amount to anything if he couldn't answer the most obvious question in the world. "All right, here's an easy one," he said. "Multiple choice. The current ratio and quick ratio are the best indicators of a company's what? A. liquidity, B. efficiency, C. profitability or D. growth rate."

William Denton's mouth began to work over that one—kind of—but his brain didn't seem to be cooperating.

Matthias shook his head in disappointment. "I'm sorry, Mr. Denton, but I just don't think you have what it takes to—"

"Wait!" he interrupted. "I know the answer to that one!"

"Unfortunately, your time is up," Matthias told him. "Tell DayTimers I'll be in touch."

And with that, he pushed the front door closed and turned away. From the other side, William Denton called out, "A! It's A! Liquidity! Right? Am I right?"

He was right, Matthias thought. But it was too little, too late. The person he hired as his assistant was going to have to be a quick thinker and unafraid to speak up, in addition to being knowledgeable and savvy. Like Kendall. William Denton just didn't have what it took to fill her shoes.

Oh, well. Another candidate lacking even the most rudimentary business skills. Another interview shot to hell. Matthias would just have to look for someone else.

Padding barefoot to the kitchen, he absently pushed the button on the coffeemaker, then went to retrieve the phone book from the same cabinet where he had discovered it the day before. Bypassing DayTimers this time—since, if William Denton was the best they could do, they were obviously a fly-by-night operation—he selected the next agency on the list. After arranging for a prospective temp to come to the lodge later in the day, Matthias turned to pour himself a cup of coffee—

Only to discover that the carafe on the hot pad was empty. In fact, the hot pad wasn't even hot. He was sure he'd filled the machine with both water and coffee the night before, but lifted the top, anyway, to make sure. Yep. Coffee on one side. Water on the other. Just like the directions said. He checked to make sure the machine was plugged in. Yep. It was. He made sure the cord was attached to the coffeemaker, as well, ensured that the light switch on the wall nearest the appliance was switched to the on position, in case that was necessary, inspected everything he could possibly inspect to see what the problem was. To no avail. He pushed the on button again. Nothing.

Dammit.

Matthias wasn't one of those pathetic caffeine addicts who couldn't function without their crack-of-dawn coffee and suffered ugly mood swings when denied. No way. But, like any civilized human being, he liked to enjoy a cup or two in the morning, maybe three if he had time, possibly four or five, if he had a meeting or something, and, okay maybe another jolt or two or three in the afternoon when he needed it. He didn't *have* to have coffee. He just wanted it. A lot.

He stared at the coffeemaker intently, drumming his fingers irregularly on the countertop, willing the machine to work. With great deliberation, he pushed the on button again. Nada.

Damn. His gaze lit then on a short stack of papers he'd placed on the countertop the night before. It was the last assignment Kendall had completed before she'd tendered her resignation, a contract she'd typed up for an agreement between Barton Limited and a new consulting firm with whom he'd be doing limited business for the rest of the year. He smiled, and reached for the phone again, punching in a number he knew by heart.

"Kendall," he said when she answered her cell phone. "It's…" He started to say "Mr. Barton," but halted. "Matthias," he identified himself instead. "There's a problem with the Donovan contract you typed up before you left. Can you spare a couple of hours this morning to go over it?" He listened to her objection, then said, "I realize that. But this is a problem you're responsible for, one you need to rectify. And it's urgent. When can you be here?" He grinned at her reply. "Good. I promise not to keep you any longer than I absolutely have to. And, Kendall," he added before she had a chance to hang up, "I saw a coffee shop in town. Would you mind swinging by it on your way?"

Kendall stewed as she waited for Matthias to answer the doorbell she'd just rung, and switched the enormous cardboard cup of coffee from one hand to the other as it began to burn her fingers. It had been awkward, to say the least, explaining to Stephen DeGallo on her first official day of training why she needed to take part of the morning off. And although he hadn't exactly been happy about the request, he'd told her to go ahead, that they could meet again after lunch.

Lunch, she thought now, that she should have been having with her new boss, not the one she'd left behind.

As if conjured by the thought, Matthias opened the door, smiling with what looked like profound relief when he saw her. She softened some at his expression, flattered that, in spite of everything, he still seemed to need her. It was always a nice feeling to have.

Then he reached for the massive cup of coffee in her hand, popped off the top and lifted it toward his face, inhaling deeply to enjoy a long, leisurely sniff. Carefully, he lifted it to his mouth and sipped, closing his eyes as he savored it. Then he opened them again, stared down into the dark brew and said, "Oh, God, that's better."

That was when Kendall realized it was the coffee for which he was grateful, not her. And she wondered again why she'd bothered.

Because she was conscientious about her work, she told herself. It had nothing to do with Matthias needing her. If there truly was a problem with the Donovan contract that was her fault, then it was, as he'd said, up to her to rectify it. Although she couldn't imagine what she'd done wrong. She'd triple- and quadruple-checked the document before she'd given it to Matthias to look at. And why was he just now looking at it, anyway? she wondered. It was supposed to have gone back to Elliot Donovan two weeks ago.

And what was up with his appearance? she wondered further. Okay, she knew he was on vacation, but she'd never seen him looking like this. Here it was, almost ten o'clock in the morning, and he looked as if he'd just rolled out of bed. His black sweatpants were rumpled from sleep, as was the white V-neck T-shirt stretched taut enough across his chest that she could see the dark hair beneath— besides what was visible around the neckline. A day's growth of beard shadowed his face, his dark hair was shaggy and uncombed and his brown eyes were hooded and soft. He looked…

Well, actually, Kendall thought as a coil of something warm and electric unwound in her belly, he looked kind of…hot.

No! Not hot! she immediately corrected herself. Slovenly. Yeah, that was it. Seeing him looking the way he did made her think of some lazy hedonist lolling in bed on a Sunday morning. Some dark-haired, sleepy-eyed pleasure monger, waking slowly and stretching his brawny arms high over his head, then smiling down at the woman lying next to him, who—Hey, how about that?—looked a lot like Kendall, then gliding a slow finger across my…I mean, *her*…naked shoulder, then leaning down to trace the same path with his mouth before rolling me…I mean, *her*…over onto her back and sliding his hand beneath the covers, down along my…I mean, *her*…naked torso and settling it between my…I mean, *her*…I mean…I mean…I mean…

She stifled a groan and stopped thinking about how Matthias looked. Until he lowered the cup of coffee again and ran his tongue along the seam of his lips to savor the lingering taste of it, wherein all Kendall could do was think about how it would feel to have his tongue running along the seam of her lips, too.

Oh. No.

The Donovan contract, she reminded herself. That was why she was here. Not for…anything else. "So, um…what's the, uh…the problem with the, ah…the Donovan contract," she finally got out.

For a moment, he looked at her as if he had no idea what she was talking about. Then, "Right," he finally said. "Come on in."

He stepped aside to let her enter, and as Kendall pushed past him, she tried not to notice how the fragrance of the coffee mingled with a scent that was distinctly Matthias, something spicy and woodsy whose source she'd never been able to identify. It was probably from the soap or shampoo that he used, though she'd never known another man to smell the way he did—or as good as he did. And smelling him again now, after being deprived for two weeks…

She sighed. What was the matter with her this morning? She was reacting to Matthias as if he were an old boyfriend she hadn't been ready to break up with.

She reminded herself again that she was nothing more to him than a former employee, and that he was nothing more to her than a former employer. She'd come here because of a professional obligation, not a personal one. The sooner she fixed whatever she'd done wrong with the Donovan contract, the sooner she could get back to work. Her new work. At her new job. With her new boss. One who appreciated her business degree and knowledge. One to whom she owed the greater obligation now. Matthias was her past. No, Barton Limited was her past, she corrected herself. And OmniTech Solutions was her future.

Period.

She spun around as Matthias closed the front door. "What's the problem?" she asked point blank.

Instead of answering her, he tilted his head toward the sweeping staircase behind him and said, "This way."

She rankled at the order, but followed him, noting how beautiful the lodge was. Wow. Whoever'd furnished the place had great taste. And they knew a thing or two about making a home comfortable without making it too feminine. Although the colors were bold and the fabrics a little masculine, Kendall would have felt perfectly content staying here herself. And the view of the lake beyond the picture windows was spectacular.

She wondered again about the details of the bequest that required him to be here. It must have been a pretty major requirement to make him take an entire month away from the office. Especially in a place like Lake Tahoe, where there were so few corporate concerns, and no one she could think of that Barton Limited did business with. Then again, in the whole time she'd worked for him, she couldn't remember him ever taking a vacation of more than a couple of days. So maybe it would do him good to be here for a month. Maybe he'd learn to relax a little. Realize there was more to life than work.

Yeah, right, she thought. And maybe the next World Wrestling champion would be named Stone Cold Sheldon Abernathy.

As her foot hit the stairway landing, her gaze lit on a photograph that was hanging there, and Matthias's reasons for being in the lodge became clearer. Unable to stop herself, Kendall halted for a moment, smiling at the picture of the—she quickly counted—seven men, all college-aged, one of whom was obviously Matthias. But one was his twin brother, Luke, too, so she wasn't sure, at first, which was which. Then she noted the way one of the boys' smiles curled up a little more on one side than the other, and she knew, without question, it was Matthias. Interestingly, he was the one with the longer hair, and was the more raggedly dressed of the two. Funny, because Matthias had always talked about his brother as if Luke were the black sheep of the family, the rebel, the one who wanted to make waves. Looking at the photograph, however, it was Matthias who better fit that description.

"The contract is in the office," she heard him say from some distance away.

Looking up, she saw that he had continued to the second floor and was striding down the hall without realizing she had stopped. "Hey!" she called after him, surprising herself. She'd never said *Hey!* to Matthias before. It had always been *Excuse me, sir* or *Pardon me, Mr. Barton,* something that had been in keeping with their relationship—which had always been fairly formal. It was just that, being here in this beautiful, comfortable lodge with him, seeing him in sweats and a T-shirt and finding a picture of him from his youth, formal was the last thing she felt.

He spun around at the summons, at first looking as surprised by the casual address as she'd been. Then he saw what she was looking at and...

Huh, she thought. She would have thought he would smile in much the same way as he was smiling in the photograph. Instead, he looked kind of annoyed. Probably because he didn't want an employee—even a former one—seeing him as anything but the businessman that he was.

Well, tough, she retorted silently. If that was the case, he shouldn't have made her drive down here. And he certainly shouldn't have answered the door in his jammies.

He walked slowly back down the hall, and then the stairs, until he stood beside her, hooking his hands on his hips in a way that made him look very put out. "What?" he asked. Interestingly, he didn't look at the picture, even though he had to realize that was why she'd called him back.

Unfortunately, she suddenly realized she wasn't sure what she'd intended to say when she'd called him back. She'd mostly just wanted to look at him now and compare him to the boy in the photograph. So she pointed to the picture and said, "Who are these guys you're with?"

It was with obvious reluctance that Matthias turned to look at the picture. He studied it for only a moment, then turned back to Kendall. "Friends from college. We called ourselves the Seven Samurai."

"Akira Kurosawa fans, were you?" she asked, proud of herself for knowing the name of the director of the film made half a century ago.

"Actually, I think Hunter was the only one of us who even saw the movie. He's the one who named us. God knows why."

"Which one is Hunter?" Kendall asked.

With even more reluctance than before, Matthias lifted his hand and pointed at the young man who was laughing right at the camera. He looked the happiest of the bunch, and gave the impression, even on film, of being their ringleader.

"Where is he now?" Kendall asked.

Matthias hesitated a telling moment before revealing, "He died."

Something hard and cold twisted in Kendall's belly at hearing the flatness of Matthias's voice. Even more than he sounded sad, he sounded…tired. As if the weight of his friend's death was too much for him to bear.

"What happened?" she asked softly. "He was so young."

"Melanoma," he said. "This is his lodge, even though he never lived to see it completed."

"I'm so sorry, Matthias," she said quietly. Impulsively, she extended a hand and curled her fingers over his upper arm, giving it a gentle, reassuring squeeze. His skin was warm beneath her fingers, solid, strong. But in that moment, he didn't seem any of those things himself. "I didn't mean to bring up bad memories," she told him.

He shook his head. "Actually, since coming here, I've had one or two good memories," he told her. "Things I'd forgotten about." He did smile then, albeit sadly. Still, it was better to see that than the look of desolation that had clouded his features a moment ago.

She waited to see if he would elaborate on his memories, but he didn't. And Kendall didn't want to pry any further than she already had. Even if she was massively curious about the other young men in the picture. And even more curious about the young Matthias.

"So the rest of you will share the house now?" she asked.

"None of us owns the place," he told her. "But each of us is spending a month here before it goes to its rightful owner. Which will be the town of Hunter's Landing."

Kendall smiled. She hadn't made the connection until now. "So Hunter came from here? Or he's named after the place?"

Matthias shook his head. "No, I think he just stumbled onto the town and liked that it shared his name. And since it was on the lake, he thought it was the perfect spot for the lodge. We'd all talked about doing something like this in college, building a big party house we'd share someday, but after graduation, we never followed through. We were all too *busy*," he said, the last word sounding as if it left a bad taste in his mouth. "Busy *working*," he added, emphasizing that word in a way that was even less complimentary. Which was strange, since Matthias was the kind of man for whom busyness was one of the seven virtues and for whom work was sheer Nirvana. "Too busy working for useless things like following dreams," he concluded softly.

His expression had gone soft, too, as he spoke, Kendall noticed, and when he turned away from the picture to look at her again, there was something in his eyes she'd never seen before. Melancholy. It was almost tangible.

"So do you still see the other Samurai?" she asked. "Besides your brother, I mean?"

Who, she had to admit, he hadn't seen much of. It had only been a couple of months ago that the brothers had even spoken to each other after years of estrangement. And then only because Matthias had needed Luke to switch months at the cabin with him so he could take his trip to Stuttgart. It had been that or break the terms of the will, and Matthias hadn't wanted to do that. Neither had Luke, which was the only reason he'd gone along with the switch. Ultimately, once everything with Lauren Conover had been smoothed out, the Barton brothers had renewed their relationship. But it was still, Kendall knew, a little strained at times.

Matthias looked at the picture again, seeming to take in each of the men one by one. "I haven't seen any of them for years," he said. "Though we'll all be here for the dedication in September."

"What dedication?" Kendall echoed.

He nodded, still looking at the photograph. "Once each of us has spent a month here, the house will go to the town, and I think the plan is to turn it into some kind of medical facility or something. Anyway, there's going to be a big ceremony with the mayor and chamber of commerce or something. All of us will be here, too."

She smiled. "Sounds like Hunter was a good guy."

"The best," Matthias immediately replied. " He was the very best of all of us." This time, when he smiled, there was genuine warmth, and genuine happiness, in the gesture. Then the smile fell, and he grimaced a bit. "I'm sorry. I'm keeping you longer than I meant to."

Actually, Kendall thought, *she* was the one who was holding up things by asking all these questions. *She* was the one who would make herself even later than she'd intended getting back to Stephen DeGallo. Funny, though, how she hadn't given Stephen a thought since entering the lodge.

"Hey," she said again when he started to turn away, more softly than she had the first time.

He spun around again. "What?"

She smiled and pointed to him in the photo. "You looked good with long hair."

He looked at where she was pointing and asked, "Are you so sure that one's me? It could be Luke."

She shook her head. "No, I know it's you."

Now he crossed his arms over his chest, as if in challenge. "How do you know?"

She wasn't about to tell him she knew him by his roguish smile. So she said, "I can tell by the twinkle in your eyes."

Oh, bravo, Kendall, she congratulated herself. *Telling him that was so much better than telling him you recognized him by his smile.*

Matthias arched his eyebrows at the comment, his eyes… Oh, damn. They were twinkling. "Really?" he asked with much interest. Way more interest than he should be showing, actually.

"I mean…" Kendall started to backtrack.

But he wasn't going to let her. "You think my eyes twinkle? Since when?"

"Well, since you were in college, anyway," she hedged. She pointed at the photograph again. "Obviously."

"No, I mean, since when did *you* notice it?" he asked.

If she were going to be honest, she would have to admit that she first noticed it when he interviewed her for the job. Naturally, she wouldn't tell him that. "I don't know," she hedged again. "And really, it's not like they twinkle a lot or anything."

He smiled. "They must, if that's how you knew it was me in the photo and not Luke."

"Okay, I lied," she said. "That's not how I knew it was you in the picture."

His smile grew broader. He was enjoying this, she thought. Enjoying seeing her uncomfortable. Enjoying putting her on the spot. She eyed him carefully. Or was it that he was enjoying the fact that she'd noticed his eyes? she wondered.

Nah, she assured herself. He couldn't have cared less what she noticed about him. He was just having fun at her expense.

"Then if it wasn't my twinkling eyes," he said, "what was it?"

She sighed with exasperation. At herself, because if she'd been put on the spot, it wasn't Matthias who'd put her there. She'd gone willingly by opening her mouth in the first place. Oh, hell, she thought. She'd already blown it. So she answered honestly this time, "It's your smile, okay? I could tell it was you because of your smile."

A smile that bloomed full force when he heard that. Honestly, Kendall thought. There should be a vaccination for the way Matthias could make a woman feel by turning on the full wattage of his smile.

"Really?" he asked. "What's so special about it?"

"Oh, you're just fishing now," she told him.

"Damned right. It's not every day a beautiful woman compliments a man's smile."

It was for him, Kendall thought. She was sure of—

Then the rest of what he said hit her. "You think I'm beautiful?"

His smile faltered at that. "Did I say that?"

She nodded. Vigorously. "Yes. You did."

He shifted his weight from one foot to the other, clearly not feeling as confident as he'd been a second ago. "Are you sure?"

"Yes. I am." What, did he think she didn't notice it when a man said she was beautiful? Especially a man like him?

"Well, I…" he began. "I mean…" he continued. "It's just…" he hedged this time.

"What?" Kendall demanded.

He jutted his thumb over his shoulder and said, "The Donovan contract. We really need to take a look at that."

She opened her mouth to object, but Matthias had already spun around on his heel and was headed down the hall. Knowing it would be pointless to continue—for now—Kendall followed him.

She found herself in an office decorated as nicely as the rest of the house, all warm wood paneling and hardwood floors and bold colors and boxy, but comfortable, furniture. There was a desk on which sat Matthias's laptop—she'd recognize it anywhere, even without the San Francisco Giants wallpaper—a chair, some shelves and a massive bulletin board onto which someone had tacked and taped more old photos of Matthias and his other six Samurai.

Then her gaze lit on a handwritten note that was tacked up alongside them. "Matt," it began—Matt? Kendall thought.

Good luck, bud. You're about to begin your month at "the Love Shack." Remember the universal truths about women we came up with on New Year's Eve our senior year? Scrap 'em. Here are the new universal truths about The One: She'll set you free. Loving her is the most dangerous thing you'll ever do.

It was signed, "Ryan."

Matt? Kendall thought again. She couldn't imagine anyone calling Matthias *Matt.* Then she remembered the way he'd looked in the photograph and altered her opinion. She supposed, once upon a time, he could have been a *Matt* after all. But what was with this "love shack" business?

"Here it is," Matthias said, picking up the document in question and dispelling any further ruminations she might have had on the love shack thing. "There are actually three places where I found errors," he added as he flipped up the top page.

Three? Kendall wondered. How could there have been that many? She'd gone over it a million times.

"The first one is on page two," he said.

She moved to stand beside him, so she could see what he was talking about, and tried again to ignore the luscious fragrance that was coffee and Matthias Barton.

He pointed to the middle of the second paragraph and said, "You left out a comma here."

Certain she'd misunderstood, she looked up at him and said, "What?"

He pointed again. "A comma," he repeated. "You left one out here. This is a compound sentence. There should be a comma before *and* here. And then on page three," he said, quickly turning the next page, "in the first paragraph here, this semicolon should be a comma, too. I'm sure of it. And on the last page," he continued, flipping back to that, "you didn't make the signature line long enough.

There should be at least another quarter inch there, to allow space for Donovan to sign. His first name is Elliot. You don't want to add insult to injury, not giving the man enough room to sign his name."

Kendall couldn't believe her ears. *This* was the problem with the Donovan contract? A comma? A semicolon? A signature line? For *this,* she'd risked hacking off her new boss? For *this* she'd driven a half hour one way? For *this* she'd bought him coffee using money out of her own pocket?

But even more offensive than all that was the fact that he was completely wrong. There was absolutely no need for a comma where he said there was—that wasn't a compound sentence—and the semicolon was perfectly fine. As for the sig line, she'd seen Elliot Donovan's signature before, and a more cramped bit of writing didn't exist anywhere. There was more than enough room for the man to sign his name.

She narrowed her eyes at Matthias. "You brought me all the way down here for a comma, a semicolon and a signature line?"

He clearly didn't see anything wrong with that. "It's details like that, Kendall, that people notice."

"Not unless they're wrong. Which these aren't," she told him.

He looked surprised at that. "Really?"

"Really."

"You're sure?"

"I'm sure."

"Oh. Well. Then I guess I brought you down here for nothing."

If looks could kill, Kendall thought, Matthias would be radioactive wind just then.

"But now that you're here," he said, "why don't you stay for lunch? The caretaker left some great stuff in the fridge."

There were so many ways Kendall could have answered his question—not the least of which was head-butting him, something she very much wanted to do just then—so she settled on a simple, "No. Thank you," and hoped he would hear the edge in her voice. And then, you know, fear for his life.

Instead, he smiled and asked, "Then how about if I offer you your old job back, and then you won't have to worry about getting back to Stephen DeGallo on time, because you'll already be where you need to be."

At that, Kendall decided that head-butting was too good for Matthias. What he really deserved was being hit with a brick. No, two bricks. Oh, what the hell. The same number of bricks it took to build the British Museum. However, she again managed to reply, "No. Thank you." And then she added, "Now, if you'll excuse me, I have to, as you said, go where I need to be. Which is *not* here."

And with that, she spun on her heel and exited the office. Without looking back once. Without even saying goodbye.

Five

Matthias watched Kendall through the front window of the cabin as she descended the steps toward her car.

He'd told her the truth about having good memories of Hunter and the rest of the gang since coming to the lodge. But he'd been plagued by even more bad ones. Not just of Hunter's death, but of how he and Luke had let their own relationship fall apart. Hunter had been the one in college who'd somehow managed to help the brothers turn their competition with each other into affection for each other. When he died, it was almost as if the bond that had held Matthias and Luke together died, too.

Matt and Luke, he corrected himself. Back then, he hadn't been Matthias. He'd been Matt. A regular guy, an easygoing student, the kind of kid who liked keggers and Three Stooges movies and games of pickup rugby in the park. It had only been after college, when he'd heard the terms of his father's will, that he'd begun to go by his given name of Matthias. Matthias had sounded more studied than Matt, more serious, more seasoned. Matthias had sounded like a grown-up. And, thanks to the terms of his father's will, Matt had been forced to grow up fast.

Even in death, the old man had pitted the twin brothers against each other, decreeing that whoever was able to make the first million would win the estate in its entirety. The one who didn't would be left with nothing. When the attorneys had read the stipulation to him and Luke, Matthias had been able to picture their father in the afterlife, leaning back in his celestial Barcalounger, rubbing his hands together with relish and saying, "Let the games begin."

And at first it had kind of been a game. Luke and Matthias had each good-naturedly joked that they would leave the other in the dust. Both had started their own companies, and then got down to business. Literally. For the first couple of months, they'd gone at it as they had every other competition they'd indulged in over the years, be it for a game, or a grade, or a girl. Then, little by little, Matthias had started edging ahead. A deal here, an acquisition there, and the money had begun to pile higher. A hundred thousand. Two hundred and fifty thousand. Half a million. Until that final deal that had cinched it for him and ensured he would win.

The problem was that the final deal had been tainted—unbeknownst to Matthias at the time—by some shady dealings inside his own company. Luke, suspicious, had cried foul and accused Matthias of cheating, an accusation Matthias resoundingly denied for years. An accusation that had split the brothers to the point of not speaking. Until Matthias discovered—only recently, in fact—a rat in his own corporation who had double-dealed him and Luke both and then disappeared with his own ill-gotten gains. And even though the two brothers realized now that they'd both been taken advantage of back then—even though the lines of communication were open now—things still weren't quite settled. Yeah, Matthias had helped his brother win the woman he'd once planned to marry himself. That the help had come in the form of a punch to Luke's eye had just been cake. But Luke had apologized for being an ass. Matthias, in turn, had apologized for being an ass *and* not trying harder to keep the lines of communication open.

Those lines were open now, he reminded himself. But things with Luke still weren't where they should be. He supposed there would never again be a day when they were the carefree college kids Hunter had helped them to be. But they could be brothers again.

And they would, he vowed. He would start calling his brother on a regular basis and make sure they saw more of each other. Hell, they both lived in San Francisco. It wasn't as if it was a hardship for them to see each other.

Kendall had folded herself into her car by now and started the ignition, and was looking over her shoulder as she backed out of the drive. She stopped to wait for a dog to trot past before pulling out, and when she did, for some reason, she looked back up at the house. Her eyes immediately connected with his, but she'd donned sunglasses, so it was impossible to read her expression. Matthias lifted a hand to wave it in halfhearted farewell and, after a moment, she lifted a hand in response. But she didn't wave, and she didn't smile, so the gesture felt more final than it should have.

And then she was rolling out of the driveway and putting

the car in gear, and heading down the road that would take her back to the highway. She didn't turn around again, even when she braked for the stop sign. Matthias watched her car until she was out of sight, then stood at the window a little longer, watching the empty place in the road where last he'd seen her. He told himself to get busy, that he had a lot of work to do today. He reminded himself he had another temp coming by in a few hours.

He reminded himself of a lot of things as he stood at the window looking at the place where Kendall wasn't. But all he could remember was the way her hand had felt, curled tentatively over his arm when she'd expressed her sympathy over Hunter's death.

She was going where she thought she needed to be, he told himself, recalling the words he'd used first, and which she'd turned back on him in an entirely different—and erroneous—way. But she was wrong. She didn't *need to be* with Stephen DeGallo, a man who would only use her long enough to pick her brain about Matthias's business and then manufacture some excuse to let her go. The man didn't like people working closely with him whom he hadn't brought up himself from scratch. Matthias knew DeGallo fairly well—What was the old adage? Keep your friends close, your enemies closer?—and Kendall, to DeGallo's way of thinking, was tainted. She was used goods, sloppy seconds. No matter how much she liked and trusted the guy, DeGallo would, once he got the information from her he wanted, consider her a liability, and he would let her go.

And *that*, Matthias told himself as he continued to watch the empty street, was why he needed—no, *wanted*— Kendall to come back to work for Barton Limited. Because

DeGallo didn't appreciate her the way Matthias did. Because DeGallo wouldn't offer her the security and benefits Matthias would. Because DeGallo didn't care about her any more than he would care about a new printer or phone system or hard drive.

It *wasn't* because of the warmth that had spread through him when she'd curled her fingers around his arm. And it wasn't because of the way she'd looked at him as he'd talked about his old friends, as if she wanted to hear more—about them *and* him. And it certainly wasn't because the lodge had come alive while she was here and felt dim and somber now that she was gone. That was ridiculous. Houses didn't live and they didn't have feelings.

Then again, there were those who would say the same thing about Matthias.

He sighed heavily and pushed a handful of hair back from his forehead. He didn't have time for this, he thought. He had work to do and an interview to perform. Because as much as he knew Kendall wasn't where she needed to be, she was the one who would have to realize that. In the meantime, he needed—no, wanted—someone else.

Even if no one else would ever come close to her.

By the end of the week, Matthias had run through every temp agency in the Tahoe area without finding even a marginally acceptable candidate to replace Kendall, even temporarily. The one who had just appeared at his door was his very last hope, and already he knew she wasn't going to work out, either. She had no concept of how to dress for a job interview, even one conducted in a nonoffice environment. She'd actually paired a crisp white shirt with a pair of pin-striped trousers and flat loafers, and had knotted her dark hair on the top of her head like a tennis ball. Her little black glasses were tailored and elegant, and her makeup—if she was even wearing any—was understated and clean.

What the hell was she thinking, showing up for a job interview looking like this? She was even more over-the-top and under-a-rock than the first guy had been.

He expelled a restless sigh and gestured halfheartedly toward the living room, indicating she should take a seat on one of the chairs beside the fireplace while he folded himself perfunctorily into the other. The sooner they got this interview over with, the better. Then Matthias could...

Well, okay, he could be alone. At least he wouldn't be wasting his time interviewing people who obviously had no clue how to interact in the world of big business. Instead, he'd be wasting his time dreading the fact that he'd have to set up another interview with someone who would almost certainly be as unqualified to fill Kendall's position as this woman was.

"So, Ms...." He glanced down at the résumé the temp agency had e-mailed him to inspect in preparation for her arrival. "Ms. Carrigan," he finished. "I see you're a graduate of Stanford Business School."

She smiled a small, unobtrusive smile that made Matthias flinch, so blatantly inappropriate was it for a job interview. "I am," she said. "I graduated in May with honors."

Yeah, yeah, yeah, Matthias thought. Honors schmonors. If he had a dollar for every honors degree places like Stanford and Harvard issued, he could paper the whole top of his desk.

"And what interests you about the position as my personal assistant?"

She sat up straighter, crossed her legs at the ankles,

wove her fingers together loosely in her lap, then tilted her head thoughtfully to one side. Matthias mentally shook his own head and somehow refrained from rolling his eyes. Her entire posture just screamed indolent slob. What an incredible waste of time this was.

"May I speak frankly, Mr. Barton?" she asked.

"Of course," he told her. Adding to himself, *Making presumptions already?*

"Ultimately," she began, "I'd like to move higher on the corporate ladder, but I think this would be a good entry level position for me, because it would offer me the opportunity to learn from, well, if you'll forgive my momentary gushing, a legend in the business world."

Suck-up, Matthias thought. But he kept his expression bland.

"University courses," she continued, "can only go so far in imparting information. I'm hoping that by coming to work for you fresh out of college, Mr. Barton, I could gain some professional experience that would enhance what I learned in the classroom at Stanford. At the same time, I'll do an excellent job keeping your schedule organized and making sure you have everything you need at any given moment. All modesty aside, my organizational skills are exemplary, and as you can see from the letters of recommendation I've supplied from five of my professors, I routinely led my classes when it came to completing assignments promptly and neatly."

Bighead, Matthias thought. Megalomaniac was more like it. Not to mention she was barely articulate enough to string two words together.

"I see," he said. "Well, that's all good information to have, and I appreciate your coming in today." He stood and extended his hand to her. "I have your résumé. I'll be in touch."

She was obviously surprised by the quickness with which he'd concluded the interview, but there was no reason for Matthias to waste any more time—hers or his. The woman had absolutely nothing to recommend her and was in no way suitable.

What was up with business schools these days? Matthias wondered as he watched her leave. Between Tahoe and San Francisco, he'd interviewed more than two dozen people to fill Kendall's position, and each person had been worse than the one before.

Well, there was nothing else for him to do, he thought. He couldn't afford to wait for Kendall to come to her senses. He'd just have to do or say whatever it took to get her back. Give her another raise, better benefits, whatever it took. Never mind that he'd already tried to do that. Twice. Never mind that he'd failed. Twice. Matthias Barton hadn't risen to the level of success he had by taking no for an answer. Unless, you know, no was the answer he wanted to hear. No *wasn't* a word he'd heard often from Kendall. Until, you know, recently. He was sure if he made her the right offer, she'd come around. Everyone had their price. Even Kendall. All Matthias had to do was find it.

Fortunately for him, he knew exactly where to look.

Kendall had been waiting for Stephen in the dining room of the Timber Lake Inn for fifteen minutes when she looked up at the restaurant's entrance once more, hoping to see her new employer there, and instead saw Matthias. He was dressed casually again, this time pairing his khaki trousers with a chocolate-brown polo that lovingly molded his broad chest and shoulders. She was surprised to see that he'd left his shirttail out, a casual affectation he normally didn't adopt. Then again, there was something about him tonight that suggested it wasn't an affectation at all.

She waited for the irritation that should have come at seeing him, but instead, she was filled with a strange sort of relief. Her orientation this week hadn't been quite what she'd thought it would be, filled as it had been with mostly one-on-one meetings with Stephen. Meetings that had taken place more often in restaurants than in a conference room at the hotel—conference rooms that were better suited to serving high tea than conducting business, anyway. Worse, the meetings had seemed to veer off course on a fairly regular basis, shifting from the policies and procedures of OmniTech to Kendall's experiences working with Matthias.

She didn't want to believe Matthias was right about Stephen DeGallo's only hiring her to uncover information about him. But after the way the week had gone, with her having to sidestep every effort Stephen made to shift the conversation to Barton Limited, Kendall couldn't quite dissuade herself of the idea that Matthias knew what he was talking about. At best, her new employer's training methods were unconventional. At worst, her new employer's intentions were underhanded. Either way, Kendall wasn't sure she was working for the right man. Either way, she wasn't sure she was where she needed to be.

Matthias caught her eye just as she completed that last thought, and a thrill of something hot and electric shuddered through her. She recognized it as sexual, but was surprised by its strength. Surprising, too, was how much it differed from the sexual responses she'd had to men in the past. Because joining the physical sensations that were rocketing through her body was an emotional reaction that was blooming in her heart. She had feelings for Matthias she hadn't had for other men. And they were stronger, she realized now, than she'd allowed herself to believe.

But this was *Matthias*, she tried to remind herself. As recently as a few weeks ago, he'd been Mr. Barton. Yes, she'd known she was attracted to him. But she'd thought removing herself from him would put an end to that attraction. Remove the appetite by removing the temptation. But the only thing removing the temptation had done was make her hungrier.

As long as she'd been working for him, Kendall's ethics hadn't allowed her to cross the line into intimacy. Office romances, she knew, were a Very Bad Idea, no matter how you played them. So as long as she was working for Barton Limited, her conscience had allowed her to find her boss attractive, but hadn't permitted her to act on that attraction. By leaving the office environment, any obstacles that had stood in the way of her feelings for him had disappeared. Simply put, now that she wasn't his employee anymore, her conscience and her brain—not to mention her heart— were letting in things they had locked up tight before.

Not good, she thought as he came to a stop behind the chair across from her and curled his fingers over the back of it. Because how wise would it be to let herself start feeling things—things beyond attraction—for a married man? Especially when what the man was married to was his business?

"Hi," he said. And with that one word, her troubled thoughts completely evaporated.

There would be plenty of time for thinking later, she told

herself. Especially if Stephen DeGallo never showed up. Where was he, anyway? It wasn't like him to be late. Then again, why did she care when Matthias was here?

That thought, more than any of the others she'd had this evening—this week—told her more than anything else could about herself. And her feelings. And her wisdom. Or lack thereof. What told her even more was how she quickly smoothed a hand over her ivory shirt and brown trousers before running it back over her head to make sure her hair was in place. Somehow, she knew she wouldn't have bothered for Stephen. Nor would she have removed her glasses to get a better look at him, as she did with Matthias now.

"Hi," she replied, tucking her glasses into her shirt pocket.

"Meeting DeGallo?" he asked.

She hesitated before telling him she feared her new boss had stood her up. Because then Matthias would ask her why, and she'd have to tell him she didn't know, unless maybe it was because Stephen had decided she wasn't a team player, even without first letting her into the dugout. So she only said, "Actually, I'm here alone." Which was true. She was alone. She just wasn't *supposed* to be alone.

And boy, was that a loaded statement she would just as soon not leave hanging. So she hurried on, "What are you doing here? Again?"

She hadn't meant for that *again* to sound as pointed as it had. Matthias either didn't notice or chose to pretend he hadn't heard it himself, because he only smiled and replied, "I actually came here to see if you wanted to have dinner with me. When you didn't answer my knock at you door upstairs, I took a chance that you'd be down here."

She nodded sagely, but said nothing.

He looked at her expectantly, but said nothing.

It occurred to her that he was waiting for her to invite him to sit down. Then it occurred to her that, with her luck, the minute she did, Stephen DeGallo would walk through the door with a perfectly legitimate reason for being so late, and whisk her off to a PowerPoint presentation of some of OmniTech's most arcane secrets, then apologize for it taking so long to invite her into the loving bosom of his inner sanctum.

And she thought, Ew. That sounded really gross.

Not to mention it was almost certainly *not* going to happen. At least, not that last part. But there was still a possibility that Stephen would show up with a legitimate reason for being late, and it wouldn't look good for her to be sitting here with Matthias.

"If you're waiting for Stephen," he began, as if he were able to read her thoughts.

"I'm not," she quickly interjected.

"Good," he said. "Because I saw him driving off with a breathtaking blonde as I was coming into the inn."

She gaped at him. "You did not. We had a dinner…" She started to say "date," realized that hammered home even better—or, rather, worse—what her orientation this week had felt like, and immediately corrected herself by finishing, "Appointment."

"So you *were* expecting him," Matthias said, a note of unmistakable triumph in his voice.

She flattened her mouth into a thin line to keep herself from saying anything else.

"Looks like your new boss stood you up, Kendall," Matthias said. "Which isn't a very sound business plan on his part." He hesitated a beat before adding, "The man's an idiot if he doesn't realize how lucky he is to have hired you."

The momentary thrill of surprise and pleasure that came with Matthias's compliment was quickly replaced by other things she felt for Stephen DeGallo. Resentment, frustration, disappointment. She was sure the two of them were supposed to have met for dinner here tonight. Positive. In fact, he'd told her barely three hours ago that he'd see her at six-thirty in the dining room.

She looked at her watch. It was ten till seven now. There was little chance the man would be this late when he was staying at the same hotel. Obviously, he'd discovered something—or someone—in the last few hours who had seemed a more profitable return on his investment.

She braced herself for Matthias's *I told you so,* but all he said was, "How about I buy you dinner instead?"

She told herself to say no, that all she really wanted to do was go up to her suite for some room service and a long bubble bath. Then she realized that was the last thing she wanted to do. She was tired of going to her room alone at night. Tired of wondering what Stephen's motives were in hiring her. Tired of not knowing if she'd made the right choice in coming to work for him.

Work, hah, she thought. Nothing she had experienced with Stephen DeGallo so far had felt anything like work. It had felt like…

Bribery, she thought. And snooping. And something kind of smarmy and icky.

She sighed again, but this time there was less resentment, frustration and disappointment in it. They were replaced instead with a sad sort of resolution that she had made a mistake. Not in leaving Matthias's employ, but in taking the job with OmniTech. She'd talk to Stephen tomorrow, ask him point-blank if he'd offered her the job because he'd expected her to tell him about the workings of Barton Limited. If he had, she would tender her resignation immediately. And if he hadn't…

Well. She'd wait to make plans until the two of them had had a chance to talk. In the meantime, she had another choice to make. And she told herself she'd better make the right one this time.

But instead of responding to Matthias's dinner invitation the way her brain told her to—by declining—she listened to her heart instead. Even knowing her heart was wont to get her into trouble. Hey, it wasn't as though her head had been doing such a good job lately.

"Dinner would be nice," she told him.

He smiled, and the heat inside Kendall sparked a little hotter. "Not here, though," he told her. "The steak I had the other night left a lot to be desired."

That wasn't the only thing at the Timber Lake Inn that was like that, Kendall thought.

"But I do know just the place. It's a bit of a drive, but you'll love it. Nice ambience, and the food is excellent. And the service can't be beat."

Before giving her a chance to agree or decline, he moved behind her chair and gave it a gentle tug. Then he lowered a hand to help her out of it. Without thinking about what she was doing, Kendall curled her fingers over his, marveling at how the heat inside her began to purl through her entire body.

This wasn't good, she told herself again as she rose. She should have told Matthias she couldn't go to dinner with him. It would be a mistake to think anything that might happen between them would ever go anywhere. Even if the two of them did get involved—and oh, wasn't she presuming a lot there?—whatever happened would flare up and fizzle out, probably in a very short time. Matthias Barton wasn't a man for relationships. He wasn't even a man for affection. The only thing he would ever love to distraction was his business.

As long as Kendall reminded herself of that—over and over and over again, she told herself—she would be fine. Right?

Of course, right.

Six

"You'll change your mind about this place, Kendall, the minute you taste your first glass of wine."

Matthias realized his concerns were unfounded when he turned from unlocking the lodge's front door to see Kendall gazing back at him with a smile. "That's okay," she said. "I like this place. It's nice. It makes you feel comfortable as soon as you enter."

So she'd noticed it, too, he thought. Interesting.

"Not to mention it's Friday night," he added. "Every decent place along the lake is going to be packed by now. We wouldn't get seated until after ten."

"It's nice that you have this place for a month," she said as she circled around him into the foyer. "It'll do you good."

It had already done him good, Matthias thought. And just by inviting Kendall inside, the good had become better.

"Remind me after it gets dark to go out onto the deck,"

he said as he closed the door behind them. "There's a telescope out there. It's incredible, the things you can find in
the sky out here."

She smiled. "You've been looking through a telescope at night?"

He eyed her warily. "You sound surprised."

"I *am* surprised," she told him. "Matthias, you've never
taken time out of your days—or nights—for something
like that."

"Sure I have. I do it all the time."

She shook her head. "No, you don't."

"Yeah," he countered, a little more defensively than he
would have liked. "I do."

Still smiling, she crossed her arms over her midsection. In-
evitably, he noticed how, when she did that, the outline of her
bra was just discernible enough through the pale fabric of her
shirt to allow him to see that it was lace. He never would have
pegged Kendall as the lacy lingerie type. She seemed like the
Hanes-all-over type. Hell, there'd been times when she was
working for him that she seemed like the boxer short type.
And during one particularly daunting week, the jockstrap
type. But now that he realized she *was* the lacy lingerie type…

Hmm. Actually, he found the idea kind of arousing. He
also found himself wondering if she was the type to match
bra to panties. Or, better yet, bra to thong bikini.

"Name one frivolous thing you do in your spare time,"
she challenged.

Figuring Kendall meant *besides* pondering the mysteries of her underwear, he opened his mouth to rattle off a
dozen things he did for enjoyment, then realized he
couldn't think of even one. Other than looking through the
telescope, which he'd done only since coming here.

Finally, "I play squash," he said. "And tennis. And I play an occasional round of golf."

"And you use them all for networking and wheeling and dealing."

Yeah, okay, she had a point. So sue him.

He bristled at her suggestion that he was a man who found no enjoyment in life outside his work. Mostly because he couldn't honestly deny it. "Frivolity is overrated," he finally said. "And there's no point to it. I like working. It gives me pleasure. I don't need anything else in my life."

Her smile fell at that, and he realized he had been speaking with more vehemence than he intended—not to mention more than he felt. She'd just hit a sore spot with him, that was all. Why did everyone criticize people who were enthusiastic about their work? So what if he defined himself by how successful he was, and how hard he worked? So what if he was the kind of person who *would* be lying on his deathbed worrying that he hadn't worked enough during his life. There was nothing else in his life but work. Why was that such a terrible thing?

Kendall dropped her hands to her sides, her smile gone now. An awkward moment followed where neither seemed to know what to say. So Matthias forced himself to relax and said, "So how about dinner?"

For a minute, he thought—feared—she was going to decline and ask him to take her back to the inn. Finally, however, she nodded.

He roused a smile for her, tilting his head toward the kitchen. "Come on," he said in a lighter voice. "I'll have it on the table in ten minutes."

It actually only took about half that time, since all

Matthias had to do was remove food from containers in the fridge and arrange them on two plates. Opening the wine was the most time-consuming part of the task, but the cork left the bottle of Shiraz with a nice crisp *pop*. He poured them each a glass and carried those, too, to the table.

Kendall surveyed the food on the plate—a strip steak, green beans and new potatoes he'd picked up at a gourmet carryout place about ten miles down the road—a little warily.

"It's cold," she said.

"No, it's tartare," he countered as he sat in the chair on the side of the table that was perpendicular to hers. To show her it was fine, he lifted his fork and knife and sliced through the tender beef, then halved a potato with the side of his fork. "See? Looks delicious, doesn't it?"

"Tartare means uncooked," Kendall corrected him. She pointed at the plate. "This has been cooked. It just hasn't been heated up. I mean, even the vegetables are cold. Why don't you just pop the plates into the microwave for a couple of minutes?"

He sighed heavily. "The microwave is broken," he admitted. "And so is the oven," he added when she was about to mention that.

She looked over her shoulder at the appliances in question, the former set into the cabinets above the latter. "They look brand-new," she said as she turned back around again.

"Yeah, well, whoever built this place obviously cut corners on the appliances, because none of them work. But trust me, food like this tastes great cold."

Kendall smiled. "In other words, you've been eating your meals cold all week because you can't figure out how the microwave or stove work."

His back went up at that—figuratively *and* literally.

"No, I've been eating my meals cold because the microwave and stove *don't* work."

She gazed at him with an expression he couldn't decipher, then stood and picked up both their plates. She strode over to the microwave, set one plate on the stovetop as she opened the door and inserted one, then picked up the other and put it in beside the first. Then she looked at the keypad—which Matthias knew was completely incomprehensible to anyone except the rocket scientist who designed it—punched a few buttons with a beep-boop-beep and the microwave suddenly came alive.

He rose from his chair and crossed the kitchen to where Kendall stood. "How did you do that?" he demanded. "That thing hasn't worked since I got here."

"Well, it's fine now," she said. Then, with another little smile he wasn't quite sure how to figure out, she asked, "What else have you been having trouble with?"

"Why do you assume I've been having trouble with anything else?"

"Well, you did just mention that none of the appliances work."

"Right." He'd forgotten about that. He thought Kendall was insinuating that he had problems with small appliances. Which was completely ridiculous. He was, after all, a captain of industry. Now, if someone would just promote him to colonel of technology, he'd be all set.

He pointed over his shoulder, at the most pressing of his concerns. "The coffeemaker," he said.

She nodded knowingly. "I should have figured that out when you cooked up that bogus contract problem to trick me into bringing you coffee."

"I never—"

But she ignored him, only smiling more sweetly, as if in sympathy. "Poor Matthias. Not getting his morning coffee every day. It's a wonder you're not a drooling mess."

"Drooling mess?" he echoed. "I've never been a drooling mess. Over coffee or anything else."

"Of course you haven't."

He eyed her narrowly but said nothing. Hey, he knew he wasn't a slave to caffeine. He could quit any time he wanted. Caffeine addicts were weak. He was strong. Hell, there were days when he didn't even go near a Starbucks. He just, you know, couldn't remember the last one, that was all. Besides, real caffeine junkies drank cheap, grocery store coffee, and they drank it all day long. Matthias bought only the premium gourmet blends, and he drank only in the morning. Except on days when he needed a little extra something to get him through the afternoon. Hey, he could afford it. He still looked good. He was still healthy. Besides, there had been plenty of studies that said it was good for you. Plus he had all those issues with his father, and coffee helped take the sting out of those.

Ah, hell. What were they talking about?

"Then I guess you don't care that I have a coffeemaker like that myself," Kendall said, "and know how to fix it. If there is, in fact, anything wrong with it," she added in a way that he knew was meant to ruffle him.

It did.

"It doesn't work," he repeated, more emphatically this time. "I've done everything. Even the clock on it is wrong."

She patted him on the shoulder—something that sent a strange ripple of warmth through him—and crossed to the counter where the coffeemaker sat. Mocking him. Again, she pressed some buttons that made a couple of quick beeps. Then she pushed the big red button Matthias hadn't wanted to push himself, fearing it might trigger a nuclear strike over North Korea, and a little green light came on. But there was nothing to indicate the machine was working, no whirring of the grinder, no hiss of water as it heated, no gurgle of coffee as it dripped into the carafe.

"See?" he said. "It doesn't work."

"I set the timer for you," she told him, sidestepping his insistence that it didn't work. And it didn't work, Matthias was sure of that. "As long as you fill it with coffee and water every night, it'll start brewing at six-thirty in the morning."

He gaped at her. "How did you do that?"

She pointed to the little green light. "I set the clock to the correct time, then pushed the button that says, 'Timer.' The machine walks you through the steps after that."

Matthias hooked his hands on his hips and said nothing, only stared at Kendall in wonder, trying to figure out how the hell he was supposed to manage for the rest of his life if she was working for someone else. Because he had no choice but to admit then that he needed Kendall. *Really* needed her. What was beginning to scare him was that he was starting to suspect it wasn't only in the office where he had that need.

She smiled at him and extended her hand. "Okay, give it to me," she said, her voice tinted with laughter.

He shook his head in confusion. "What are you talking about?"

"Your new BlackBerry," she said. "The one you brought to the hotel earlier this week. I'll program it for you."

Damn, he thought. She *would* ask about that now. "It's not necessary," he told her.

She arched her brows in surprise. "You programmed it yourself?"

"Not exactly."

"Then give it to me and I'll do it for you."

He expelled an exasperated sound. "I can't."

"Why not?"

"Because it's at the bottom of Lake Tahoe."

Kendall looked at him in disbelief for a second, then she started to laugh. It was a nice laugh, Matthias thought. Full and uninhibited without being an obnoxious bray. He tried to remember the last time he'd heard Kendall laugh…and realized he never had. Not until this evening. She'd always been so serious at work. So pragmatic and professional. So enterprising and efficient. He'd always thought she was so straitlaced. So somber. It had never occurred to him that there was a woman lurking beneath her gender-neutral attire.

He watched her as she made her way back to the microwave to remove their now-warmed dinners. She was dressed as she always dressed for work—dark trousers, pale shirt, her hair pinned up on her head. But she was more relaxed now than she'd been when she worked for him. She smiled more. Laughed. Spoke to him familiarly. Called him Matthias. When she wasn't working for him, she was…different. Softer. Warmer. More approachable.

He began to feel a little warmer himself as he watched her carry their plates back to the table. Though not particularly soft, he realized with no small amount of surprise. He wondered what she'd do if he…approached.

"The steak formerly known as tartare," she said as she set his plate back on the table with a flourish. "Have at it."

Matthias smiled at her wording. *Have at it* could mean anything. And there were a lot of *its* he wanted to have. Fortunately, he and Kendall had a nice long leisurely evening ahead of them.

* * *

Kendall shook her head as she watched Matthias fiddle with a knob on the telescope, wondering what had come over him this week to make him so…so…so…

Human.

Tonight, he'd been… She smiled as a word came to her. She tried to push it away, so wildly inappropriate a description for him was it, but it wouldn't budge. There was just nothing else that was as accurate. Tonight he had been…*adorable.* All evening long. Never in her wildest dreams would she have thought she would use such an adjective to describe him. When she'd been working for him, he'd been a lot of things—gruff, focused, no-nonsense, intense—but never, ever adorable.

The closest she'd ever seen him come to being soft had been when he'd returned from this very lodge two months ago, after seeing his brother Luke for the first time in years. For a few days after his return, Matthias had seemed distant and distracted and, well, soft. But the softness had still been tempered with an edge, thanks to whatever had happened between the two men while they were here. They'd even brawled at one point over something. Although Matthias hadn't confided in Kendall what the fight had been about, he'd come back from that trip with a black eye that she'd naturally asked him about.

But even with all the changes that had come over him on that occasion—as temporary as they'd been—he hadn't seemed like a normal human being, any more than he ever seemed like a normal human being. He'd still been a powerful force to be reckoned with.

Tonight, though, that force was a soothing breeze. Just like the one rolling off the lake that nudged a stray strand of hair into Kendall's eyes. She brushed it back as she continued to watch him by the telescope, tucking it behind her ear, though, instead of bothering with trying to poke it back into the bun. By now, several such strands of hair had escaped and blew freely about her face. Short of freeing her hair and starting all over again, there wasn't much she could do about them. Not to mention there was something about the languid, peaceful evening—and okay, something about Matthias, too—that prevented her from wanting to be her usual buttoned-up self.

The broad deck stretched along the length of the back of the house, dotted here and there by sturdy wooden furniture and the occasional potted greenery. The sun hung low over the mountains behind them, spilling a wide, watery trail over the lake as it left the sky, bisecting the rippling water with a shimmer of gold. The temperature had dropped with the sun, tumbling from the eighties into the sixties, and she knew that, with full nightfall, it would go lower still. She wished she'd thought to wear a jacket. But then, she hadn't planned on leaving the hotel, had she?

Which was ironic, she thought now, because suddenly she didn't feel like going back to it.

It was just surprisingly pleasant being with Matthias now, when they were on more equal footing. No, she wasn't a corporate bigwig or hotshot industrialist, as he was. Not yet, anyway. But neither was she his assistant anymore. She could speak to him as an equal now, and did. What was nice was that he spoke to her as an equal, too.

But then she realized that wasn't exactly right, either. Because equals in business spoke to each other about business. And she and Matthias hadn't even touched on that tonight. Over dinner, they'd discussed Lake Tahoe and the lodge, the small town in Washington state where Kendall had grown up, Matthias's favorite dog when he was a boy, and how they'd both been high achievers throughout school. The sort of things people talked about when they were getting to know each other. Personally, not professionally.

"Okay, here we go," he said now, drawing her attention back to the matter at hand. "I found Venus. Come have a look."

Kendall drained the last of her wine and set her empty glass on a table next to his, then covered the half-dozen steps to where he stood by the telescope.

"You'll see it better once the sun has completely set," he added, "but even now, it's a beautiful sight to behold."

When she came to a stop beside him, he moved to one side, far enough that she would have room to look through the telescope, but still close enough that he could give her instructions, or a hand, if she needed one.

"Look through here," he said, pointing to a piece that jutted up from the enormous scope.

The thing must magnify a billion times, she thought.

"And you can focus in and out with this," he added, pointing to a knob next to the one he'd been turning to find the planet. He looked at her and smiled. "It's amazing the detail you get with this thing. When I look at the moon at night, it's like if I just stretched out far enough, I could fill my hand with moondust."

Fill my hand with moondust, Kendall repeated to herself, marveling at the phrase. Had Matthias actually said that? It was just so…so…so un-Matthias.

He seemed to realize that, too, because he suddenly looked uncomfortable. His gaze, which had been focused on hers, ricocheted off, and he began to look at everything on the deck except her. Finally, his focus lit on something behind her, and he pointed in that direction.

"Our glasses are empty," he said. "I'll open another bottle of wine." Then, still not looking directly at her, he dipped his head toward the telescope and said, "Enjoy the view. I'll be right back."

She took him at his word, but instead of enjoying the view through the scope, she instead enjoyed the view of Matthias as he strode over to collect their glasses, then made his way back into the lodge. His shirttail flapped in the breeze, rising at one point to give her a lovely view of a surprisingly nice derriere. Since it had generally been covered by a suit jacket whenever she was around him, she'd never had the chance to notice what a nice tush Matthias had. Or maybe she just hadn't allowed herself to notice, because she was working for him. Now, however, she noticed.

Boy howdy, did she notice.

Almost as if he'd heard the thought forming in her brain, Matthias spun quickly around and caught her ogling him. Heat flooded her face at being caught in such a flagrant position, and she waited for the icy look she was sure he'd shoot her way. But the look he gave her wasn't icy. In fact, it was kind of hot. For a moment, his expression didn't change. Then, gradually, an almost invisible smile curled his lips. The kind of smile he didn't want anyone to see. The kind of smile someone who knew him well—like Kendall—couldn't miss. Then it was gone, and he was turning again to make his way back inside the lodge.

But something in his smile lingered, even after he was gone. And it lingered inside Kendall. A thrill of warmth that had sparked in her belly when she first saw his smile, then gradually eased through her entire system, warming her even as the breeze off the lake began to grow cool.

Too much to drink, she decided. She and Matthias both had obviously overindulged on the wine. Funny, though, how she'd never considered two glasses of wine—spread out over two hours, with dinner—overindulging before.

Absently, she curled her arms over her midsection—because she was cold, she told herself, in spite of the warmth spreading through her, and not because she was trying to hold the feeling inside a little longer. She looked up at the bright speck in the sky with her naked eye, then bent toward the eyepiece of the telescope. It took her a moment to get in the right position, but eventually, she found what she was looking for.

Wow, she thought when she saw the yellow planet streaked with bits of orange and pink. It really *was* gorgeous. But she was still surprised that Matthias would think so, too. That he would even care there were planets up there. Looking at the sky just seemed like such a frivolous thing for him to do. That he'd been spending his evenings at the lodge out here on the deck, contemplating the mysteries of the universe, instead of in the amply equipped office getting work done, spoke volumes. And it wasn't in a language he'd ever been able to master before—that of leisure enjoyment.

Something warm and heavy slipped over her shoulders then, and she glanced up from the telescope to find Matthias settling a jacket, clearly one of his, over her shoulders.

He smiled at what must have been her obvious surprise at the gesture and said, "The temperature's dropping. I don't want you to get cold."

There was certainly no chance of that happening,

Kendall thought, as long as he looked at her the way he was looking at her now. She smiled gratefully and murmured her thanks, then pressed her eye to the eyepiece of the telescope once again.

"So what do you think?" he asked.

"You're right," she told him. "It's as if you could just reach right out and touch it."

"When it gets a little darker, I'll see if I can find Jupiter, too," he told her. "It's even more incredible. You can actually see the big red spot with this thing."

Kendall pulled her head back and looked at Matthias again. In the few minutes he'd been inside, the evening had grown noticeably darker, and now the flicker of candlelight danced in his hair, setting little gold fires amid the dark tresses. He must have lit the ones scattered about the tables and the railing while she was so rapt over the image of Venus. His gaze fixed intently on hers as he extended a glass of wine toward her, and she took it without really paying attention, automatically lifting it to her lips for a sip. It tasted different from the last glass, its flavor smoother, more mellow, more potent. Or maybe, she thought, it was just Matthias who was suddenly all those things. She'd better pace herself, or he'd go right to her head.

"So," he said, the word coming out slowly and softly, "how are things going with the new job? Do you like OmniTech so far?"

Kendall was surprised he would ask. Not just because of the whole former employer-employee thing, but because the evening had just been so pleasant and enjoyable with the absence of any talk that was work-related. Still, she knew Matthias wouldn't have asked if he didn't expect an answer. An honest one, at that.

"Actually," she said, her own reply coming out even slower and more softly than his, "so far, it's not exactly what I expected."

His expression changed not at all, but he asked, "How so?"

She shrugged, nudging back another strand of hair that blew into her face and pulling his jacket more snugly around herself. "Well, for one thing, Stephen's idea of orientation seems to be asking me a lot of questions about my old position at Barton Limited and dodging any questions *I* ask about my *new* position at OmniTech."

She waited for a smug *I told you so,* but Matthias's reply was instead a very careful, "I see."

Even though he didn't ask for more information, she found herself continuing anyway. "Orientation will be over after tomorrow, and I know almost nothing about Omni-Tech, save the history of the company and its mission statement and where its national and international offices are located and—" She halted abruptly. "Anything I could find out myself by an online search."

Matthias sipped his wine, but again said nothing, just waited for her to continue, should she want to. The sky behind him was smudged dark blue, the fat full moon hovering over his left shoulder. The only other light came from the candles flickering inside the hurricane globes on the tables, but it was enough to allow her to see his expression. Unfortunately, she couldn't tell by his expression what he was thinking, and that bothered her a lot. Not that she wanted to know what he thought about her situation with OmniTech, but because she wanted to know what he thought about *her.* If he considered her naive for not realizing what he had about Stephen DeGallo, or foolish for having disregarded his warning,

or ridiculous for clinging to the idea that she had made
the right choice.

Especially since she was no longer clinging to that idea.
With every new meeting she had with Stephen, her suspi-
cions about the man and his motives grew stronger. His
having blown off their dinner meeting tonight—regardless
of his reason for doing so—had only cemented her fear that
what Matthias had told her was true. Stephen DeGallo had
hired her because he'd hoped she would give him insight
into Matthias's business. Which, of course, she would
never do. Her job performance at Barton Limited was pertinent to Stephen only in so far as assuring him she had
achieved enough experience to perform the job for which
he had hired her, that her record was stellar, and that she
was committed to her professional obligations. Period.

Now that he had realized she had no intention of playing
corporate spy, he was no longer interested. She wouldn't be
surprised if, before her alleged orientation even ended
tomorrow afternoon, he manufactured some reason to let her
go. Thanks to reorganization, the position for which he'd had
her in mind was no longer viable. Or he'd discovered something in her work history that presented a conflict of interest.
Oh, he'd find some way to make it sound plausible. He
might even give her a generous severance package—though
she doubted it. But there was certainly reason to believe her
new position at OmniTech wouldn't be hers for long.

She looked at Matthias. "You were right," she said,
forcing herself to admit the truth. "I think the only reason
Stephen hired me was because he assumed I would share
what I know about Barton Limited with him."

Matthias eyed her warily now. "Did he ask you about
the Perkins contract?"

She shook her head. "Not specifically, no. Not yet, anyway. But he did ask an awful lot of questions about you and the company. I wouldn't be surprised if the particulars of the Perkins contract was next on his to-do list."

"And what did you tell him about Barton Limited?" Matthias asked, his voice revealing nothing of what he might be thinking about.

She smiled. "I told him about the history of the company and its mission statement and where its national and international offices are located. You know. Anything he could discover by doing an online search."

Matthias smiled back. "That's my girl."

Something about the way he said it, so soft and intimate, sent a ripple of awareness shimmying through her unlike anything she had ever felt before. The breeze chose that moment to pull another strand of hair from the knot at the back of her head and nudge it across her eyes. She started to reach up to brush it away, but Matthias intercepted her, dipping his index finger beneath the disobedient tresses and brushing them back from her forehead. Then he surprised her even more by moving his hand to the clip that held the mass of hair in place and pulling it free.

"You might as well just leave it loose," he told her as he completed the action. "The wind is only going to pick up as the evening goes on."

Which, Kendall thought, was all the more reason to keep her hair anchored. Matthias obviously thought differently. Because as her hair tumbled down around her shoulders, he dragged his fingers through it the way a stylist would, pushing it back over her shoulders, then forward again, then back, as if he wasn't sure how he liked it best. But where a stylist would keep his touches dispassionate and economical, Matthias took his time, stroking the straight, shoulder-length tresses again and again. Kendall finally had to reach up and circle his wrist with her fingers to stop him. When she did, he immediately halted, his gaze connecting fiercely with hers.

For a moment, neither of them spoke, neither of them moved, neither even seemed to breathe. Matthias dropped his gaze from Kendall's eyes to her mouth, then looked into her eyes again. She felt her lips part almost of their own volition, though whether it was because she intended to say something, or for another reason entirely, she wasn't sure. The moment stretched taut, and still neither spoke or moved. Then, for one scant, insane instant, it almost seemed as if he were dipping his head toward hers, tilting it slightly, as if he intended to...

Kiss her? Kendall thought frantically. Oh, surely not.

But her heart began to hammer in her chest all the same, and heat flared in her belly, and her pulse rate quickened, and her entire body caught fire, and then...and then...

And then Matthias suddenly, but gently, pulled his hand from her grasp and leaned back again, and the moment full of...whatever it had been full of...evaporated. He looked down at his glass and lifted it to his lips, filling his mouth with the dark red wine, savoring it for a moment before swallowing. Kendall was still too keyed up and confused by what she was feeling to say anything, so she watched him instead, noting how his strong throat worked over the swallow, feeling warmth spread through her belly as if she were the one who had drunk deeply from her glass.

When Matthias looked at her again, his expression was bland and unreadable, as if there had been nothing about the last few minutes that was any different from the millions of minutes that had preceded them. As if wanting to emphasize that, he asked a question guaranteed to dispel any strange sensations that might be lingering.

"So what do you plan to do about Stephen?"

Kendall wished she had an answer for all the questions—both spoken and unspoken—that had arisen this evening, but most especially for that one. Her future, at the moment, was shakier and more open than it had ever been before. And she wasn't the sort of person who found the unknown exciting. On the contrary, she couldn't function if she didn't have a thorough, well-thought-out plan. The only plan she had at the moment, though, was to have another sip of her wine. Which she did.

Then, "I don't know," she finally said. "I feel like Stephen hired me under false pretenses, and I don't want to work for OmniTech if that's the case. I'd like to be hired on the merit of my knowledge and potential, not because I might have juicy gossip."

"You could resign," Matthias said.

She studied him in silence for a moment, wondering why he'd made the suggestion he had. Was it because he wanted to be proven right? Or was he looking out for Kendall's best interests? Or was it simply because he wanted to stick it to Stephen DeGallo?

Not long ago, she would have assumed it was either the first or last of those reasons. Now, however, she couldn't help thinking maybe he really did want to help Kendall do what was best for herself.

"It will probably be a moot point," she said. "If he decides I'm not going to be beneficial to him in the way he first thought, I wouldn't be surprised if he manufactures some excuse to let me go."

She raised a shoulder and let it drop, hoping the half shrug hid the turmoil roiling inside her. What was weird was that the turmoil was less a result of the prospect of being unemployed, and more the result of the way Matthias continued to look at her.

He dropped his gaze into his glass again, swirling the dark wine around the sides of the bowl in thoughtful concentration. "Well, if you do decide to resign," he began, "or if Stephen is stupid enough to let you go, I have a position at Barton Limited that needs filling." He glanced up at Kendall again, fixing his gaze on hers. "If you think you'd be interested. You'd be perfect for it."

For some reason, his offer of her old job back didn't rankle her as much as it had before. Maybe because this time he wasn't being such an arrogant jackass about it. No, this time, his tone was solicitous, his body language inquisitive. This time, it was indeed an offer, not an order. But Kendall was no more interested in accepting it now than she had been before. She still wanted—needed—more than to be Matthias Barton's assistant. She was too smart and too ambitious, and she wanted to do more—with her life and herself.

"Matthias, I can't be your assistant anymore," she told him. "We've been through this. I need something that will challenge me to be the best that I can be."

"I'm not offering you your old job back," he told her. "I'm offering you a new one."

Kendall wasn't sure if she should be suspicious or not. Ultimately, she decided on being cautious. "What kind of position?"

He turned toward the deck railing and leaned over to

prop his arms on it, then gazed up at the moon as he spoke. "There's no title for it yet. But I'm getting ready to acquire a technology company that's been failing due to mismanagement and carelessness. I'm going to need someone to work side by side with me getting it whipped into shape."

Kendall told herself not to make anything of his body language—that he was looking at the moon and might be, figuratively anyway, offering her something that didn't exist—and consider what he was saying. "Tell me more about the company," she asked carefully.

He did, describing its rise and fall and the problems that had led to its faltering. She nodded as he spoke, turning over in her mind the possibilities and potential, and the various avenues they could take to put the company back on its feet. When Matthias finished, she asked, "What's the salary and benefits for this position?"

"Quadruple what you made as my assistant," he told her.

Her eyebrows shot up at that. That was two times more than the position at OmniTech.

"Full medical and dental," he added, "contributions to an IRA and 401(k). And, if you want, we can talk stock options."

"I want," she said readily.

By now he had straightened again and was lifting his glass to his mouth. But he stopped so abruptly when Kendall said what she did that some of the ruby wine spilled over onto his hand. Hastily, he took the glass in his other hand and tried to shake the wine from his fingers, then looked around for something to wipe the rest of it off. Kendall, always prepared, pulled a clean handkerchief from her trouser pocket and handed it to him. He set his glass down, wiped his hand clean, then, out of habit, she guessed, deftly tucked the scrap of cotton into his own pocket.

When he looked at her again, he seemed agitated about something. But all he said was, "Then let's talk."

Kendall met his gaze levelly. "Okay. I'm listening."

Seven

The coffee shop where Stephen had scheduled their "morning meeting," which he'd deemed "unavoidable" on a Saturday because Kendall's "orientation" had "fallen behind" this week—yeah, Stephen, since some people blew off "essential dinner meetings" to instead chase after breathtaking blondes—was located a couple of blocks away from the inn. But it was every bit as quaint and charming. Even though it was early—and also *Saturday,* in case Kendall hadn't mentioned that part—there were a number of people out and about, ambling down the walkways, waiting for the shops to open and sipping their morning lattes. But, unlike Kendall, who was dressed in her usual business trousers and shirt—in this case beige for the former and cream for the latter—everyone else sported vacation clothes, mostly shorts and T-shirts or loose cotton dresses coupled with sneakers or sandals. Because they, unlike Kendall, didn't have to work today. On account of it was Saturday. In case she hadn't mentioned that part.

She looked longingly down at her pointy-toed, three-inch ivory pumps, then at the beat-up Birkenstock sandals on a woman passing by, and she sighed. Someday, she thought, she was going to be the big cheese at her own successful corporation. And the first policy she planned to put in place was a Casual Friday. Then she'd add a Casual Thursday. And a Casual Wednesday, Tuesday and Monday, too. And then she'd decree that no work ever took place on the weekend.

She knew her business philosophy was an unconventional one. Most corporate big shots had gotten where they were by working overtime, downtime, double time and time and a half. She knew it was traditional to keep employees toeing a conservative line in all things business-related. And she knew power suits made a more imposing impression than well, beat-up Birkenstock sandals. But she also knew that the *real* secret to success was loving what you did for a living.

And Kendall loved big business. She just wasn't that crazy about all its trappings. She didn't think the image was as important as other people did. As far as she was concerned, actions spoke louder than power suits. She would rather have a force of casually dressed, happy, productive employees working for her than she would a bunch of polished corporate drones. It wasn't enough to be smart and energetic in today's business world. Creativity was absolutely essential. And creative people were *not* a suit-wearing tribe. So Kendall was going to cut her workforce a little slack.

She toed off one pointy-toed high heel and let it drop to the sidewalk. And she would cut herself some slack, too.

Matthias hadn't had a title or description yet for the job he'd offered her, but she wasn't worried. No matter what it was, she would do it well. She would play by his rules for as long as it took to get the business off the ground, and then she would tailor it to her policies and procedures and put her own personal stamp on it. Matthias, for all his conservative bluster, had always been an open-minded and farsighted businessman. It was part of what had made him so successful. He would allow—no, expect—Kendall to be her own woman with whatever he gave her to direct. And she couldn't wait to get started.

As if cued by the thought, Stephen DeGallo turned the corner just then, catching Kendall's eye and raising a hand in greeting. He was having a Casual Saturday, she noticed, wearing faded jeans with a brightly patterned tiki shirt and, she noted with some wistfulness, sandals.

"You didn't have to dress for work," he said by way of a greeting as he sat down across from her.

Kendall eyed him with what she hoped looked like terseness, since terse was suddenly how she felt. "Well, since we're *supposed* to be *working*," she said meaningfully, "I dressed for work."

"But it's Saturday," he said with a smile. Then he looked past her and waved to catch a waiter's attention. "You don't have to be all buttoned-up and battened down. Live a little."

Yeah, like you did last night, huh, Stephen? Kendall had to bite her lip to keep the words from tumbling out. Instead, she was the picture of politeness when she asked, "What happened to you last night?"

He looked genuinely puzzled. "Last night?"

She nodded. "We were supposed to have a dinner

meeting. To discuss which OmniTech health-care plan would be best for me."

He shook his head. "No, we're doing that this afternoon."

Kendall turned her head and tugged lightly on an earring. "No, it was supposed to be last night, Stephen. In fact, when we parted ways yesterday afternoon after our session on the new sweetheart agreement you made with one of the subsidiaries I'd be working with, you distinctly said, 'I'll see you at six-thirty.' But I waited twenty minutes, and you never showed."

He looked a little taken aback, presumably by her tone, which, she had to admit, wasn't the sort of voice one normally used with an employer. Particularly a brand-new one. No, it was more the tone of voice one used with a dog who had just peed on the carpet.

His eyes went flinty. Then he smiled, a gesture that fell well short of making him look happy. "I meant six-thirty *tonight,*" he said.

"No, you meant Friday," she countered with all confidence. "I don't make mistakes like that."

"Neither do I."

"You did last night," Kendall told him pointedly. "Or maybe you just found yourself…preoccupied by a better prospect. A blond prospect."

His smile disappeared, and his eyes hardened even more. "What I do in my private time is none of your business, Kendall."

"It is if it affects my job."

He expelled a soft sound of undisguised contempt. "What job?" he demanded. "You're fired, effective immediately."

Not that Kendall minded, since it would save her the trouble of resigning and get her out of OmniTech more quickly, but she felt compelled to ask, "On what grounds?" Mostly because she didn't want to leave any loose threads hanging. And, okay, also because she wanted to goad him.

"What grounds?" he asked incredulously. "How about insubordination for starters? You're also completely unsuited to the position I hired you for."

Ridiculous, she thought. She was perfect for the job of vice president. And in a few years, once she got her legs, she'd be perfect for the job of CEO. After that, she wasn't sure, but she might take over the universe. At the moment, she felt perfectly capable—she was that confident of her abilities.

Evidently, Stephen didn't have such an inflated opinion of her, however, because he continued, "You're also withdrawn and uncooperative, and you're *not* a team player."

Kendall nodded at this. By his definition of those words, he was right, and she told him so. "In other words, I'm ethical to the point that I won't roll over on my former employer and tell you all his best-kept business secrets."

Stephen's mouth shut tight at that, but he said nothing.

"That's why you hired me, isn't it, Stephen? Because you thought I'd speak freely about Matthias Barton. You thought I'd make you privy to all his personal quirks and habits and reveal the details of any of his dealings that I might have been in on."

For a moment, Stephen said nothing. Then he sneered at her and said, "As if Matthias Barton would allow his *secretary* to be in on any of his dealings. I don't know what I was thinking to assume a nobody like you would have any insight into a rival corporation."

Kendall smiled sweetly. "For one thing, Stephen, secretaries are the backbone of any good business. They're not nobodies. For another thing, you're wrong. I know more about Matthias's business than Matthias does. He'd tell you himself he couldn't operate without me. So much so, that he's offered me a job. An executive position," she added confidently, even though she was confident of no such thing. Matthias had made clear that the job—whatever it was—*was* important. Essential. Valuable. And it was hers, the moment she was free of Stephen DeGallo.

Which was going to happen more quickly than she initially thought.

"You can't fire me, Stephen," she told him as she stood. "I quit." Much better than resigning, she thought. As she slung her purse over her shoulder, she added, "Thanks for the coffee. And the reality check. I assure you both were *much* appreciated."

And then she turned and strode confidently down the sidewalk, back toward the Timber Lake Inn. She had an unexpected day off, she thought with a smile. Well, okay, maybe not all *that* unexpected. She'd planned to tell Stephen this morning that she wouldn't be coming to work for OmniTech, and she'd been fairly sure he would terminate her on the spot. She'd just thought it would go a little more smoothly, that was all. She truly hadn't meant for things to end as abruptly as they had, or with as much chilliness.

But Stephen *had* deliberately skipped their meeting last night, something that had illustrated his disregard for her as both a person and an employee. And he *had* hired her under false pretenses to begin with. It hadn't exactly been a situation that lent itself to air kisses and toodle-oos. If she'd been too pushy or blunt—

Her steps slowed and her back straightened. She smiled. If she'd been too pushy and blunt, then it just meant she was a solid businesswoman. Any man who'd been pushy and blunt would have been applauded and called assertive and candid. So she was going to applaud herself, too.

Boy, what a couple of days for changes and epiphanies, Kendall thought. So far, she'd accepted a new power job, resigned from an old dubious job, told her sleazy ex-employer what a sleazy ex-employer he was, discovered what an assertive businesswoman *she* was, and now she could go back to her hotel and—

She halted in her tracks, her confidence fleeing completely. Because she realized then that her hotel wasn't her hotel anymore. Stephen DeGallo wasn't going to foot the bill for her room now that she wasn't in his employ. And he'd probably cancel her return ticket to San Francisco, not to mention the rental car. And with it being the peak of the summer tourist season, finding a flight *or* car right away might prove to be a bit daunting.

She was going to have to check out of the Timber Lake Inn. She had nowhere else to go and no way to get there.

She sighed and gave her forehead a good mental smack. So much for being the assertive, candid businesswoman who could take over the universe at will. In a matter of hours, Kendall was going to be living on the streets.

Matthias was reading a political thriller he'd found in one of the spare bedrooms when he heard the front doorbell ring. He set it facedown on the sofa and went to answer, automatically brushing the dust from his jeans and pin-striped, untucked oxford, even though the house wasn't old enough to have accumulated any dust, and even though, if it did, Mandy or Mindy or Maureen or whatever the hell the caretaker's name was would make quick work of it.

Mary, he remembered as he stepped into the foyer.

Mary, who had seemed strangely familiar for some reason, even though, at the moment, Matthias couldn't even remember what she looked like. For all he knew, it was she who was at the front door right now. He hadn't seen her since the day of his arrival. Not that he'd expected to. He wasn't even sure if she lived here in Hunter's Landing. But something about her had made him think she had a vested interest in the house and would check on it from time to time to make sure none of the Seven Samurai was trashing the place with wild parties and wilder behavior.

Even though the days of their trashing anything—like the furniture they'd nailed to the ceiling in the dorm their freshman year—had long since passed. These days the Seven Samurai, in addition to no longer being seven, were no longer the soldier of fortune types they'd fancied themselves when they'd assumed the nickname for the group as young men. They'd all made their fortunes in one way or another, and now they were all too busy trying to protect those fortunes and make them grow larger to have time for wild parties and wilder behavior.

And why that realization made Matthias's mouth turn down in consternation, he couldn't have said.

But his mouth turned up again when he opened the front door, and his step felt lighter—even if he was standing still—when he saw that it wasn't the caretaker who stood on the other side, but Kendall.

Her appearance surprised him. Not so much her appearance on his doorstep, but rather her *appearance* on his doorstep. She was dressed in the kind of thing he'd never seen her wear before—blue jeans that were faded to the point of being torn in places, and a pale lavender T-shirt that was brief enough to allow a glimpse of creamy flesh between its hem and the waistband of her jeans. Even more surprising than Kendall's appearance, however, was her luggage's appearance, since, by virtue of its appearance, it was apparent that it would be visiting, too. It was scattered about her feet in a way that made it look as if she'd just dropped it there in frustration before ringing the bell.

She sounded frustrated, too, when she said, by way of a greeting, "Can I ask you a favor?"

Matthias tried to tear his gaze away from that very alluring strip of naked flesh…and failed miserably. Still gazing at the hem of her shirt, he mentally willed it to leap up again the way it had—all too briefly—when she'd shoved her hands into her back pockets. And somehow he conjured the presence of mind to reply to her question. Unfortunately, that reply was a very distracted, "Huh?"

She shifted her weight from one foot to the other, an action which, although not the one he was mentally willing her to complete, nevertheless had the desired result. For another scant second, that band of naked flesh widened, causing the heavens to open up and a chorus of angels to sing, "Hallelujah, hoo-ah."

"Can I ask you a favor?" Kendall said again.

But she said it without moving her body, unfortunately, so her shirt stayed in place. Then again, that at least allowed Matthias to be coherent enough to answer her question this time. Kind of. At least he got out an "Mmm-hmm" that sounded vaguely affirmative in nature. The problem was, by then, he couldn't remember what the question was that he was answering.

His reply seemed to be fine for Kendall, though, because

she continued, "Would it be possible for me to crash here for a couple of days?"

The question was unexpected enough to command a much larger chunk of his attention. So unexpected, in fact, that he wouldn't have been more surprised if Kendall had just asked him if it would be possible for him to pull the Empire State Building out of his pocket. Then again, the way he was beginning to feel watching the comings and goings of her shirttail, that might not be such an unreasonable request in a few more minutes.

He managed to cover his reaction well, though—he hoped. And through some herculean effort, he also managed to bring his gaze back up to her face. "Problems at the inn?" he asked.

She shook her head. "Problems at OmniTech."

Hey, that sounded promising, he thought. "What kind of problems?"

"I sort of quit. Effective immediately."

He was wrong. That wasn't promising. It was perfect.

Before he could say anything more, she hurried on, "But I sort of didn't take into consideration until too late the fact that, by quitting, I was also ending any reason for Stephen to pay my hotel bill. In the time it took me to walk from the café where we had our morning meeting back to my room, the lock had already been changed on my door. The only reason I was able to get my stuff out was because housekeeping showed up, and the housekeeper was nice enough to let me change my clothes and pack while she was in there cleaning."

Thank God for small favors, Matthias thought. Inescapably, his gaze had dropped to her midsection again when he'd noticed—how could he miss it?—that as Kendall had spoken, she had used a lot of hand gestures, and the hem of her little T-shirt rose and fell with every one, once even high enough to allow him a peek at a truly spectacular navel. So spectacular, in fact, that he enjoyed a quick impression of dragging a line of openmouthed kisses across her flat abdomen before dipping his tongue into the elegant little cleft for a taste....

Until he remembered it was Kendall's navel he was tasting in his fantasy. Kendall, he reminded himself emphatically. This was *Kendall* he was thinking about, for God's sake. *Kendall's* midsection. And *Kendall's* navel. All of them were strictly off-limits because... Because... Because...

Well, because she was Kendall, Matthias told himself. That was why. A trusted employee. A trusted employee he didn't want to compromise with some kind of messy workplace involvement. A trusted employee with an excellent work record. A trusted employee with strong business ethics and sound professional judgment.

A trusted employee with silky dark blond hair that was tumbling free around her shoulders in a way that made him want to reach out and touch it. A trusted employee with enormous green eyes a man could drown in. A trusted employee with a luscious navel he really, really wanted to taste.

"So if the offer of that new position is still open," his luscious, tasty, trusted employee said now, "I'd like to come back to work for you."

The word that should have registered most in that sentence was *work*. But Matthias's brain had gotten so caught up on *position* that it never quite made the leap to *work*. And the position that came to mind just then, although it definitely involved Kendall, had absolutely nothing to do with work. Well, okay, maybe there would have to be a little work involved—it was kind of an unusual position—but that work would have definitely been a labor of lo—

Lust, he hastily corrected himself. A labor of lust.

"Matthias?"

His name, spoken in her voice, a voice so rife with concern, made him push the thoughts out of his head completely. "What?" he asked.

She eyed him curiously. "Is everything…okay?"

He nodded. "Yeah, fine," he said with some distraction. "I was reading when you rang the bell, and I guess my mind just hasn't caught up with the rest of me."

Actually, that wasn't true, he knew. His mind had not only caught up, it had raced right past him and was now in an entirely different time zone. The Navel Zone. Where time moved at a totally different pace than it did in Lake Tahoe.

"So is it okay if I crash here for a couple of days?" she asked again. "I had to change my flight back to San Francisco, and I couldn't get one out until Monday. I tried to find a room at another hotel, but all the good ones are booked solid, and—"

"It's fine, Kendall," he interrupted her. "Of course you can stay here. There's plenty of room."

Though the minute he said that, somehow, for some reason, the huge lodge suddenly felt very crowded.

"Thanks," she said, breathing a sigh of unmistakable relief.

She bent to retrieve her bags, but Matthias intercepted her, scooping up all three before she had the chance. When he looked at her again, he could tell she was surprised by the gesture. Or maybe it was just that she was usually the one doing things for him, not the other way around.

It hit Matthias then, like a two-by-four to the back of

the head, how very true that was. When she was working for him, Kendall had done so many things for him to keep him on track. Granted, that was what he paid her for, but still. What had he ever done for her in return, other than pay her wages and benefits? Yeah, there had been the Godiva chocolates for her birthday every year and the gourmet food baskets every Christmas. But those had been things he'd had his secretary order for her—and he hadn't even picked them out himself.

Then again, Kendall had never seemed to expect anything more, he told himself. Then again—again—that was no excuse for not showing his appreciation more often.

Note to self, Barton. Show Kendall a little appreciation this time around. As a reluctant afterthought, he made himself add, *And appreciate something* besides *her navel.*

It would be a tough job, but he was pretty sure he could do it.

She followed him up to the second floor where Matthias had a choice of guest rooms in which to house her. Not asking himself why he did it, he made his way immediately to one near the master bedroom, where he was sleeping himself. The room was furnished in varying shades of green and gold, the stout four-poster covered with a light-weight patchwork quilt, the hardwood floors broken up here and there with rag rugs. It was what Matthias had come to think of as the Rustic Room. Though it was every bit as luxurious as the rest of the house. The wide windows opened onto a thick patch of pine trees, beyond which was a spectacular view with a finger of lake on one side. At night, he thought, she could do what he'd been doing—lie in bed and listen to the wind gliding through the trees, and wait for the melancholy hoot-hoot-hoot of a solitary owl.

Hey, it wasn't as if there was much else to do around the lodge at night. At least, there hadn't been before.

"Why don't you stay more than a couple of days?" he asked impulsively as he tossed Kendall's bags onto the bed.

When he turned, he saw that she had stopped in the doorway, and she didn't look as if she planned on coming in anytime soon.

"I mean, you quit OmniTech," he pointed out unnecessarily, "and I'm not going to be coming back to San Francisco for a few more weeks. I don't expect you to report to the office before I get back myself. When was the last time you took a vacation?"

She threw him a funny look. "I just had one. Two weeks between leaving Barton Limited and going to work for OmniTech."

"Oh. Right. Well, what did you do during those two weeks?" he asked. "I bet you didn't spend them out of town, did you?"

"No," she admitted. "I did some work around my condo that I'd been putting off for a while."

"Well, there you go," Matthias said. "You need a vacation. I have a vacation home. At least for a few more weeks."

She crossed her arms over her midsection and dropped her weight to one foot. "And besides," she said, "you brought a lot of work with you from the office, and you could use someone to help out with it while you're here. Right?"

He gaped at her, shocked that she could think such a thing of him. What shocked him even more was that what she'd just accused him of had never once crossed his mind. "Of course not," he denied. "Yeah, I brought work with me, but I'm getting it done just fine by myself."

Well, except for how his laptop kept eating his files and

how he couldn't figure out how to open Excel and how every time he tried to send e-mail on the desktop in the office upstairs, a box kept popping up with all kinds of weird symbols in it that he was reasonably certain were the equivalent of digital profanity. Really bad digital profanity, too. Other than that, everything was fine.

She smiled at him in a way that made him think she knew exactly what kind of problems he was having. Then she surprised him by saying, "Okay, I'll stay a couple more days. It is a beautiful place. And I could use some downtime."

Matthias wasn't sure what to make of the ripple of pleasure that wound through him at her acceptance of his invitation. So he decided not to question it. In fact, he decided not to think about it at all. Because Kendall's smile grew broader then, and she crossed her arms in a way that made her little T-shirt ride up on her torso again, giving him another delicious glimpse at that navel. The ripple of pleasure turned into a raging tsunami at that, and he was suddenly overcome by the absolute conviction that his life would never get better than it was in that moment, standing in the same room with Kendall and her navel, knowing she would be around for a few more days.

But he was wrong. Because what she said to him after that multiplied his pleasure tenfold and nearly sent his body into paroxysms of ecstasy.

Because what she said then was, "You know, I need to run into town to pick up a few things. Why don't we look for a new BlackBerry for you while we're there? And I'll get it all nice and programmed for you, just the way you like it."

That was when Matthias knew, without doubt, that Kendall Scarborough was the only woman in the world who would ever be able to make him happy.

"But, Matthias," she added, more soberly this time, "you have to promise me you won't contact that guy in Nigeria or the woman with the Web cam."

He narrowed his eyes in confusion. "Why not?"

"Just don't. Trust me."

Strangely, he realized he already did. Implicitly. Though, thinking back on their history together, maybe that wasn't so strange after all. What was strange was that, suddenly, for some reason, he realized he also trusted Kendall in ways that went beyond the professional. But what was strangest of all was that he found himself wanting her to trust him, too. In ways that had nothing to do with the professional.

"C'mon," she said. "You'll have to drive. Let's pick up some groceries, too. I'm tired of hotel food and carryout. Let's cook tonight."

Eight

They weren't able to find a BlackBerry for Matthias in tiny Hunter's Landing. They did lots of other things there—shared a banana split at the ice-cream parlor, played air hockey at the arcade, selected fresh produce at the farmer's market and enjoyed a late-afternoon beer at the pub—but the little community was fresh out of sophisticated gadgetry by the time they arrived. Interestingly, Matthias wasn't even halfway through the banana split when he forgot all about it. And when Kendall made mention of it again halfway through the afternoon beer, he had to take a minute to remember that, oh, yeah, that was one of the reasons they'd gone into town, wasn't it? Because by then, he was enjoying himself so much with Kendall that he couldn't even remember why he'd wanted a BlackBerry in the first place.

Nor could he remember the last time he'd played air

hockey. Probably because he had played with Luke, and it had probably been one of those death matches the two of them never seemed able to avoid. With Kendall, they hadn't even kept score. Matthias couldn't remember the last time he'd had a banana split, either, and he'd certainly never shared one before, thanks to the I-got-mine mentality he'd grown up with under his father's misguided tutelage. Even the afternoon beer was unusual for Matthias. He never took time out of his day to engage in things that had no purpose other than to make the day a little nicer.

And the thing was, the day would have been nicer even without all those things, simply because Kendall was a part of it.

Why had he never realized before how much he liked having her around? he wondered as they drove back to the lodge, chatting amiably the whole way. She'd worked for him for five years—five years—and not once had it occurred to him that the reason his life was as good as it was was due in large part to Kendall's simple presence in it. All that time, he'd thought he valued her for her efficiency and organizational skills. It was only after she'd left that he'd realized she'd brought so much more to his life.

He *liked* Kendall. He liked her a lot. Not just as an employee, but as a person. As a friend. As a companion. The two of them had an easy camaraderie with each other after all these years that he hadn't even realized had developed. A give and take, an ebb and flow, an itch and scratch that was as well orchestrated and choreographed as a Broadway show. And now he understood that that camaraderie transcended their working relationship. Today, they'd enjoyed an ease of conversation Matthias didn't share with people he'd known twice as long as Kendall.

And last night, out on the deck with the telescope… That had been one of the most enjoyable evenings he'd ever had.

Even as they unpacked and put away their groceries, they spoke easily and moved in concert with each other as if they did this all the time. The preparation of dinner, too, was another perfectly executed team effort, as was the cleaning up afterward. As Matthias opened a second bottle of wine, Kendall reached into the cupboard for two fresh glasses. As he poured, she dimmed the lights, and, together, they retreated to the lodge's lush living room.

The sun was setting over the mountains, leaving the lake midnight-blue and smooth as silk. Matthias watched Kendall head for a lamp, then hesitate before turning it on. He understood. The lighting outside this time of evening was just too beautiful not to appreciate it. When she moved to the massive windows to look out on the vista, he joined her. But it wasn't the lake and mountains that drew his eye. It was Kendall's expression as she looked at them, all soft and mellow and contented. The way he felt himself.

"This place is truly gorgeous," she said.

He nodded, still looking at her. "Gorgeous," he echoed.

"I can't believe your friend had it built and isn't able to be here to enjoy it."

Matthias sighed, turning to look out at the view now. "Oh, I imagine Hunter's enjoying it, wherever he is. I think he's enjoying seeing the effect the place has on all of us. Somehow he knew all those years ago what kind of men the Seven Samurai would turn out to be."

"And what kind of men did you all turn out to be?" she asked.

Matthias inhaled a deep breath and let it out slowly. "Men who are too busy building our empires to remember why we wanted to build them in the first place. Men who work so hard, we've forgotten how to live."

But he realized as he said it that that hadn't been true of him today. Today, Matthias had forgotten all about work. Today, he'd forgotten all about empires. Today, he'd thought only about Kendall. And today, more than any other day of his life, he had *lived.* He'd lived, and he'd enjoyed living. He'd enjoyed it a lot. More, even, than work.

From the corner of his eye, he saw Kendall turn toward him, but he continued to gaze out the window, looking for…something. He wasn't sure what.

"You miss him, don't you?" she said softly.

He nodded. "It happened so quickly. By the time the doctors found the cancer, it was too late to do anything to save him."

"It must have been hard on you and your other friends."

Hard wasn't the word, Matthias thought. "Devastating," he said instead. "It tore us apart, in more ways than one. Hunter was the glue that kept us together. I think that was his gift—that he knew people. Knew what made them tick. Knew what made them behave the way they did. I mean, look at what he did for me and Luke."

"What?" Kendall asked. "I thought you guys didn't get along."

"We don't. Didn't," he immediately corrected himself. "But in college, we did. Somehow Hunter made us see past all the animosity and one-upmanship our father generated in us. Luke and I were friends—real friends—in college. But after Hunter died…"

He didn't continue. What had happened to Matthias and Luke was complicated and unsettled, and he didn't want to talk about anything complicated or unsettling tonight.

So he only said, "We all drifted apart after college. We all did well, at least professionally, but we lost each other."

He did turn to look at Kendall then. "Until now," he said, smiling. "This lodge, Hunter bringing us all here, it's getting us together again. There's going to be a reunion in September, once Jack has fulfilled his obligation to spend the month here." Although he had no idea what possessed him to do it, Matthias added, "Would you like to come back with me for that?"

Her eyes widened in surprise at the invitation. And truth be told, Matthias was surprised he'd extended it. But once said, it seemed perfectly natural. Perfectly normal. Something about having Kendall there with the friends from his past—the people who had always been more important to Matthias than anyone else—felt right.

She nodded slowly, smiling. "I'd love to come," she said. "It would be nice to meet all your old friends. And your brother, too."

Matthias wasn't sure why he did what he did next. Something about the moment, about the lodge, about the woman, just made it feel right. Dipping his head toward Kendall's, he covered her mouth with his and kissed her.

Lightly at first, gently, a part of him fearing she might pull away. But she didn't pull away. She tilted her head to the side a little, to make it easier for him, and then she kissed him back. Slowly, sweetly, almost as if she'd been expecting it, and as if she wondered what had taken him so long.

Kendall wasn't sure when the line between her and Matthias disappeared, whether it had happened just now, or during the banana split, or when she finally quit, or if it had happened years ago at a point she didn't even notice.

But when he kissed her, the way he did, she knew that line would never be back again. And then she stopped thinking about any of that, because the feelings blooming inside her, and the sensations twining through her body, were just too delicious to ignore. All she knew was that, one minute, Matthias had been looking out the window and talking about Hunter, and the next, he was surrounding her.

As he kissed her, he plucked her wineglass from her hand, and she followed his mouth with hers as he bent slightly to place both their glasses on an end table beside them. Then they were both straightening again, and he was pulling her into his arms completely, opening his mouth over hers now, tasting her deeply. She felt his hands on her back, first skimming along her spine, then curling around over her nape, then tangling in her hair. Instinctively, she raised her own hands to explore him, too, touching his rough face, his hard shoulders, his silky hair, savoring the different textures and reveling in the heat, the strength, the power she encountered beneath her fingertips.

He towered over her, seeming to touch her everywhere. Every time she inhaled, she filled her lungs with the scent of him and her mouth with the taste of him. His heart thundered against her own, the rapid beating of both mixing and mingling, until she wasn't sure which was his and which was hers. Their breathing, too, grew fierce and ragged as the kiss intensified, until Kendall felt as though their breath had also joined and become one.

One hand still tangled in her hair, he moved the other to her hip, inching it slowly downward to curve over her fanny, pushing her body forward into his. Kendall responded instinctively, rubbing her pelvis against his, sinuously, seductively, loving his growl of satisfaction in response. He moved his hand higher again, bunching the fabric of her shirt in his fist and pushing upward. She felt the cool kiss of air on her heated back with every new bit of flesh he exposed. When his fingers had crept high enough for him to realize she wasn't wearing a bra, he groaned again, splaying his fingers wide over her naked skin before deepening the kiss even more.

Thinking turnabout was fair play, Kendall dipped her hand under the hem of his shirt, too, steering her fingers over the silky swell of muscle and sinew that crisscrossed his back. Then she brought her hand forward, caressing the springy hair of his chest and the taut musculature of his torso. He was hard in all the places she was soft, angled in all the places she was curved, rough in all the places she was smooth. But his skin was as hot as hers was, and his heart beat every bit as rapidly. Their differences complemented each other, but their similarities were what brought them together. They wanted each other equally. That was enough.

She felt his hand move to her waist then, squeezing between their bodies long enough to deftly flick open the fly of her jeans and tug the zipper down. Then he was at her back again, tucking his hand into the soft denim and under the fabric of her panties, curving over her bare flesh, stroking her sensitive skin again and again and again. Heat and dampness bloomed between her legs as he stroked her, then exploded when he dipped one confident finger into the delicate cleft of her behind.

"Oh," she murmured against his mouth. "Oh, Matthias..."

But he covered her mouth again before she could say more. Not that she really knew what else she wanted to say. At the moment, she only wanted to do. Do things to and with him, and have things done to her in return.

Things she had never even allowed herself to dream about, things that felt so natural, so right, now. He seemed to realize that, because he filled her mouth with his tongue, then palmed and kneaded her tender flesh, pushing her harder against his ripening erection with every stroke.

No longer content not to be able to touch him, she wedged her hand between their bodies to cup the full length of him in her palm. He murmured a satisfied sound in response and moved his hips against her hand, silently encouraging her to take her strokes farther still. Eagerly, she unfastened and opened his jeans, too, dipping her hand inside to cover him more intimately. Bare skin on bare skin, the way he was touching her. He felt so big, so powerful, so masterful in her hand, so hot, so hard, so smooth.

For long moments, they only kissed and touched each other, their pulse rates and respiration multiplying with every one that passed. When they finally started moving— slowly, deliberately, carefully—Kendall wasn't sure if it was she or Matthias who was responsible. Somehow, though, they kissed and touched and danced their way across the living room, through the door and up the stairs, until they stood in the upstairs hallway, surrounded by bedrooms. Surrounded by choices.

Only then did Matthias pull back, as if he wanted to give her time to make whatever choice she was going to make. His hesitation surprised her. Usually, he was a man who, when he wanted something, did whatever he had to do to get it. No cajoling, no seducing, no petitioning, only full-on frontal attack, damn the torpedoes or anything that got in his way. She wouldn't have been surprised if he had swept her up at the bottom of the stairs the way Rhett had Scarlett, and carried her to his room to ravish her. Especially since she'd made it clear how very much she wanted to be ravished.

Evidently, though, Matthias pursued his personal affairs with more finesse than he did his professional ones. And for some reason, realizing that just made Kendall that much more certain that allowing this next step between them, however suddenly it had come—though, somehow, it didn't feel that sudden at all—was the right thing to do.

When she said nothing to object to what he was so clearly asking her, he did take the initiative, weaving his fingers through hers and guiding her to the master bedroom. Once inside, he slipped an arm around her waist and pushed her hair aside, bending his head to place a soft, chaste kiss on her nape that, ironically, was infinitely more arousing than all the desperate hungry ones put together. He pulled her body back against his, his hard member surging against her backside, something that shot heat through her entire body. When he nuzzled the curve where her neck joined her shoulder, Kendall tilted her head to facilitate his action, then reached behind herself with both hands to thread her fingers through his hair. She purposely put herself in a vulnerable position, knowing Matthias would take advantage, which he did, covering her breasts with both hands.

As he dragged his mouth along the sensitive flesh of her neck and shoulder, he gently kneaded her breasts through the fabric of her T-shirt, bringing a sigh of pleasure from Kendall. Then he dropped his hands to the hem of the shirt and tugged it up, up, up, pulling it over her head and tossing it to the floor. Then his hands were on her bare breasts, his hot palms squeezing and stroking and caressing. As he rolled one nipple under his thumb, his other hand scooted lower, down along the bare skin of her torso, his middle finger dipping into her navel as it passed. Then Matthias pushed his hand into her panties, finding the hot damp center of her and burying his fingers in the swollen folds of flesh.

She gasped at the sensation that shot through her then, her fingers convulsing in his hair. Kneading her breast with one hand, he stroked her damp flesh with the other—long, thorough, leisurely strokes that pushed her to the brink of insanity. Her body stilled as he touched her, her breathing the only sound in the room. Little by little, he hastened his pace, moving his hand backward and forward, left to right, drawing circles and spirals until finally he touched her in that one place, with that one finger, in a way that made her shatter. Kendall was rocked by an orgasm that came out of nowhere, seizing her body and sending a crash of heat shuddering through her.

For a moment, it felt as if time had stopped, as if she would exist forever in some suspended pinnacle of emotion, her body fused to Matthias's, her heart and lungs racing alongside his. Then the moment dissolved, and so did she, and she spun around to just kiss him and kiss him and kiss him.

Somehow, they managed to undress each other without ever losing physical contact, dropping clothes left and right, leaving them where they lay. On their way to the bed, Matthias slowed long enough to light a trio of candles on the mantelpiece, something that bathed the room in the golden glow of light. They paused by the big sleigh bed, the candlelight limning everything in gold. Kendall's heart pounded faster as she took in the sight that was Matthias. Strangely, he seemed even bigger when he was naked, his broad shoulders and strong arms curved with muscle, his flat chest and torso corded with more beneath the dark hair she found so erotic.

He settled both hands on her hips as she curled her fingers over his shoulders, then sat on the edge of the bed and pulled her into his lap, facing him, her legs straddling his. Roping an arm around her waist, he kissed her again, the way he had before, hungry and urgent and deep. She moved her hand to the hard head of his shaft, palming him, then began to stroke him, leisurely, methodically, as she kissed him back. Matthias curled his hands over her fanny, matching his caresses to hers and mimicking both in the movement of his tongue inside her mouth.

He turned their bodies so that they were lying on the bed crossways, Kendall on her back and he by her side, with one heavy leg draped over both of hers and an arm thrown across her breasts. He kissed her jaw, her cheek, her temple, her forehead, then moved down to her throat, her collarbone and her breast. There, he took his time, flattening his tongue over her nipple before drawing it into his mouth, confidently and completely. He covered her other breast with his hand, catching her nipple between the V of his index and middle fingers, squeezing gently and generating more fire inside her. Wanting more, she spread her legs and rubbed herself against his thigh, gasping at the new sensations that shot through her.

Matthias seemed to understand her needs, because after a few more dizzying flicks of his tongue against the lower curve of her breast, he moved downward again, tasting her navel this time as he passed and kissing the skin beneath. Then he was going lower still, pushing open Kendall's legs to duck his head between them, running his tongue over the warm damp folds without a single hesitation. He lapped leisurely with the flat of his tongue, then drew generous circles with the tip. Pushing his hands beneath her fanny he lifted her higher, parting her with his thumbs so that he could penetrate her with his tongue, again and again and again. Then he was penetrating her with his finger, too, deeper now, slower, more thoroughly.

Ripples of pleasure began to purl through Kendall again, starting low in her belly and echoing outward, until her body was trembling with the beginning of a second climax. Seeming to sense how close she was, Matthias moved his body again, this time kneeling before her. He parted her legs and, grasping an ankle in each hand, pulled her toward himself to bury himself inside her—deep, *deep* inside her. Hooking her legs over his shoulders, he lowered his body over hers, braced both elbows on the mattress on each side of her and thrust himself forward even deeper. Again and again, he bucked his hips against hers, going deeper with each new penetration, opening Kendall wider to receive him. She wrapped her fingers tight around his steely biceps as he thrust harder, taking him as deeply as she could, until finally, finally, they both cried out with the explosive responses that rocked them.

For one long moment, they clung to each other, his body shuddering in the last of its release, hers quaking with the remnants of her climax. Then Matthias was relaxing, falling to the bed beside Kendall, one hand draped over her waist, the other arcing over her head.

It was then that Kendall's confidence about what she had allowed to happen between them began to slip. Because she realized then that what she had thought was a crush on her boss was so much more. And although Matthias had certainly mellowed during his time at the lodge, to the point where he no longer seemed consumed by his work, he'd offered no indication that he considered anything else more important. Maybe he wasn't married to his business anymore. Maybe. But could he—would he—ever join himself to something, someone, else?

Kendall woke slowly, not sure at first where she was. The sun wasn't up yet, but there was an indistinct golden glow dancing at the foot of her bed whose origin she couldn't quite figure out, so groggy was she from sleep. She felt blissfully happy for no reason she could name and snuggled more deeply into the covers.

Why was her bed so much more comfortable than usual? she wondered blearily as she pulled the covers higher. So much warmer? So much more welcome? And why did she want nothing more than to stay here like this forever? Usually, the moment she awoke, she awoke completely, then immediately shoved back the covers and rose to face the day. She was even one of those people who immediately made the bed, so finished with it was she until nightfall came again. But today…

She sighed deeply, purring a little as she exhaled. Today, she just wanted to stay in bed until nightfall came again. Because something about the prospect of nightfall coming once more made a shudder of delight wind through her.

She was about to sigh again when her brain finally started to function—albeit none too quickly. It did get enough momentum going for her to finally realize what the light at the foot of the bed could be.

Fire. Her bedroom was on fire.

She jackknifed up to a sitting position, prepared to flee for her life, then was shocked to discover she was naked.

Why was she naked? In moving so hastily, she jostled the person next to her—why was there another person in her bed?—who, with a muffled groan, turned over and, with a muffled thump, landed on the floor. And she realized there was something very familiar about that groan…

That, finally, was when Kendall remembered. She wasn't in her bed. She wasn't in her condo. The fire in the room was the light of candles. It was perfectly safe. Perfectly lovely. Perfectly romantic. And the reason she felt so good was because—

Oh.

So *that* was why there was someone else in the bed.

She felt more than saw Matthias throw an arm up onto the mattress, but she definitely heard another soft groan as he pulled himself up off the floor. Then she heard a sound of exasperation as he crawled back into bed beside her. And then in a voice full of concern, he asked, "What's wrong?"

Oh, there were so many ways she could answer that question. Too many ways. And even so, none of them seemed quite right. Going to bed with Matthias last night had been the wrong thing to do, Kendall told herself. He was her employer again, and she was too smart to get involved with an office romance. But being in bed with Matthias this morning felt so wonderfully right. She would have been an idiot not to make love with the man last night, feeling the way she did about him.

Okay then, her feelings for him were wrong, she told herself. Falling in love with her boss? How stupid could she be? But then, only a brainless ninny would be immune to a man like him. How could she not love him?

And that was when it hit her full force. She was in love with Matthias. Probably had been for years. She just hadn't let herself admit it, because she'd been convinced he would never love her in return. And maybe he didn't love her, she thought. Just because they'd made love…more than once…with utter abandon…and not a little creativity…

Oh, God, she thought. Kendall had no idea what to think just then. So she did the only thing she could do. She lied.

"Nothing," she said, hoping Matthias didn't detect the note of alarm she heard in her voice. "Nothing's wrong. Everything's wonderful. Fabulous. Marvelous. Stupendous. Couldn't be better. In fact, everything is so perfect that I want to leave right now, before anything happens to change it. I'll see myself out. Call me when you get back to San Francisco. Goodbye."

Okay, so she lied *and* panicked. It was a perfectly justifiable response. Thankful for the darkness, she shoved the covers aside and started to rise from the bed.

Until Matthias clapped a strong hand around her wrist and pulled her back down again. Then he levered his body over hers and kissed her. Hard. Long. Deep. And then some of the tension in Kendall's body began to drain away.

Oh, all right, *all* the tension in her body drained away. In fact, by the time Matthias raised his head, she was pretty sure it was going to be hours before she moved again. Unless, you know, he kissed her like that a second time, in which case she would probably start moving *a lot*.

"Going somewhere?" he asked, his voice a velvet purr in the darkness.

Not sure she could get her tongue to work—well, not for talking, anyway—she only murmured, "Mmm-mmm."

"Good," he said. "Because we're not even close to being finished."

Oh, my, Kendall thought.

He chuckled softly. "First we have to have breakfast."

Ooooh, Kendall thought. Breakfast. Right.

"And I'm in the mood for something light, delectable and sweet."

Kendall was in the mood for something dark, delectable and spicy. They were going to need a smorgasbord for this.

No! she immediately told herself. They weren't going to have a smorgasbord. In fact, they couldn't have breakfast at all. They probably never should have had dinner last night. Or the dessert that had come after. Or the dessert after *that,* either.

She found her voice and softly said, "Matthias, we need to talk."

He cupped his hand over her breast and said, "No, we need to *not* talk."

When he started to lean down to kiss her again, she opened her hand lightly over his chest and held firm. Less softly this time, she repeated, "Matthias. We need to talk."

"Kendall—"

"Matthias."

He expelled a quiet sound of resolution, then rolled back over to his side of the bed. Enough light flickered from the candles to enable her to make out his expression. But where she might have expected him to be annoyed or unhappy, or even angry at her having halted his advance, instead, he looked kind of dejected.

Dejected, she marveled. Matthias Barton. He'd never looked dejected about anything. Because he'd never *been* dejected about anything. Then the look was gone, and she told herself she must have just imagined it.

"What do we need to talk about?" he asked. Sounding kind of dejected.

No, annoyed, she told herself. He must be feeling annoyed that instead of romping in the sheets a while longer, she wanted to do some girlie-girl thing like talk about their feelings. But she needed to know how Matthias felt. Especially since she understood how she felt herself.

Inhaling a deep breath, she said very carefully, "What exactly happened here tonight?"

He hesitated a moment before answering, as if he were trying to be careful in choosing his words, too. "Well," he began, "first we had a very enjoyable day in town, and then we came back here."

Actually, Kendall hadn't intended to go back quite that far, but he seemed to need to stall for a little more time, so she let him off the hook. Hey, it wasn't as though she knew exactly what to say, in spite of being the one who said they needed to talk.

"Then we fixed a great meal here, with a very nice cabernet—"

In which they'd probably overindulged, she couldn't help thinking.

"And then we went into the living room and looked out at the lake," he continued. "And then you kissed me—"

"No, you kissed me," she corrected him.

"And then we kissed," he went on as if she hadn't spoken, "and then we came up to the bedroom and had sex."

She was about to say something in response to that, when he continued, "Then we got hungry and went downstairs to have a snack. Only we stopped in the hallway to, um…have an appetizer."

Kendall opened her mouth to speak, but Matthias continued, "And then we had another appetizer on the landing. And then on the stairs. And then on the living room floor."

She started to talk again, but he went on. "And then we had a snack and came back upstairs and had sex in the bed again. And then we slept. And then we woke up. And now we're talking. Can we do something else now? Something *I* want to do? Like have sex?"

By the time he finished, Kendall was only half listening. Because she'd heard what she'd wanted—or, at least *needed*—to hear halfway through. "So then, it was all just sex?" she asked.

When he hesitated again, she studied his face closely, wishing the light were better. Because no matter what he said next, she wouldn't know if it was true or not unless she could look him in the eye. One thing she'd learned working closely with Matthias for five years was how to tell when he was being serious or when he was bluffing. But if she couldn't see his face…

"What do you mean *just* sex?" he asked in a voice that was void of any emotion at all, something that bothered Kendall even more than it would have bothered her had it been filled with *some*thing, even annoyance. At least then she would have known it meant something to him. "Sex isn't a *just* thing. Sex is a *spectacular* thing. And we had some pretty spectacular sex, Kendall. To reduce it to a cliché, wasn't it good for you, too?"

Oh, it had been more than good, she thought. It had been more than spectacular. Because to her, it had been special. Matthias, she feared, felt differently. And Kendall felt…

Well, she felt different, too. That was what falling in love did to a person. It made them feel different. About everything. Remembering he'd asked her a question that needed an answer, and without thinking, she told him, "It was nice."

"Nice?" he echoed incredulously. "Kendall, my great-

aunt Viola is nice. The Beaujolais Nouveaux last year were nice. Raindrops on roses and whiskers on kittens are nice. Sex with Matthias Barton? That's not nice. That's phenomenal."

In spite of the way she was feeling inside, Kendall smiled. Then, unable to help herself, she reached over and cupped his jaw in her palm. "You were wonderful," she told him.

"Phenomenal," he corrected her.

"Phenomenal," she repeated dutifully.

He had been phenomenal, she thought. But she still didn't know if he was in love. So she turned the conversation to a topic she knew he would understand.

"Matthias," she said carefully, "have you come up with a title for the new position I'll be filling at Barton Limited?"

It wasn't as strange a question as it may have seemed. He wasn't accustomed to talking about his feelings. Although she was confident that he did indeed *have* feelings for her, she wasn't sure if they mirrored hers for him. Asking Matthias how he felt in that moment would only make him clam up. Asking him about work, on the other hand, would make him talk. After five years with him, Kendall had learned to read the subtleties of his business-speak. Matthias's reply to the question she'd just asked would tell her infinitely more than the one to "How do you feel?" would tell her.

"That's kind of a strange question to ask right now, isn't it?" he asked. "I mean, aren't you going to ask me how I feel?"

She shook her head. "I want to hear about the new position. Details this time. Not vague promises."

He expelled a soft sound of resignation, but replied, "Actually, I still haven't come up with a title."

She nodded slowly, her heart sinking a little. "Okay. Then what does the new position involve?"

He hesitated a telling moment, then said, "It's really going to challenge you. The responsibilities are awesome. There will be days when you meet yourself coming and going."

Well, that certainly sounded…vague. "Such as?" she asked.

"Well, your day will begin early," he told her. "I'll expect you at the office by seven-thirty."

"Matthias, that was what time I arrived when I worked for you before. It's not a problem." And, she couldn't help thinking a little sadly, it wasn't very awesome, either.

"Right," he said. "Of course. A typical day for you at this new job will consist of a lot of different things," he continued. "Lots of responsibilities. Awesome responsibilities."

Her heart sank more. "So you've said. You just haven't told me what the responsibilities are."

"Sure I did. They're awesome."

She expelled an impatient breath, her sadness turning to exasperation now. She was pretty sure where this was leading. Now she just wanted to get it over with. "Could you be more specific?" she asked halfheartedly.

"Well," he began in the voice he used whenever he needed to stall, "for instance, every morning, you'd be in charge of sustenance acquisition."

Any hope she might have still been harboring fled with that, and something hard and icy settled in her stomach. She eyed Matthias flatly. "Sustenance acquisition," she repeated.

"Sustenance acquisition," he told her in a more confident voice.

"In other words, getting you your coffee."

He uttered an insulted sound at that. As if he was the one who should be insulted, she thought. Right.

"No, not just getting coffee," he denied.

"Okay, a Danish, too," she conceded. "Or maybe a bagel, if you're on a health kick." He opened his mouth to object, but she cut him off with, "What other awesome responsibilities would I have?"

Not that she couldn't already guess. But she wanted to make sure before she declined the position. And then packed her bags and headed back to San Francisco. She didn't care if she had to hitchhike all the way home.

"Well, let's see," he said, feigning deep thought.

Kendall knew he was feigning it, because if he was having the thoughts she was fairly certain he was having, they weren't in any way deep. Unless they were in something for which she would have to wear waders, which, now that she thought about it, was entirely possible.

"You'd also be in charge of technology aggregation," he told her.

"You mean buying software for your laptop."

"That's way oversimplifying it," he told her.

"Right," she agreed. "Because I'd have to do all the paperwork on the warranties, too. And that sure can be awesome."

He continued gallantly, "You'd also be responsible for environmental augmentation."

"Keeping your desk tidy and well supplied," she translated.

He frowned, but added, "And client satisfaction."

"Planning cocktail parties."

"You'd be my sanitary health liaison."

"I'd make appointments for you at your barber and the gym."

"And you'd be in charge of equipment enhancement."

"Pencil sharpening," she said brightly. "Yeah, can't get enough of that."

"Kendall, it's not—"

"Yes," she said vehemently. "It is. What you're describing is exactly the job I left behind."

"All right, all right," he relented. "I want you to come back to work for me in the same capacity you were when you left. As my assistant. But I'll pay you four times what you were earning before."

"To do the same job?"

"Yes."

"Why?"

He didn't answer right away, only met her gaze levelly and studied her with a look she had no idea how to decipher. Finally, though, he told her, "Because you're the best assistant I ever had, that's why."

She closed her eyes. "I'm not an assistant, Matthias," she said. "I'm a businesswoman. That's where I want to make my mark in the world. That's what brings me satisfaction. That's what I want to be defined by." She opened her eyes again and held his gaze with hers. "I don't want to be anyone's assistant. Not even yours."

"But I can't get through the day without you, Kendall."

"Of course you can get through the—"

"No." He cut her off with even more vehemence than she'd shown herself. "I can't. You've seen me. Look, I know I'm good at what I do for a living. Hell, I'm phenomenal at that. But I can't do it by myself. If I have to be bothered with all the mundane, everyday tasks that consume so much time, I can't get anything done."

"And you think I *like* doing those things?" she asked. "You think I'm suited to that?"

"No, that's not what I meant at all."

She shook her head, not bothering to hide her exasperation now. "Face it, Matthias, you just think you're more important than me. You think you're smarter than me, and more essential than me, and more valuable than me. But here's a news flash for you. Everyone's important in some way or another. Everyone's got smarts of one kind or another. Everyone's essential in some capacity. And everyone's valuable, too." She inhaled a deep breath and finished, "I'm valuable, Matthias. For more than getting you coffee and tidying your desk and planning your parties. I can make as big a mark on the world as you have. And I will. Just watch me."

Nine

Matthias felt panic well up inside him when he realized Kendall was going to leave. Really leave this time. Not just her job, but him. And this time there would be no convincing her to come back. How could she think her job wasn't important? The work she did was crucial. And how could she think he didn't consider her valuable? She meant more to him than anything.

Anything.

And that was when it hit him. It wasn't that he needed Kendall as his assistant to keep him on track. And it wasn't that he needed her as his assistant to be successful. And it wasn't that he needed her as his assistant to make him happy. He just needed Kendall. Period. In his work, in his life, in his…

In his heart.

"Kendall, wait," he said as she pushed back the covers and scrambled out of bed.

But she ignored him, jerking the top sheet from the mattress and wrapping it around herself with an awkward sort of fury that generated a sick feeling in the pit of his stomach. After everything they'd enjoyed last night, after everything they'd discovered, she wanted to cover herself up now. She wanted to get away from him.

She wanted to leave.

"Kendall, you don't understand," he added as he rose from the bed, too. He grabbed his navy silk bathrobe from the back of the bedroom door as he followed her into the hall.

"Oh, I understand perfectly," she snapped as she went into the guest room where the bags she hadn't even unpacked still lay on the bed.

Good God, Matthias thought. She didn't even have to pack her bags. All she had to do was get dressed, and she'd be out of there. He had mere minutes before she was gone for good.

"No, you don't," he told her. "You can't understand, because I just figured it out myself."

She spun around so quickly, her hair flew over her face. Brushing it fiercely aside with one hand, her other tightened where she clutched the sheet until her knuckles were white. Her entire body quivered with her anger, he noted. Or maybe it was with something else. Maybe it was the same thing that was making his body shudder, too. The realization that he'd just found something wonderful—the most wonderful, stupendous, spectacular thing in the world—and were about to lose it, before he even had a taste.

Finally, coldly, she said, "What, Matthias? What don't I understand?"

He opened his mouth to try and explain, to try and put

into words, as eloquently as he could, all the things he needed to tell her. How much she'd come to mean to him. Not as an employee, but as a woman. How he couldn't live without her. Not because she helped him work better, but because she helped him live better. How he couldn't get through another day without her. Not because she knew how to work his BlackBerry, but because she knew how to fill all the places inside him he'd thought would be empty forever. But all he could think to tell her was—

"I love you."

She went completely still at that. But her fingers on the sheet relaxed, and her expression softened. "What?" she said, her voice a scant whisper.

"I love you," he said again.

She stiffened once more. "Don't you dare say something like that just because you're trying to—"

"I mean it, Kendall," he said. "I may be heartless when it comes to getting my way in business, but I would never put my heart on the line like this unless I was telling the truth."

He took a few experimental steps into the room, taking courage in the fact that she didn't back away from him. But neither did she reach out to him. Nor did she say a word.

"I thought I needed you to come back as my assistant, because I thought that was why you were good for me." She frowned at that, so he hurried on, "You know me, Kendall. I've always been married to my business. It never occurred to me that anything else could make me happy. I'm an idiot," he admitted. "But I'm not so stupid that I can't learn. And I finally realize, it doesn't matter what job you do, whether you program my BlackBerry or mop the floors at Barton Limited or…or come aboard as my new VP in charge of Public Relations."

She narrowed her eyes at him. "What are you talking about? You have a VP in charge of Public Relations. Mitchell Valentine."

"Yeah, well, Mitchell's wife is pregnant with twins, and he wants to be a stay-at-home dad, so he's leaving at the end of August. I was going to hire a headhunter to find someone to fill the position, but I think I already have the perfect candidate working at Barton Limited."

Her expression was cautious. "Who?"

Did she really have to ask? Well, okay, he supposed she did, since she had asked. "You," he told her. "I'd like you to come work for me as my new VP."

She said nothing in response to his offer, something he wasn't sure was good or bad. So, thinking, what the hell, he decided to go for broke. "There's just one problem," he told her.

Now her expression turned wary. "What's that?"

"Barton Limited has a policy that bars spouses from working together."

Her eyes widened at that.

"Fortunately," he added, "it's just a policy, not written in stone anywhere. Besides which, I'm the CEO, so I can do whatever the hell I want. Should, you know, two of the executives want to get…married."

It occurred to Matthias then that Kendall had never actually said she loved him, too. Not that he wasn't pretty sure she at least had *some* feelings for him. He just wasn't sure if they were as strong as his were for her.

"You really want to marry me?" she asked.

He nodded. "Yes. I do."

"You really love me?"

He nodded again. "More than anything."

This time, she nodded, too. But it was a slow nod. A thoughtful nod. The kind that indicated she was thinking, not agreeing. Finally, though, she told him, "Then I think, Matthias, before we go any further with this, we need to talk about the terms."

Good businesswoman that she was, she insisted they be dressed for their discussion. Conceding the point, Matthias decided they should also have access to coffee. So after dressing and having breakfast, he and Kendall took their coffee out to the deck, where a warm summer breeze skidded off the lake, and where the golden sun washed over them.

They took their seats on the big Adirondack love seat, settling comfortably into the patterned cushions. Matthias took solace in the fact that Kendall sat close enough to touch him, tucking her bare foot under her denim-clad leg comfortably. Her white cotton shirt was embroidered with white flowers and edged with lace, feminine enough to be unprofessional, another good sign. He, too, was barefoot, his blue jeans as worn as hers, his polo an old, lovingly faded green one that was his favorite for those few occasions when he kicked back and relaxed. They were talking terms, he thought, but for something much more important than business.

"Where would you like to start?" he asked.

She sipped her coffee and gazed out at the lake. "It occurs to me that if I agree to this merger, it's not the first time you've attempted this kind of thing. And I want to be clear that, although I'm not the first candidate for the position you've offered me, I'm your first—your only—choice."

He looked at her, confused. "I'm not sure I follow."

She sighed, then turned to face him. "Two words. Lauren Conover."

He smiled a little self-deprecatingly. "Ah. I guess that's my signal to tell you about my botched wedding attempt, isn't it?"

Kendall nodded. "I tried to be subtle, but you men just don't have the subtlety gene."

He nodded. "That explains a lot, actually. Like how my engagement happened in the first place."

He looked at Kendall, who had placed her hand on the seat cushion between them, so that her thumb touched her own thigh and her pinky touched his. Her eyes glistened in the morning light, the sun flickered in her hair, first orange then red then gold, and her cheeks had bloomed pink from the warm breeze. Her entire being seemed illuminated from within, as if it were she, not the sun, that brought warmth to the day. And to Matthias, too. Because he'd sat in the sunshine plenty of times, but never had he felt the way he did in that moment. As if everything in his life that had come before it was only preparation for this moment. As if this moment signified the beginning of something new and wonderful that would last forever.

How could he have missed Kendall's beauty all those years? he wondered. How could he have missed Kendall? How could he have not seen what should have been obvious from the first? That she was a rare, exquisite jewel amid the meaningless rubbish of his work. How could he have thought his work was the most important thing in the world, when every day she was with him was a sign of how there was so much more?

"Matthias?" she said softly.

He lifted a hand to thread his fingers through her hair, then hesitated, in case she didn't want him to. But she leaned her head forward, toward his fingers, toward him, and he closed what was left of the distance gratefully, loving the way the soft, warm tresses felt cascading over his fingertips. "Hmm?" he replied absently.

"The engagement?" she prodded gently. "You were going to tell me why it happened."

Right. He had been planning to tell her about his now-defunct engagement. Which was weird, because there was another engagement he wanted to talk about so much more. Of course, that engagement hadn't happened—yet. So maybe it would be best to divest himself completely of the old one. Then he could move ahead to the new.

"It was actually Lauren's father's idea," he began. "He and I were talking about merging our companies over dinner one night, and when the food came, the conversation turned to more personal subject matter, because it's hard to talk business when you're eating." He adopted his best professor voice as he added, importantly, "Because as everyone knows, it's an unwritten rule of business etiquette that you should never talk about important things with your mouth full. So talk about unimportant things with your mouth full instead."

Kendall chuckled at that. "Yeah, personal matters are so much less important than professional ones."

He nodded. "You learned well at my knee, grasshopper. Unfortunately, a lot of what I taught you was wrong."

She smiled at that. "As long as you understand that now."

"Oh, I understand a lot now that I was clueless about before."

She lifted her hand and cupped his cheek affectionately. A very good sign. "We can talk about that, too," she said. "In fact, I look forward to it. But first, you're talking to Conover…"

"Right. He mentioned that his daughter had just returned from Paris having canceled her wedding for the third time. Not the same wedding, mind you," he hastened to add, "but the third wedding with a third fiancé."

"Lauren Conover was engaged three times before she agreed to marry you?"

Matthias nodded. "Which was why she let her father cajole her into the whole thing. She'd gotten to the point where she didn't trust her own judgment. And Conover took advantage of that to convince her an arranged marriage would be best."

"And how did he convince you of that?" Kendall asked. "Somehow, I've never pictured you as the sort to mistrust your own judgment."

"Too true," he said. Except that, like so many other things, he'd been wrong about that, too. His judgment, at least when it came to matters of the heart, stank. Or, at least, it used to. "But Conover is a very persuasive man, and he made some excellent points about why it would be beneficial to merge our families as well as our businesses. And since I'd never planned to marry, marrying Lauren Conover made sense."

"Whoa, whoa, whoa," Kendall said. "I don't follow that logic at all."

"Of course not," he said. "You don't have the convoluted logic gene that men have."

"Ah."

"The convoluted logic goes like this," he told her, smiling. "Try to keep up. I'd never planned to marry, because I never planned to fall in love." Something else he'd been wrong about, he thought. Man. Where had he ever gotten the idea that he was savvy? "So marrying for love made no sense to me. Marrying for business, however…"

Now Kendall nodded. "Right. Got it. It's all coming clear now. Anything done for the sake of one's business makes perfect sense."

"It used to," he said. "Back before I realized what was really important. I guess I just never really thought marriage was such a big deal. And when I did think about it, it seemed like the things that screwed up a marriage always resulted from the emotional investment people made in it. I concluded that by not investing emotionally, my marriage to Lauren would be successful. As long as she and I looked at it pragmatically, everything would be fine."

"And what did Lauren think?"

"At that point, she agreed with me. Like I said, she'd been engaged three times because she thought she'd been in love, and all three times, she ended up abandoned. She hadn't wanted the arrangement to be based on love any more than I had. Until she came to her senses one day and realized how unrealistic she and I both were being about it."

"And until she met up with your brother, Luke."

Matthias waited for the stab of…something…that should have come with the comment. A stab of jealousy maybe, even if he hadn't been in love with Lauren when Luke set out to seduce her. Or a stab of anger that his brother, even though the two of them had barely been speaking at the time, would misrepresent himself as Matthias and deliberately seduce his brother's bride. Or even a stab of resentment that Luke had won some misguided competition between the two men over a woman.

But all Matthias felt was relief. Profound, unmitigated relief that Lauren, at least, had been smart enough to know they'd be making a huge mistake if they married. Then he met Kendall's gaze again, and he felt something else, too.

Something he'd never felt before, but he recognized none-theless. Something his brother had ultimately found with Matthias's ex-fiancée, something that had made him pro-pose to Lauren instead. Something that made Matthias realize there was a lot more to life than work.

"Love," he said aloud. "Lauren didn't just meet up with my brother, Luke. She fell in love with my brother, Luke."

Kendall said nothing in response to that, only gazed at Matthias in silence. She had to know, though, he thought. Not only had he told her, but her hands were placed right over his heart, and the way his heart was racing now, as he looked back at her, feeling what he felt, knowing what he knew, she had to feel it. She had to.

Finally, softly, she asked, "And how do you feel about that? That your brother, Luke, is going to marry a woman you once planned to marry yourself?"

"I'm happy," he told her. "Lauren's a nice woman. I'm glad she finally found someone who allows her to realize that about herself."

"And Luke?" Kendall asked. "Are you happy for him, too?"

Matthias recalled the last time he'd seen his brother, how desperate and terrified Luke had been when he thought he'd lost Lauren. Helping Luke win her back was the first time he and his brother had worked together to gain something since... He smiled. Wow. That had probably been the first time in their lives they'd ever cooperated together by themselves to achieve a common goal. That it had been to enable one brother to win the heart of the woman who'd been engaged to the other...

Well. That was actually pretty cool, now that Matthias thought about it.

Things between him and Luke were better than they'd been a few months ago, but they still weren't quite settled. Matthias wasn't sure if he and his brother could ever go back to the glory days of college, the one period in their lives when they'd been as close as, well, brothers. But he was willing to put forth the effort if Luke was. In addition to reuniting what was left of the Barton family, burying the hatchet with Luke would be a nice way to honor Hunter's memory. Hunter had been the one who reconciled the two of them at Harvard, by convincing them that brothers were supposed to be at each other's sides, not at each other's throats. Hunter had, in his way, made all of the Seven Samurai feel like brothers. Shame on all of them for not maintaining that brotherhood after his death.

And shame on Matthias and Luke in particular for allowing the gap Hunter had helped close to open again.

"I'm happy for Luke, too," Matthias said.

"Really?" Kendall asked.

He nodded. "Really. He's a good guy, even if he's acted like a lunkhead over the last several years. I guess, in a way, he had his reasons."

Of course, his reasons had been totally misguided, since he'd thought Matthias had cheated him—both years ago and as recently as a few months ago. They'd cleared the air about that two months ago, here at this very lodge. Now it was time to clear the air about everything else, too.

"Luke and Lauren both deserve to be happy," Matthias said. He smiled at Kendall. "Just like you and I deserve to be happy."

"You should call him," Kendall said.

Matthias nodded. "I will. I have a few things to talk to him about, not the least of which is to build a bridge that we should have built years ago." He met her gaze levelly now, wanting to gauge her reaction when he said the rest. "I also want to ask him about being best man at the wedding. My wedding, I mean, not his." He held his breath as he added, "Provided there's going to be a my wedding in addition to his."

She studied him in silence for a long time, her eyes never leaving his. He had no idea what she could be looking for but she must have finally found it, because she smiled. Not a big smile, but it was enough to tell Matthias that everything was going to be okay.

He hoped.

Finally, she said, "What do you mean *your* wedding? I assume there will be someone else at the altar, too, right?"

"God, I hope so," he told her. "It wouldn't be much of a wedding without her."

"It wouldn't be much of a marriage, either," she pointed out. "Since, I assume you're taking into consideration that after the wedding ends, there will be a marriage hanging around your neck."

He tilted his head to the side, feigning consideration. "Mmm, I don't know. I thought I might wear my marriage on my sleeve. Next to my heart."

Now she rolled her eyes. "No one could ever accuse you of wearing your heart on your sleeve, Matthias."

"Maybe not before," he told her. "But I do now."

She bent forward and craned her head to look first at his left arm, then at his right. "I don't see it anywhere."

Catching her under her arms, he lifted her from the love seat and into his lap, then looped both arms around her waist. Oh, yeah, he thought. Everything was going to be just fine.

"Sorry, my mistake," he said as he pulled her close. "My heart isn't *on* my arms. It's *in* them."

She smiled at that, cupping her palm softly over his cheek. "What a coincidence," she said. "My heart is surrounding me."

"So is my love," he told her.

She smiled. "I love you, too."

Very, very fine, he thought, relief—and something even more wonderful—coursing through him.

"Enough to marry me?" he asked.

"As long as it's not convenient," she replied.

He brushed his lips over hers, once, twice, three times, four, enough to get both their hearts pounding, but not enough to scramble their brains—at least not yet. Then he pressed his forehead to hers and pulled her closer still.

"I think I can safely say there will be no convenience in our marriage," he told her. "Love, honor and cherishing, but no convenience."

"Good," she said. "Because convenience just gets too messy sometimes."

He sighed. "I must be absorbing the subtlety gene through osmosis," he said, "because I'm pretty sure you just told me you won't be running Public Relations conveniently, either."

"Oh, don't you worry your handsome little head about that," she told him. "I know what I'm doing. Trust me."

He wasn't much surprised to discover that he did. He trusted Kendall implicitly. And not just with the business, either. Which meant he was so far gone on her, he was never coming back. All the more reason, he thought, to stay together forever.

"I love you, Kendall Scarborough."

"I love you, Matthias Barton."

"Then you'll marry me?"

She nodded. "As long as you promise me you'll never let anyone program your BlackBerry but me."

He chuckled and kissed her quickly on the lips. "It's a deal."

The first deal he'd ever made that would enrich his personal life instead of his professional one. A very sweet deal indeed. Starting today, Matthias Barton was no longer a man who was married to his business. Starting today, he was a man who would be marrying his love. His life. The love of his life.

Life was good, he thought as he dipped his head to Kendall's again. And from here on out, it was only going to get better.

Epilogue

"So tell me more about this picture," Kendall said.

She and Matthias stood on the stairway landing their last day at the lodge, having made their final run through the house to make sure they hadn't left anything behind. Well, other than some wonderful memories. Which, she supposed, they would actually be taking with them after all. They were dressed for the drive back to San Francisco in blue jeans and T-shirts, hers pale yellow and his navy blue, a stark contrast to the suits they'd be donning the following Monday, when they went back to work.

It would be strange, she thought, having an office on a different floor from Matthias. But at least they would still be in the same building. And the Public Relations office was only one floor down from his. They could meet for lunch regularly. And, it went without saying, play footsie under the table whenever there were meetings.

"Tell me about each of the Seven Samurai," she said now. "I know about Hunter," she added. "And obviously, I recognize you and Luke. But who are the others? Which one is Ryan?"

He looked at her askance. "How do you know Ryan's name?"

"I saw the note in the office," she confessed.

He nodded. "It was waiting for me on the desk when I arrived. Ryan obviously knew that would be the first place I went once I got settled. I tacked it up with the photographs because I figured I'd need a laugh. All that stuff about finding The One."

"You think finding 'The One' is a joke?"

He smiled down at her. "Well. I did then. She was, after all, being so uncooperative."

Kendall gaped at him. "Uncooperative? Me?"

"Hey, what else do you call a woman who leaves you high and dry when you've come to depend on her?"

"You fired me!"

"You quit!"

"But I wouldn't have left you high and dry," she told him. "If you hadn't fired me, I would have wrapped up everything I needed to before going. I tried to give you two weeks' notice, but noooooo."

"And what else do you call a woman," he continued, ignoring her, his smile growing broader, "who refuses to come back to work for you, even when you offer her her job back not once, not twice, but three times, even for quadruple her previous salary?"

"It was the job I quit," she pointed out. "Why would I come back?"

"And what would you call a woman," he went on, still

smiling, still ignoring her objections, "who makes you feel things you never thought yourself capable of feeling, who makes you think things you never thought you'd think, who makes you question everything you thought you knew about yourself, everything you thought was universally true."

She brushed her lips lightly over his. "You guys were in college when you made those universal truths," she reminded him. "You didn't know jack about women then."

"We don't know jack about women now," he told her with a laugh.

She shook her head. "You know enough. Because you know how to make us happy. Now, then," she added, pointing to the photo again. "Tell me who all these guys are."

He sighed, but this time when he looked at the picture, the sadness she'd seen in him before was gone, replaced by an unmistakable wistfulness that was captured in his voice. "This is Ryan," he said, pointing to the young man on the far right. "He was here last month and met a woman named Kelly Hartley, who I understand decorated the place."

"She's good," Kendall said.

"Ryan seems to think so, too. They're engaged."

Kendall grinned at that.

"This guy—" he went on to the next young man in the group "—is Nathan Barrister. He was the first one to stay here at the lodge. Then he stayed longer out of the lodge, because he ended up marrying the mayor of Hunter's Landing."

"That was fast," Kendall said.

"Nathan's always been the kind of guy to know what he wants, and he does whatever he has to to get it. Her," he quickly corrected himself. "You know what I mean."

"Boy, do I," she said with a laugh.

6

"And this," Matthias continued, smiling at the comment and moving to the guy next to Nathan, "is Devlin Campbell. He was always the dutiful one. Still is, evidently. He just got married to a woman who's having his baby. Not that he married her out of duty," he hastened to add. "When Ryan called this place a 'love shack' it was for good reason. Dev met Nicole because she was working in a casino near here."

"Hmm," Kendall mused, "and didn't Luke meet Lauren because she came to the lodge looking for you?"

Matthias nodded. "He did indeed."

"So then this *is* a love shack."

"Only in the literal sense," he said.

"So who's this last guy?" Kendall asked.

"That's Jack Howington. Excuse me. I mean Jack Howington the third. Gotta get those three *I*s in there. He was Special Forces after college, but these days, he owns a consulting firm where he takes what he learned in the service and helps people keep their businesses safe in dangerous parts of the world. Interesting guy."

"Sounds like it."

"He'll be staying here after I leave."

Kendall studied the man in the picture carefully. He was, like the rest of them, very handsome. But where the others all seemed to be generous with their smiles, Jack's was a bit more reserved. Maybe mysterious, she decided. Hard to tell.

"I wonder what his experiences in the love shack will be," she said.

Matthias shook his head. "I don't know. But that reminds me. I need to leave him a note, too."

He turned and made his way up to the office loft, Kendall following in his wake. He withdrew a pad of paper from the desk drawer and plucked a pen from a container full of them, then folded himself into the chair. He tapped his mouth lightly with the pen as he thought about what to write, then smiled. Kendall moved to stand behind him, watching him as he wrote, his strong hand moving slowly, as if he were giving great thought to what he was writing. As he moved down the page, she read what he'd written so far.

Jack—

When I read Ryan's note that called this place a "love shack," my first thought was, "What a load of B.S." But now I think he may be on to something. He was also right about how wrong we were when we compiled our universal truths about women. Remember those? Yeah? Well, now you can forget 'em. We had no idea.

Kendall smiled at that, then continued to read.

As for me, here's what I learned during my month at the lodge: The most important work you'll ever do has nothing to do with the job. And it's work you can't do by yourself. But when you find a partner you can trust, and the two of you do that work together, it pays better than any career you could imagine. And perks? You have no idea…

Have a good month, pal.

She noticed that he hesitated before signing it, then finally dashed off, "Matt."

"Matt," she said aloud. "When I first saw that on the note Ryan wrote to you, I couldn't imagine anyone calling you that. But now I think it kind of fits."

"No one but family and close friends has ever called me that," he told her. Then, after another small hesitation, he added, "But if you'd like…"

She didn't have to hesitate at all. "I do like," she told him. "Matt."

She pushed herself up on tiptoe to kiss him, then, as one, they turned to make their way down the stairs. The car was packed, the lodge was empty. They'd left the key on the kitchen table, as the caretaker had asked them to. Kendall told herself not to feel too sad as they closed the front door behind them and checked to make sure it was locked. She would be coming back in a couple of months to see the place again. To meet Matthias's—no, Matt's—friends. To see fulfilled the dream the Seven Samurai had made in college. She was a part of that dream now, she realized as they made their way down the steps. Part of Matt's dream. Part of his life, just as he was part of hers.

No, not part of it, she realized. And not two lives. They were one now. In work. In life. In love.

And that, she thought, was exactly where they needed to be.

* * * * *

Don't miss the exciting conclusion of the
MILLIONAIRE OF THE MONTH *series,*
Susan Mallery's **In Bed with the Devil***,*
available August 2008 from Desire™.

SIX-MONTH MISTRESS

by
Katherine Garbera

Dear Reader,

I'm a native Floridian born in South Florida. During the turbulent early seventies, my family left Miami and moved farther north, first to Fort Pierce and then eventually to Lake Alfred. But my maternal grandparents moved only as far as Okeechobee and settled there.

As a young girl I would visit them. My grandmother would always plan a special shopping day for my mum, my sisters and me. A day that involved driving to West Palm Beach and Palm Beach and shopping at the luxury stores.

When I sat down to write this book, I was missing Florida as I always do! And I started to think about locations. Visiting the ritzy Palm Beach area was always fun for me, because my grandmother would buy us something and we'd have adventures. Then I thought about what it would be like to live there and *not* have money.

Or…to have money and lose it all. And then Bella was born in my imagination. I knew immediately that her hero had to be someone who was a part of the world that she no longer belonged to. I knew that he had to be someone who had something she wanted – besides his hunky physique. And I knew that there would be some scandal from her past to overcome. I hope you enjoy the luxury and drama of *Six-Month Mistress*!

Please stop by my website at www.katherine garbera.com for a behind-the-scenes look into *Six-Month Mistress*.

Happy reading!

Katherine

KATHERINE GARBERA

is a strong believer in happily ever after. She found her own after meeting her Prince Charming in Fantasyland at Walt Disney World. She's written more than thirty books and has been nominated for a *Romantic Times BOOKreviews* career achievement award in Series Fantasy and Series Adventure respectively. Katherine recently moved to the Dallas area where she lives with her husband and their two children. Visit Katherine on the web at www.katherinegarbera.com.

This book is dedicated to my sisters...
Donna and Linda, sisters by birth. Nancy, Mary
Louise, Eve and Beverly, sisters by chance.

One

"Jeremy Harper is here to see you."

"Send him in," Isabella McNamara said, even though he wasn't on her calendar. She hung up the phone and settled back in her leather executive chair, blowing out a long breath. This was just another meeting. She faced heads of Fortune 500 companies all the time—facing Jeremy would be no different.

Yeah, right.

She wiped her sweaty palms on the fabric of her silk skirt and immediately regretted it. She wanted to look her best, to pull off some of Angelina Jolie's charm and confidence. Taking a deep breath, she repeated a few words in her head—calm, cool, clever.

Everything was always different with Jeremy. She'd seen him exactly twelve times in the last three years. And each of those meetings had left her shaken, hungry and wanting more of the man. Of course, since she'd pretty much signed away her body to him, every time they'd met all she could think about was what it would be like to feel his naked skin rubbing against hers.

Oh, God, he'd turned her into a sex fiend. She knew that being a man's mistress wasn't about sex; it was about money. But Bella had never been able to think of anything to do with Jeremy as only business.

She didn't have to guess why he was here. Three short years ago, she'd made a deal with Jeremy and now it was time to pay up. She didn't kid herself that he was here for any reason other than to collect on that debt.

The door to her office opened and she stood to greet him. He wore a Dolce & Gabbana suit with the same ease that teenagers wore jeans and T-shirts. He sauntered into the room as if he owned it.

She caught her breath, wishing for a minute she didn't find him so attractive. But she always had. And that was probably why she was in the position she was: Owing this man a debt she had no idea if she would survive paying.

The door closed firmly behind him, but she

barely noticed. Instead she tried to ignore the spicy scent of his aftershave and the way his bluer-than-blue eyes watched her.

He was her devil. The man she'd sold her soul to—and he was here to collect. She twisted her fingers together, trying desperately to believe that she wasn't scared of a six-foot-two man. But she was.

"Hello, Bella."

His voice was deep and low-pitched. She'd spoken to him on the phone countless times, yet his voice always sent little shivers of awareness pulsing through her veins.

"Jeremy," she said, then remembered a very important lesson that her mother had taught her. *Never let them see you sweat.* Of course, her mom had been referring to the Palm Beach jet set they'd once been a part of, but Bella figured the same rule applied to sexy billionaires. "Please have a seat."

He moved farther into the room, seating himself in one of her guest chairs. She sank down into her leather chair, opening her center desk drawer and touching the jewel-encrusted Montblanc fountain pen that had once been her mother's and was now Bella's lucky charm. She rubbed her fingers over it before taking it out of the drawer and placing it on the desk.

"What can I do for you?" she asked carefully. He might be here for another reason. Maybe he wanted her to cater an event for his company or his family's annual Fourth of July bash.

"I think you know."

She sighed. Not an event after all. "Time's up."

He laughed, a rich sound that filled the room, and for a moment she forgot to be afraid. Forgot that he held all the cards in this situation by her own design.

"I was hoping time would have helped alleviate your fears."

"I'm not afraid of you," she said, very aware that her words were a lie.

She didn't care if Jeremy knew it, either. She'd spent most of her life dealing with people she was afraid of, ever since her father had died when she was fourteen and they'd gotten the news that his entire fortune was gone. She'd learned to deal with the fear of being mocked by the same people she'd once called friends.

She'd faced fear again when her mother died four years later and the sole responsibility for raising her fourteen-year-old brother, Dare, had fallen to her. She'd known real fear—survival fear—and she'd never once admitted to it out loud.

Jeremy arched one eyebrow at her—an arrogant gesture that fit him to a tee.

She forced a smile. "Dare is still in college."

"He's graduating at the end of summer. And he has a job lined up with Fidelity starting in the fall."

"How do you know that?" she asked. Dare had only just called this afternoon with the job news. She'd known then that she needed to call Jeremy.

To let him know that she was now ready to fulfill her part of the bargain.

"I told you I'd make sure your brother's future was taken care of."

"I thought you meant the scholarship." But she'd suspected he'd done more. Dare had mentioned a few times that Jeremy had visited him at school.

He shook his head. "I'm not here to discuss your brother."

No, of course he wasn't. He was here to discuss her and the contract she'd signed three years ago. A contract in which she'd agreed to be his mistress for six months in return for the help he'd given both her and her brother.

"So, it starts tonight?" she asked at last. For three years he'd been waiting for her to be free of her obligation to her brother. For three years she'd seen him every three months to affirm that the deal was still on. For three years she'd dreamed of his passionate embraces…and the hope that, once they started their affair, she'd be able to convince him that she was meant to be more than his mistress. Because she wanted to be Jeremy's wife.

"I believe you're free," he said.

She was available tonight. The new manager she'd hired had proven himself capable of handling all the events, so she was taking a rare night off. How did he know? "Did Dare tell you?"

"He didn't have to. I asked your assistant."

"You're a very thorough man." She was going to have a talk with Shelley about giving out personal information. Her hands were shaking and she clenched them together so he wouldn't notice. He was just a man. But for some reason he'd always been more to her.

"When I see something I want…" he said.

"And you want me?"

"After the kisses we've shared, I know you don't doubt that."

She didn't. But by the same token, she'd always sort of wished she'd just imagined the intensity in Jeremy's eyes when he looked at her.

She had no real idea how to respond to that. "Um…I…"

He stood up and walked around her desk to stand next to her chair. She tipped her head back to look up at him. "Changed your mind?"

She couldn't read the emotion in his eyes—there wasn't any. For all the reaction she saw, he might not care either way. And that was why she was afraid. She'd been desperate when she'd agreed to the contract, wanting to stop feeling so alone in the world. People she knew left but, if she had the chance, she knew she could convince Jeremy to stay.

Jeremy had gone beyond what he'd said he would do, introducing her to business partners of his and recommending her party-planning services before she had any real references. He'd helped tremendously to get her business off the ground, and to ensure its success.

And she wanted him, she did. She was just afraid that the secret crush she'd always had on him would make it too easy for her to believe there was something more between them than a contract.

She was attracted to Jeremy. She'd been in lust with him since she'd first met him when she was sixteen. She'd been working at the Palm Beach Yacht Club as a waitress and he'd been dining with a bunch of his college friends. He'd been tan and fit and incredibly handsome. And polite—the nicest to her by far.

When he'd finally approached her a few years later, she'd been thrilled at first. Until she realized that what he was offering was a business arrangement. An arrangement that she'd never regretted not turning down.

"I haven't changed my mind. I gave you my word." She didn't feel guilty about the contract she'd signed. A lot of women married for money and then divorced and married again. In essence she was doing the same thing.

"And your word is your bond?"

"It has to be. I didn't have anything else when you made your offer." She didn't like to remember those days, the despair and the sense of failure that she'd been mired in.

"You had your pride," he said softly, running one finger down the side of her face. He cupped her jaw in his hand and she held her breath.

His gaze fell to her mouth and stayed there. She licked her dry lips and his gaze narrowed. Silly as it sounded, she could feel his eyes on her lips.

"I still do."

"Good."

She leaned away from him. "It would make me feel more comfortable if everything you said didn't sound so arrogant."

"I can't help that."

"You can, you just choose not to."

"I've had thirty-four years to get this way."

"And no one has ever complained?"

"Not to my face."

"I don't think I'm going to be able to keep my comments to myself."

"I wouldn't want you to. I'm not asking you to pretend to be someone you aren't."

But he was. The woman she was today was different from the one she'd been three years ago. And at twenty-six she wasn't sure she could pretend they were dating when she knew the truth. That she was his mistress. That the relationship was stamped with an expiration date. And that he was planning to walk away from her without looking back or leaving any of his emotions behind.

* * *

Jeremy stared down into Bella's big brown eyes and felt like he'd taken a punch to the gut. He'd waited lifetimes for this night. True, he knew it had been only three years, but they seemed long—too long. His skin felt too tight and if she didn't lose the nervous look, he wasn't sure what he was going to do.

She was his. For the last three years that knowledge had been in the back of his mind. His life had gone the same as always. But in the back of his mind he knew that Bella McNamara belonged to him. Finally he could claim her.

He had a contract with her signature on it. A legal document that proclaimed she'd be his mistress for six months. But even he wasn't that big of a bastard—he wouldn't force Bella into his arms and his bed if she didn't want to be there.

Still, he'd have absolutely no qualms about seducing her into his bed. About using the passion that had always been between them to gain her acceptance and get her where he wanted her.

"Um…how is this going to work? Will we go to your place right now?" she asked. A strand of her hair had escaped the clip at the back and curled against her cheek. She tucked it behind her ear absently.

She bit her lower lip. Her mouth was full and enticing. It was the second thing he'd noticed about her. He had tasted her lips before, when he'd held her in his arms. But the way he felt about her was…hell, he couldn't define what he felt for her. He wanted to groan out loud.

"No, not now. We're attending the Tristan-Andrew Cancer Institute charity benefit tonight. Our arrangement will stay private. In public, it will seem like we're dating."

"Thank you," she said.

"For?"

"For keeping our arrangement private. I don't really want the world to know," she said, her words breathy. A soft little confession.

Jeremy didn't pretend he understood women but he did know that socially a girlfriend and a mistress weren't in the same league. He'd seen that firsthand with his own father's women. Bella had enough marks against her socially. But this was the only arrangement she would accept from him. And mistresses he understood.

He'd hoped for a different sort of evening—an intimate dinner for two on his yacht, followed by dancing under the stars. But at least at the charity benefit there would be music and he could hold her in his arms.

The last three years had been the longest of his life. He hadn't been celibate, but every woman he'd slept with had become Bella in his head. He wanted *her.* When he woke in the morning he imagined her soft brown eyes opening to meet his. She'd become an obsession—and a successful businessman couldn't afford to be obsessed with anything other than business.

She licked her lips again and his body clenched. He wanted to know the taste of her mouth. It had been too long since he'd last kissed her. This time he did groan out loud.

"What?"

He shrugged. The safe bet would be to play it off as not wanting to go to the charity event. He liked social events, normally. Tonight he was being generous in letting her have this time to adjust to being in a relationship with him.

The event had been organized by his mother. His family was a major benefactor to the local cancer institute. They were hosting the charity fashion event this evening at Neiman Marcus. His mother had called to remind him that plenty of single ladies would be in attendance, all of them suitable to become Mrs. Jeremy Harper III.

Which made this the perfect night to be seen with Bella.

He rubbed the back of his neck to keep from reaching out and capturing that strand of hair that was once again curled against her cheek. "Are you familiar with the event?"

"We lost the bid to cater it." She said it almost absently. She straightened some papers on her desk and only then did he notice the fine trembling of her hand.

"Forget about your business for one night," he said, trying to process her reaction. His own hands shook at the thought of being alone with her. The feelings she evoked in him were that intense.

"I don't think that's a good idea."

"Why not?" he asked.

"Business is all we have between us," she said, staring up at him. He knew he was missing something in the words and her expression, but he couldn't figure out what it was. If it *was* just business between them, then he couldn't have her. He never wanted to be more involved than his partner in an intimate relationship.

"Our business is very personal," he said at last, capturing that curl and wrapping it around his finger. It was what he wanted to do with her. Wrap himself in her curvy body and silky limbs.

"Yes, it is. And, oh God, I'm not sure—"

He covered her mouth with his fingers. Her lips were plump and moist from her breath. "You can change your mind."

She shook her head. "I don't want to."

He smiled then, hoping his relief didn't show. It was unnerving to be so attracted to a woman. He'd jumped through hoops for Bella that he wouldn't have for any other woman. After all, he'd waited three years for her.

"Then let's go to the party and see where the night leads."

"What about the contract?" she asked, clearly still uneasy with him.

He struggled for a way to put her at ease. He knew he could be charming, but with Bella he wasn't his usual self. From the moment he'd suggested that she become his mistress, he'd been out of control.

At the time she'd seemed so young—only twenty-three—and so fragile.

"We can discuss it over dinner after the party," he said. He wasn't ready to let her out of the contract. He knew a better man would have torn the document up a long time ago, but frankly it was the only leverage he had with Bella. Leverage he didn't want to let go of.

"Okay. I can have my secretary make us a reservation," she said, trying to take control of the situation.

He held back a smile. He admired her bid for power but there was no way he was letting her take charge. "I'll take care of that. Just get your purse or briefcase and we can leave."

"Leave?" she asked. Her face flushed and she looked like she wanted to tell him off. Finally he felt like they were getting somewhere. He saw the real Bella in that instant. The woman he'd first been attracted to. The woman of passion and pride and determination. Not someone who was biddable and afraid of him, something he didn't want.

"Yes. My driver is waiting out front."

She smiled sweetly at him. "Thanks for the offer of a ride, but I have to go home and get changed."

"I have a dress for you."

"That's nice, but I'd prefer to wear my own clothes."

"And I'd prefer you to wear the dress I selected."

"I think we're at a stalemate."

"No, we're not."

"We're not?"

"No."

She shook her head. "I know you think you're going to get your way, but—"

"I don't think it, Bella, I know it."

"Why?"

"Because as my mistress you'll put my preferences first."

Two

Bella laced her fingers together under the desk to keep from doing something she was sure she'd regret. She wished she had a mentor when it came to filling the role of a mistress, but she didn't. She sensed it would be easier to just let her pride go. *Once you agree to be a man's mistress, your pride means nothing.*

If only. Suddenly it wasn't the sex that concerned her, but the attitude that she'd have to pretend to have. She tried to smile, but couldn't force herself. If only she owed him money, then she could go to the bank and take out a loan, but he'd given her a lot more than money. He'd given her contacts, business advice and provided a male role model for Dare. Those were things that couldn't be paid back in dollars.

"This isn't going to work. I'm sorry that I didn't realize it before, but I'm not the kind of woman who can—"

He put his fingers over her lips again. Her tongue brushed his skin for a second before she closed her mouth, staring up at him.

She felt her resolve melting and it had absolutely nothing to do with not wanting to be in breach of the contract she'd signed. It had to do with his eyes.

His touch was featherlight and almost tentative. Like he wasn't sure he had the right to touch her, but couldn't help himself. That reassured her. No matter what he'd said before, there was more to this than a contract.

He must know he was pushing her. Did he want her to renege? Had that been his plan all along? She wanted to take his arrogance down a peg or two.

She had no idea how to handle herself with him. He had something she wanted. Something he *knew* she wanted. That elusive stamp of approval from the crowd that had tossed her out without a backward glance—and the only sure way to get that back was to marry into the crowd. And she was willing to do anything to make that happen.

If she had to swallow her pride and her temper, then she would. Being a mistress should be easy enough. She had to do nothing but live for pleasure and smile at her man. Make him feel like he was the sexiest, smartest, wealthiest man in the room.

God, she didn't think she could do it. Even for the chance to walk into a room with him, that most elusive of men, the ultimate bachelor. A man whom every single woman in that elite social jet set wanted to claim. And she thought—no, knew—she could win him over for a lifetime.

It was small and petty, but that thought made her tip her head to the side and smile up at him. "Of course, I'll wear the dress you selected."

"Let's go then."

"I'll need a few minutes to get ready. I'll meet you in the waiting room."

He nodded and walked out of the room. She collapsed into her chair as soon as he was gone.

There was a brief knock on the door and then it opened again.

"Bella?"

"Yes, Shelley?"

"He asked me to give you this."

Shelley handed her a small, gold-foil-wrapped box. "I had no idea the two of you were dating."

And so it starts. "We've known each other for years."

"I know that. Are you going to open it?"

She didn't want to know what was inside. A gift for a mistress might be different than a gift for a girlfriend. She thought maybe she should open it by herself, but Shelley didn't look like she was leaving. Her assistant was also the closest thing that Bella had to a friend.

"Yes, I'll open it."

She didn't let herself dwell on the fact that it had been almost ten years since she'd received a wrapped present. Dare gave her gifts, but generally left them in the bag from the store they'd come from. She slipped the ribbon off the box and set it aside.

"Oh, man, I can't wait to see what it is. How can you go so slowly?"

"I don't get that many gifts."

"Me neither. Not like this. Not from men."

Bella slipped her fingernail under the seam in the paper and ripped it away. The box was long and narrow, and when the paper fell away she saw it was that distinctive Tiffany blue. *Jewelry.* He'd gotten her jewelry.

Shelley perched her hip on the desk and leaned forward as Bella lifted the lid. It was a platinum, diamond-encrusted choker.

Shelley gasped a little and reached out to touch it. "It's gorgeous."

"Yes, it is," Bella said. She realized that he'd done her a favor, insisting she wear a dress he'd purchased. She would have worn one of her mother's old haute couture dresses and costume jewelry and all the time she'd have felt like a fraud.

Did he realize that? Or had buying her a dress and, she assumed, a wardrobe simply been part of preparing her to be his?

She closed the jewelry box and slipped it into her leather Coach bag. She'd skimped and saved until she could afford the large, classy bag that she wanted and needed for work.

Her stomach was still a knot of nerves, but she refused to think about it. Instead she fell back on her business. "Remind Randall to call me when the event tonight is over. I want to know how it went."

"Are you sure about that?"

"Of course I'm sure."

"If I was going out with someone like Jeremy Harper I wouldn't want my phone ringing."

"Shelley…"

"None of my business, I know. Have fun tonight, boss lady."

Bella knew she'd have a lot of things tonight and wasn't sure fun was one of them. But she was excited and nervous and a million other things that she'd never expected. It wasn't just Jeremy. It was her return to Palm Beach society and the ten long years it had taken to get there.

Jeremy escaped from his partner's spouse, who desperately wanted to find him a wife. Despite the fact that he'd arrived tonight with Bella on his arm, Lucinda wasn't deterred. She had a friend she wanted him hooked up with and nothing would stop her.

Ever since Daniel and Lucinda had married, Lucinda Cannon-Posner had been trying to pair him up with her oh-so-proper society friends. The moment Bella had stepped away to powder her nose, Lucinda and her friend Marianne had pounced.

Jeremy eased deeper into the shadows, waiting for Bella to reappear. He was surprised by how much he was enjoying the evening. Normally these events were a total bore. But tonight, with Bella at his side, he'd been enjoying himself—until Lucinda and her friend had made their move.

"Hiding from Marianne?"

Jeremy glanced over at Kell Ottenberg. He and his cousin had been best friends forever. Their mothers were sisters and the two men had been raised together. Kell handed him a martini glass.

"Waiting for Bella."

"Ah, the mystery lady. Rumor has it she's been hired for the evening."

Jeremy knew Kell was trying to get a rise out of him. The fact that he'd hit so close to the mark was something Jeremy chose to ignore. "You're the one who has to pay for companionship."

"I don't have to pay, but it does make life easier. None of those messy entanglements that come from getting involved."

Jeremy shrugged. Kell had a bad attitude toward

women and it was understandable. He'd been raked over the coals by a first-class, gold-plated bitch.

"So who is she?"

"Isabella McNamara," Jeremy said. Kell leaned back against the wall. The fashion show was going on next door and this room was relatively quiet.

"Where did you find her?" Kell asked.

"Hiding." She'd been living in a small duplex in Fort Pierce. Not that many miles from Palm Beach, but a world away.

"Ah, so that's what you two have in common."

Jeremy punched Kell on the arm. "I'm not hiding, I'm waiting."

Kell glanced around the area. "In the corner?"

Jeremy shrugged.

"Why don't you tell Daniel to have a talk with Lucinda?"

"I have. He doesn't want to upset her."

"After seven years of marriage he shouldn't be so concerned about that."

Jeremy knew from observing Daniel with his wife that he loved Lucinda and he'd do anything to keep her happy. Frankly, Jeremy didn't understand Daniel and Lucinda's relationship. His own parents had been happiest apart. His father had always kept a mistress on the side and everyone had seemed pleased with that arrangement.

"She is beautiful," Kell said.

"Marianne? I'll tell Lucinda you think so."

"No, thanks. I meant your lady," Kell said, gesturing to Bella, who was walking slowly toward them. She glanced up, caught him watching her and smiled.

"Later."

"Later? Don't I get to meet her?"

"I'm taking her to the dance floor. I think three would be a crowd."

"I'll just cut in."

Jeremy glanced at his friend. "Why?"

"I want to meet her."

He knew from Kell's tone that he wanted to question her. "She's not like—"

"I'm sure she's not. I'll be good, I promise."

"Somehow I doubt that," Jeremy said under his breath.

He went to meet her, aware that Kell was only a few steps behind him. Jeremy cupped his hand under her elbow and drew her away from the fashion show into a third room where the DJ and dance floor were set up, ready for the party to spill over once the fashion show ended.

"I'm sorry if I kept you waiting," she said.

"No problem." He heard Kell chuckle behind him and suspected it was because he sounded like an idiot. What the hell was it about this woman that made his brain short circuit?

He'd dated beautiful women before, so it wasn't that. There was something else about her. The dress he'd selected was perfect for her. It was a summer cocktail dress with a slim-fitting skirt and a scoop neck.

"Hello, Isabella," Kell said, reaching past him and offering her his hand. "I'm Kell."

She took his hand. Kell lifted it to his lips, kissing the back of it and smirking at Jeremy while he did so.

Bella smiled at Kell and Jeremy felt his gut tighten. He knew she was his, and she knew it, too. But he still felt a twinge of jealousy.

"Let's dance," Jeremy said, drawing her away from Kell and tucking her up against his side.

Kell's laughter followed them as they walked away. Jeremy ignored it. He wanted to believe his reaction had absolutely nothing to do with jealousy. She was his mistress for six months, nothing more. He told himself that he only wanted to keep Bella from being hurt by Kell, who could be charming but would never be sincere.

"What was that about?" she asked, a different note in her voice. He glanced down at her and saw the smile lingering at her mouth. She was still nervous, but the exchange with Kell had relaxed her. She was teasing him.

"Kell's a goofball. Don't pay any attention to him," he said.

"You have a friend who's a goofball?"

"Unfortunately, I'm related to him."

"How?"

"Cousins. Our moms are sisters."

"Ah, so the crazy gene…"

He pulled her into his arms as the DJ played a slow song. "Skipped my branch of the family."

"Whatever you say."

He didn't say anything else, just pulled her closer in his arms. She relaxed against him, following his lead. They fit together perfectly.

He kept stroking his hand down her back, completely obliterating her thought process. She liked the strength in his arms. The way they felt wrapped around her.

For a minute Bella bought into the illusion of security that his arms offered. She closed her eyes and let the spicy scent of his aftershave fill each breath she took. The music was slow with a funky beat. With her eyes closed, she could let her worries and fears and the past years drop away.

She could just be Bella and pretend this was her teenage fantasy come to life. She thought she'd known all about Jeremy from her crush those many summers ago, but she was coming to realize there was so much more to the man.

She remembered seeing Kell back then. He and Jeremy were photo negatives of each other, both tall, one blond and outgoing, the other dark and dangerous.

More than once she'd wondered why Jeremy

had made his offer to her. What had he seen in her that had made him offer to help her?

Was it only sex, a desire for her to be his mistress?

She looked up and met his gaze. She was surprised that he was watching her. If he was pretending, then he was a better actor than she was. He held her and looked at her like she was his. His for more than six months and because of more than a contract. She knew it was an illusion, but she hoped to make it a reality.

"What?" he asked with a hint of tenderness in his voice.

"Uh…" She couldn't remember what she'd been about to say. She wrapped her arms around his shoulders, let her fingers caress the back of his neck. Held him. This was what she'd dreamed of for the last three years.

Bella realized that giving herself up to Jeremy freed her to just be herself.

He continued to stare down at her, making her wish she could remember what she'd been about to say. She started to worry that something was wrong with the way she looked. She resisted the urge to pat her hair. Oh, man, she hoped she didn't have a bit of spinach in her teeth or something like that. Something that marked her clearly as an outsider. This was the kind of event her mother had missed the most when they'd had to move out of the mansion and into that shabby apartment.

It was odd to Bella that she was actually attending this event and not working it as a caterer—or standing on the sidewalk with her mother, pretending they were window-shopping. A shiver of embarrassment crawled down her spine as she remembered arriving tonight and seeing Lucinda Cannon and friends spot her outside.

"Why me?" she asked, finally remembering what she'd wanted to say.

He brushed his finger down her cheek before he cupped her jaw. His hand enveloped the side of her face, his fingers caressing her neck. His gaze was compelling. She couldn't decipher what she saw in his eyes. He lowered his head until there was barely an inch of space between them.

"You're not like any other woman I know," he said.

That wasn't what she had wanted to hear. She didn't want to be so different that everyone could see it in a glance. She wanted to blend into the moneyed set that she'd partly grown up in. She wanted to forget that she'd ever been cast out and use Jeremy to find her place again. But that wasn't what she was doing tonight.

Instead she was enjoying his arms around her and wishing they were alone. Wishing for a minute that this entire night was real. Wishing he'd asked her because he cared for her, and not because she was going to be his mistress.

This was the very thing that woke her in the middle of the night. How was she going to make Jeremy fall for her? She knew she had to keep him from seeing that she wanted so much more than to be his mistress. Somehow, she had to seduce him into seeing her as more.

"I'm sure of that," she said at last. She *was* different from the other women in the room. She'd had to scrape and struggle to get back to this glitzy world. She doubted even Jeremy understood the toll those years had taken on her.

"I meant it as a compliment," he said, brushing his lips over hers. His lips were full and firm.

All night he'd been touching her. Accustoming her to his touch and taste. The feel of his body brushing against her.

He didn't push his tongue into her mouth, just pressed his lips lightly against hers. Someone cleared his throat, but Jeremy didn't pull away. He lifted his head slowly, caressing her face before he turned to face a man she didn't know.

"I see now why you're avoiding Marianne."

"Who's Marianne?" she asked, trying to calm her racing blood. She didn't like the fact he'd rattled her with that one brief touch of his lips on hers.

Jeremy kept his arm around her waist, but turned them toward the man who'd interrupted them. The music changed again to a more lively number and Jeremy led her off the dance floor.

"One of my wife's friends. I'm Daniel Posner," the man said, following close behind them.

"Isabella McNamara," she said.

"What do you want, Daniel?" Jeremy asked.

"To invite you and your date to join us at our table," he said, gesturing to a round of eight set near the dance floor.

Bella smiled over at the table until she recognized Lucinda Cannon. Her heart started racing and the blood drained from her face. She'd hoped to see Lucinda again, hoped to have the chance to meet her onetime friend as an equal once more. But she wasn't ready yet. It was too soon.

Daniel wrapped his arm around Lucinda as she approached. "This is my wife, Lucinda. Honey, this is Isabella McNamara."

"We know each other," Lucinda said.

Bella could only nod at Lucinda, not sure what to say or how to fill the awkward gap of silence that grew between all four of them.

She pulled away from Jeremy and then realized how cowardly that was. She wasn't at this event as part of the staff. Jeremy glanced down at her. She shook her head, afraid to open her mouth. Afraid she'd blurt out something she didn't want to say.

Jeremy took charge. "We'd love to join you, but we have a dinner reservation and have to leave now. Another time?"

"Certainly. Enjoy your dinner."

The look Lucinda gave Bella before she and
Daniel walked away was haughty and telling. And
the good feelings Bella had had about being back
in this high-society world suddenly dissipated.

Three

No one would ever call him a sensitive man, but even he could tell something was wrong when his date lost all color from her face. While they waited for the valet to bring his convertible Jaguar up, he watched Bella slowly sink deeper and deeper into herself. She wrapped her arms around her waist and kept her eyes down.

The June evening was hot and humid. He pulled Bella to his side and stepped away from the crowd waiting for their cars. She pulled away from him as soon as they were out of the crowd.

"Are you okay?"

"Yes," she said, but he knew she wasn't.

"You're pale as a ghost."

"Can't you just ignore it? I'll be back to normal in a minute."

"No, I can't ignore it. I didn't realize you knew Lucinda."

"Well, I do, and it's been years since I saw her...I thought I'd feel differently."

"How did you feel?"

"What are you, my shrink?"

"I'd like to think I'm your friend." Friend, he thought. Was that really what he wanted?

"I just expected it to be different."

"It?"

His car was brought up, but he signaled the valet that they'd be a minute more. The feeling of protectiveness was disturbing. He wanted to keep her in the safe box labeled *mistress*. He didn't want her upsets to affect him. Yet they did.

"Being back in that room was different," she said, her voice very soft.

He had the feeling she was talking more to herself than to him. For the first time he realized that he wanted more than Bella's body. He wanted her secrets, too.

"Different meaning better?" he asked.

"Not necessarily. I think I may have been feeling a bit vindictive when I imagined it."

He laughed at the way she said that. He already knew she wasn't all sweetness and light. He'd seen her temper and her sheer force of will, both of which she'd used to support herself and her brother.

He cupped her elbow and led her to his car. As he held the door for her and she slid into the seat, the skirt of her dress rose slightly on her thighs. He stared at her leg until she put her hand on the exposed skin and tugged the fabric down.

He closed the door and walked around the car, using the few seconds to regain his control. The entire mistress contract was supposed to enable him to control his feelings around her. Instead he had the feeling that it had backfired on him.

He saw Kell come outside just as he closed the car door. The expression on Kell's face wasn't a good one and he wondered what had happened after they'd left.

He lifted one eyebrow, a silent question to Kell: Should he stay? Kell shook his head and motioned that he'd call later.

Bella fixed her lipstick in the visor mirror and then turned toward him, putting her hand on his thigh.

He glanced at her. It was the first time she'd initiated contact. She scraped her fingernail over the fabric of his pants and he felt that touch echo all the way to his core.

"Thank you," she said.

He had no idea what she was thanking him for, but if she moved her hand a little bit higher she'd see how much he appreciated her touch. He shook his head, trying to clear it.

"For?"

She rubbed his leg one more time and then pulled her hand back. "For pretending you care."

He didn't like the way that sounded.

"I'm not pretending, Bella," he said, capturing her hand and putting it back on his leg. After tonight he hoped she'd have no doubts about how he felt toward her. "I've always cared for you."

She gave him a sideways look and stroked her finger up the inside of his thigh. "Most people don't consider lust caring."

She made him want to laugh at the wry way she said it. It was one of a hundred things about Bella that made him want to be around her. He knew she was scared of any intimacy between them, yet she played that down and treated the attraction with a frankness that was refreshingly honest.

"It's always been more than lust where you're concerned," he said, putting the car in gear and leaving Neiman Marcus behind. And that one crucial point disturbed him more than he thought it would. It was why he'd decided to ask her to be his mistress. His father said that the women who affected a man most deeply were the ones a man had to be careful of.

She said nothing as the miles passed. Then she turned off the radio and reached for his arm.

"Yes?"

"I'm sorry about that. When I'm not sure of myself I can be mean."

"You weren't mean."

"Yes I was. And you were really trying to be nice to me."

"So why did you have a self-confidence attack?"

"Lucinda Cannon," she said, and pulled her hand back to her own side of the car.

Bella knew she was ruining her image, but could only deal with so much at a time. She was losing control of the evening. Losing the perfect bubble that she'd managed to wrap herself in at the charity event.

Pretending she was someone else—a mysterious stranger who belonged—had helped. But one glimpse of Lucinda Cannon had brought her back to herself. Back to the girl who'd been sent home from the exclusive Swedish boarding school for failure to pay her tuition. Back to the girl whose mother had turned to her society friends for help and had volunteered her to clean the homes of people she'd once considered friends.

She could hear Lucinda's pitying words from long ago still echoing in her head. And she knew that this night wasn't about the past. This night was about establishing herself as Jeremy's mistress and securing her future so that she'd never have to endure pitying looks or charity again.

That was one of the reasons she'd signed the mistress contract. She couldn't stand the thought of taking charity from another person. She shook her head to clear it as Jeremy turned off the road and into the parking lot at the public beach.

"What are we doing here?" she asked, trying not to feel relieved that they weren't at a restaurant. She wasn't ready to face anyone, not even strangers. Her reaction to seeing Lucinda had left her raw and exposed and she had no idea how to pull her shell back around her.

Jeremy didn't say a word. He put down the windows and then the top of his car. The moon was only a sliver and stars were visible in the evening sky. It was still light enough to see.

The sound of the rolling waves hitting the shore filled the car as did the warm, ocean-scented breeze. She leaned her head back against the seat and closed her eyes, breathing in nature.

She focused internally as he fiddled with the radio. The mellow sound of the Dave Matthews Band flowed from the speakers. She loved the group and somehow wasn't surprised that Jeremy would know that. He was a thorough man. The kind who noticed details and remembered them.

"I think you need to mellow out," he said, shrugging out of his jacket and tossing it in the backseat. He loosened his tie and unbuttoned the top button of his shirt.

"Mellow out?" she asked. The words were incongruous with Jeremy. He personified hard work and drive. She'd heard his Blackberry beep a couple of times while they'd been driving, and at Neiman Marcus he'd excused himself twice to take calls from his office.

He slanted her a look as he slid his arm along the back of her seat, his hand came to rest on her shoulder. "It means relax."

She struggled to concentrate on what he was saying as his finger drew lazy circles on her upper arm. He turned toward her, his intense attention focused on her.

"I know what it means. I just didn't think you did," she said, knowing she was grasping at this conversation and trying to make something out of nothing. Anything to keep him from bringing up Lucinda again.

"Oh, honey, I know how to relax."

He was being sweet and she knew he'd deny it if she called him on it. Seeing this side of him made her believe that he could want her for more than six months. *This* was the man she could fall for, not the arrogant man who'd walked into her office this afternoon and told her that his mistresses wore what he provided.

She fingered the diamond choker at her neck. She was something he'd bought and paid for, like his fancy car with more gadgets than anything she owned. She was an accoutrement and she struggled to remember that he thought of her that way.

"Again with the lust thing."

The circles he was drawing on her arm got wider until the tip of his forefinger slipped under the strap of her dress, moving with slow sensual sweeps over her collarbone. "You're obsessed with making every conversation we have sexual."

No, she wasn't. She had just learned from dealing with men that they were easily led off topic when sex was introduced into the conversation. And hey, she was honest enough to admit that it was easier to resist him in the moonlight when she thought he was only after one thing.

"Isn't that what being a mistress is about?" she asked.

"I don't know. I suppose each woman has a different reason."

Somehow that made her feel a little better. "What about you? Why do you want a mistress?"

"My father was always happier with his mistresses than he was with my mother. I guess I just want to be happy. Does that make sense?"

"Yes," she said. More sense than she wanted it to.

Making Jeremy want more than six months with her was going to be harder than she'd first thought.

He left off caressing her arm and shoulder and traced the line of the choker. Her pulse sped up and the slow, steady rhythm of the music mirrored the beat of her heart.

She forgot about vindication and contracts. She forgot about wanting something that had been taken away from her too soon. She forgot about everything except the man sitting next to her.

The man filling her head with thoughts that she'd never had before. Thoughts of nighttime walks on the beach; thoughts of forever. The future had always been nebulous for her. As a young girl, the princess of her family, she'd awaited her future, sure that it would hold only more pampering and treasures. She'd never guessed that it could be such a harsh and cold place.

Despite what she might feel in this moment for Jeremy, she had to remember that the future wasn't a rosy, cheery place. The future, even one with him, would be filled with moments like the one she'd had tonight when she'd seen Lucinda. A moment that could make her stomach feel filled with lead.

"Don't think so much, honey."

"I can't help it."

"Yes, you can," he said, wrapping his arm around her and bending to kiss her. A sweet, gentle kiss….

Maybe the future wouldn't be so cold and harsh after all.

Jeremy's good intentions of relaxing Bella faded quickly when she melted in his arms. He held her loosely, trying to remember why he'd thought stopping at this very public spot would be a good idea.

He'd wanted to slow things down, to slow himself down and not rush his seduction. But at this moment, with her lips so tender under his, he couldn't recall why.

His cell phone rang again. Reluctantly he pulled away from Bella to glance at the caller ID. Kell. *Again.*

"I've got to take this."

She nodded and opened her door. "I'll give you some privacy."

He stopped her with his hand on her wrist. "Stay."

She sank back into the seat as he accepted the call.

"Kell, man, you know I'm on a date."

"I wanted to make sure you had all the information you needed."

"About?" he asked.

"Isabella."

He glanced over at the woman in question. She had her head tipped back against the headrest and her eyes closed. She tapped her fingers to the rhythm of the music playing. He had a sinking feeling in his gut that Kell wasn't calling to recommend Bella's event-planning company.

"And?"

Kell took a deep breath and Jeremy worried what his friend might have heard. "She's a gold digger, man. Lucinda remembers her. Don't be fooled by her designer gown or jewelry—she's penniless. And there's more you should know about her father."

Jeremy felt a twinge of guilt at the thought of his friends gossiping about them when they'd left. Talking about her gown and the jewelry that he'd insisted she wear. He had an inkling of understanding as to why Bella had blanched when she saw Lucinda. What had happened between those two?

"Thanks, I'll keep that in mind." Since they had a contractual arrangement, he wasn't too worried about any designs that Bella had on his money.

"You're still going to—"

"Do whatever I damn well please."

"It's your funeral."

"Thanks for the encouragement."

"Jeremy, I, uh, I just don't want to see you make the same mistake I did."

He knew that Kell didn't interfere unless he had a good reason. And Jeremy did appreciate his cousin looking out for him. Maybe he should set Kell straight on Bella. As soon as she wasn't sitting next to him. "Thanks, Kell. I won't. Are we still on for golf tomorrow?"

"Yeah," Kell said, and disconnected the call.

He tossed his phone into the center console and turned toward Bella. She opened her eyes and looked at him.

"Everything okay?" she asked, with a note of

caring in her voice that made him wonder yet again why she'd settle for a business relationship with him instead of a more personal one.

"Yes, fine."

"So what's next? Sorry about wigging out earlier. I'm not usually like that. You knocked me off balance by showing up out of the blue like you did."

He raised an eyebrow at her. "Glad to know that my plan worked."

She smiled. "You have a very devious mind."

"I'm a planner."

"Really? I'm more a reactor."

He had seen that firsthand. She seldom made plans for the long term. When he'd run into her three years ago, she'd been focused on getting Dare through college and hadn't thought beyond that. Even when making her business strategy, she seldom wanted to look more than six months ahead.

"I don't like to have to react. When you have a plan, you're in control."

She shook her head.

"You don't agree."

"Ah, sorry, but no. When you have a plan all you have is the illusion of control. You can't expect the unexpected."

"Like me coming to your office tonight."

"Exactly. I knew it was time to pay up, but thought I'd manage it from my end."

He'd meant to catch her off guard. When Bella

was prepared she was hard to read. She gave the scripted reactions to everything instead of letting him see a glimpse of the real woman. He'd only caught her by surprise twice, counting tonight. The first time, he'd kissed her—and offered to make her his mistress.

But then, her responses to him each time never failed to stagger him. He always built variables into his strategic plans for business and for his personal life, but she never responded the way he expected her to.

"We have two choices," he said.

"And they are?"

"We can still make our dinner reservation, or we can take a walk on the beach and then I'll take you home and cook for you."

"I'm not ready to be with other people right now," she said.

"Want to talk about it?"

"No. I'll deal with it."

"The way you always have," he said under his breath.

"What does that mean?"

"That you're too used to being on your own. I'm in your life now."

"For six months, Jeremy. When you're gone I'll be back where I started."

"I'm not gone yet."

"But you will be and I don't want to forget that."

"Until then I think we can have one hell of a ride, Bella."

She said nothing, and he wondered if this would be it. The moment when she decided that she'd had enough of him and his contract and walked away.

She sighed and put her hand on his thigh again. "I think I'd like for you to cook me dinner."

Four

Jeremy's house was plush and sophisticated. The trappings of his family's legacy of wealth were everywhere. It reminded her at once of her childhood home and she felt a pang in her heart as they walked by the pool in the back of the house.

The smell of hibiscus was thick in the air. The meal he'd prepared had been simple and delicious and she savored the novelty of having a man cook for her. He'd offered her an after-dinner drink but she declined. This wasn't the time to do too much drinking and the wine she'd had with dinner was giving her a sweet buzz.

She was a little sleepy, but wasn't ready for this

night to end. It had been a tumultuous ride, but she was getting used to that. It seemed everything with Jeremy was unexpected.

"What are you thinking of?" he asked, quietly coming up behind her.

She bit her lower lip. Honesty had been her policy since she'd realized that lying hurt her more than the truth.

"You."

"Hmm, that sounds good."

"Maybe."

"Maybe? That's all I get?"

"Yes. You're too arrogant for your own good," she said, but her words lacked heat. Tonight she'd seen a different side to him. A side that wasn't entirely unexpected. She'd been telling him the truth in the car—she was a reactor. But this situation was difficult for her. She wasn't sure how to react.

Inside she battled with her physical responses to him as a woman and what her mind was telling her. She needed to find a way to balance honesty with self-preservation. Because if she responded to him in the way she truly felt, she was so afraid she'd lose part of herself—her heart.

It would be so easy to melt into this role. To stop worrying about the future and just let the next six months bump along according to his design. But at the end of that six months what would she have left? The same things she had now…unless she planted the seeds of the future with Jeremy.

"You're thinking again."

She smiled at him and hoped her expression didn't reveal the sadness that was tingeing this moment.

"Sorry." She didn't say more than that, afraid that she'd blurt out more than she wanted him to know.

"Don't be. I do have some papers for you to go over. I've leased a luxury townhome for you to live in and I set up some accounts for you."

"I don't need any of that," she said. He'd already mentioned that he would provide housing and accounts, but the last thing she wanted was to take anything else from Jeremy. And she needed her real life. Her small home and her friends. They were what kept her grounded.

"I have certain standards."

"Just because I'm not in your financial tax bracket doesn't mean I live in a dump." To be fair, there was a time when it would have meant exactly that. But the last three years had been good to her and her business. She didn't live in the most prestigious neighborhood, like he did. But she lived in a nice area. A comfortable, middle-class neighborhood where people genuinely cared for each other, and not because of their social status or connections.

"I wasn't implying you lived in a dump."

Had she overreacted? She had no idea. Suddenly she wanted this night to end. She wanted to be back in her nice, safe little home, tucked under the quilt that used to grace her parents' bed, hidden away from the world so she could regroup.

"I can't put my life on hold for six months," she said, rubbing the back of her neck. This was the part she'd never been able to imagine when she'd thought of their contract. The part that made this temporary business arrangement all too real.

"I'm not asking you to." He brushed her hand aside and massaged the back of her neck and shoulders. His touch was just right, strong and firm.

Chills spread down her neck and arms. Her breasts felt fuller. Even though his touch wasn't sexual, she wanted it to be. She wanted more of the passion-filled kisses that had punctuated the last three years of her life.

"Relax, Bella. This is going to work out the way we both envision it," he said.

He slid his hands down her arms and drew her back against his body. His breath stirred the hair at the nape of her neck. She was completely surrounded by him and sank back against his tall, lean frame.

Why did he sound so reasonable? He was making her feel like she was being difficult, and that had never been her intention. She needed to be up front about what limitations she wanted on the relationship.

But she couldn't do it while she was in his arms.

Taking a deep breath, she stepped away from him, turning to face him. "I need to stay in my home. I'll be available for you on evenings and weekends. There will be some nights when I have to work, but I can come over here or even to that townhome if you want all of our sexual encounters to take place there."

"Sexual encounters."

"Aren't those the words you used in the contract we both signed?"

He closed the distance she'd put between them in one long stride. She couldn't help taking a step backward. Gone was the soft, tender lover. She couldn't really tell what he felt at this moment, but she suspected it was close to anger. She thought her blunt summation of their relationship might have been too baldly stated.

He'd let things get out of control in an effort to relax her and perhaps to make up for the encounter with Lucinda. But letting her boil down what was between them to nothing more than sexual encounters left a bad taste in his mouth, no matter that it was the truth.

From the very beginning the attraction between them had been electric. He couldn't explain it any other way. He knew that real sexual chemistry was rare. He had experienced it to lesser degrees with other women he'd dated, but from the first instant he'd seen her, his entire body had gone on high alert.

She'd been too thin and too tired to be interested in any advances he made, but she'd still responded. Responded and turned him down with regret because she had a teenage brother at home for whom she was responsible.

That had been part of the attraction, he admitted. Her total selflessness where her brother was concerned. He didn't have one acquaintance who would have done the same, except Kell. Kell would sacrifice himself for Jeremy, and Jeremy would do the same for his cousin.

But never for the women he'd been involved with. He'd thought perhaps that novel situation had been the driving factor in the attraction. He could have walked away from her—hell, who was he kidding? Walking away was never something he'd considered.

When he saw something he wanted, he went after it until he made it his own. And he was going to make her his. Completely his, no matter what she thought or how she tried to manage him and their time together. *Sexual encounters* was too tame a term to describe what he intended between them.

She bit her lower lip and he groaned out loud. Her mouth was full and lush and beckoned him like nothing else ever had.

He caught her hips in his hands and pulled her

toward him. Her eyes widened and she inhaled sharply but she didn't resist him.

"We're going to have more than sexual encounters, Bella."

"We are?"

"Yes," he said, lowering his head to hers. He dropped nibbling kisses along her brow and then slowly found her lips with his. All night long he'd kept a tight rein on his desire to devour her mouth. He knew how it tasted, always thought it couldn't be as lush and welcoming as he remembered. Yet it always was.

Her hands found his shoulders and she clung to him as he traced the seam of her lips with his tongue.

There had been something of a challenge in those words she'd uttered. And he didn't know if he would be able to prove her right or wrong. Part of him—the hard, hungry part of him—wanted sex. Craved the feel of her silky limbs against his.

There was a spark of wildness in her eyes that called to him. Her hands clasped his shoulders, making him feel like the strongest man in the world. He tilted his head to the side and plundered her mouth.

If she wanted this, then he'd be happy to oblige. He'd seduce her into his bed and use her until the passion between them ran its course and then send her on her way. She'd fulfill her promise to him and he'd have...he'd have Bella for a short time.

She tasted of some essence of woman that he was coming to associate only with her. She moaned deep in her throat as he thrust his tongue into her mouth. Her tongue stroked tentatively against his.

Sliding his hands down her back, he cupped her hips and pulled her more firmly against his body. He'd meant to keep the embrace light, but Bella made it too easy to forget his intentions.

He rubbed his growing erection against her and she made another soft sound in the back of her throat. Her nails dug into his shoulders through the layer of his shirt. She undulated against him.

He lifted his head. Her eyes were closed and her face was flushed with desire. He knew that it would take very little for him to persuade her to have sex with him, but with a few words she'd made him want her to admit there was more than sex between them.

He traced a path down the side of her neck to the choker he'd given her. He wanted to see her wearing just that and the moonlight. The image almost brought him to his knees.

He didn't know if she'd meant to remind him or herself with those words. Part of him wanted to just take what he needed. Show her how it would be if he really did just use her for sex.

But then her eyes opened and she looked at him and did something no woman had ever done before. Bella cupped his face and stood on tiptoe, touching her lips to his and whispering his name.

His heart beat too quickly in his chest and the lust that had taken control of his body abated as fear slowly crept through him. He wanted her more than he should.

He let his hands fall away from her body and turned on his heel, heading back up to the house. Once inside, he went to the wet bar and mixed himself a drink.

How had the evening gotten so out of control? Bella stayed on the patio for a few extra minutes, trying to gather her senses and make some kind of plan to get safely out the door without throwing herself into Jeremy's arms.

His arms around her always felt so right. She shook her head, refusing to dwell on that. They needed to come to a compromise about their living arrangements for the next six months. She'd angered him with her summation of their relationship and she couldn't blame him.

Half the time she said things just to get a rise out of him. As she belatedly followed him into the house, she smiled to herself. She'd gotten more than one kind of rise out of him just now.

"What's so funny?"

"Oh, it was kind of an inside joke."

He waited, highball glass in one hand, hip cocked. He looked so virile and masculine standing there in the dim light provided by the wall sconces.

He took her breath away with the way he moved. And his contradictions. Why couldn't he have stuck to ordering her around?

She could resist Jeremy all day long when he was arrogant, but as soon as she felt his arms around her she was lost. Or was she found? She'd been lost for so long that she'd almost accepted it as the norm. But then he reminded her that there were still things she wanted in the world that had nothing to do with money, status or business success.

"You might not think it's funny."

"Try me," he said, knocking back his drink.

"Um…I was just thinking that I said what I did to get a rise out of you…"

He gave her a wry grin, but didn't move from the doorway.

"I'm sorry about what I said earlier. I should try to remember what Shelley advised."

"Your assistant?"

"She's more than just an employee, she's a friend."

"What did she say?"

"To enjoy you," she said.

"Tell me more."

She shook her head. "I don't want to talk about my friends," she said quietly, reluctant to reveal more than she had.

"Me either."

She took a few steps closer to him. They had to

come to some kind of compromise. "I kind of want to have things my way on everything."

"Yeah, I can understand that. I've been dealing with people for a long time. And I've learned that having everything in a contract is the only way to keep all sides from getting upset."

It sounded so cold, hearing him talk about sleeping with her the same way he'd approach a deal he brokered. Guard your heart, Bella, she thought. This man could hurt you.

"I've never been a mistress before. And I haven't experienced relationships the way you have. Most of the people I deal with are good on their word."

"What if they aren't?"

"Then I'm disappointed in them."

"With a contract there's no room for disappointment."

"Do you realize how cold that sounds?" she said before she could help herself. Her doubts were circling back to her.

He shrugged a shoulder and turned to the bar, pouring himself another mixed drink. "Can I get you something?"

She shook her head. She knew how Alice must have felt when she'd stumbled down the rabbit hole. Bella only wished there'd been a talking white rabbit to alert her that she was now in an alternate universe.

"Where are the papers you had for me to look at?"

"On the table," he said, gesturing with his glass toward the dining room.

The dining room was bigger than the master bedroom in her current house and recalled images of the one from her childhood. She remembered playing on hardwood floors just like this, sock-skating around the table while her mother sang in her beautiful contralto voice.

Oh, man. What was she doing here? No matter how many times she asked the question, she still hadn't found the answer she was looking for.

There was a manila file folder with her name written across it. She drew out a chair and sat down, opening the folder. Inside was an addendum to the contract she'd already signed. It listed the start and end dates for their relationship.

He had been thorough and very generous. The accounts he'd set up would last only as long as their relationship did, but the annuity he was providing for her for the six months would continue. He wouldn't be adding money into it, but by the terms and stipulations she read, he'd given her a cushion that would ensure she'd never again have to leave her house in the middle of the night one step ahead of the creditors.

She struck out the clause about the townhome, but left the accounts with the stipulation that they be paid from the annuity. She didn't want to take any more than was absolutely necessary. She changed the start and end dates by one day because she couldn't start tonight.

And hoped he'd understand. She added one addendum of her own and then initialed her changes and signed her name.

She glanced up to where he waited in the doorway and pushed the papers across the table toward him. "I made a few changes."

He walked into the room, glanced at the changes and initialed all of them, including the clause she'd added, without any questions. "I'll have my driver see you home. And I'll pick you up tomorrow night around eight."

"I'll be at an event. I'll send the address to your secretary in the morning."

He nodded. The emotionless set of his face and his dispassionate eyes made her feel cold. She stood, rubbing her hands up and down her arms.

He cursed under his breath, closing the distance between them in two long strides. He pulled her into his arms and kissed her. Not a tentative meeting of the mouths, but the kind of kiss that went beyond the barriers of two people attracted to each other and straight to the souls of two lonely people.

In his kiss she felt a desperation that echoed what was inside her. She wrapped her arms around his waist and held on to him like she'd never let go. Only she knew, deep inside, that she never wanted to.

Five

Jeremy checked his watch for the second time, realizing that Bella was late. He got out of his car, leaving the keys with the valet, and entered the Norton Museum of Art in West Palm Beach.

"Sorry," Bella said, hurrying over to him. She wore a blue crepe dress that ended just above her knees and she had her hair pulled back in a professional-looking twist. She smiled at him but he could tell she was harried.

"Is something wrong?"

"Just horribly short-staffed. I'm going to be at least forty-five more minutes. If you want to go ahead to the restaurant I can meet you at the bar there."

Drinking alone had never appealed to him. Especially when Bella waited somewhere else. Thoughts of her had crept into his mind throughout the day until Daniel had text-messaged him to get his head in the game. It was the first time he could recall a woman interfering with his business and he didn't like it.

"No."

She put her hand on his wrist. Her slim, cool fingers rested right above the Swiss Army watch that his dad had given him. The watch was a constant reminder of his old man.

"I really can't leave right now, Jeremy."

He twisted his hand around to capture hers, rubbing his thumb over the back of her knuckles. "I'll come with you. Putting out fires is my specialty."

She didn't pull her hand free as she led the way back down the hallway to the theater room in the museum.

"It is? You don't look like a firefighter."

"Well, there's more than one kind of fire."

"I know that," she said under her breath.

"Are you feeling a few flames?"

"Don't even start. Twice today I—"

He pulled them to a stop in the doorway leading toward the service corridor when she didn't go on. "What?"

She shook her head. "I really need to go back to the ballroom."

"Then tell me what you were going to say."

She nibbled on her lower lip, a gesture that never failed to make him want to kiss her.

"Just that twice today I called one of our staffers by your name."

"Does he look like me?"

"Not at all. I was just—" She pulled away from him. "Don't let this go to your head, but you were on my mind."

How could he not? He tugged her back toward the main hallway. "Let's get your problems solved so we can go somewhere private. Then you can tell me all the details."

"I don't need you to solve my problems."

"I know that. It's just that I'm rather effective at it."

"Really? What's the most effective way?" she asked, tipping her head to the side in a flirtatious gesture. "I've never had a billionaire businessman give me advice on managing my workforce before."

"Keep being sassy and you still won't."

"Sassy?"

"Sassy."

"Hmm…no one's ever called me that before. Is that the key to keeping the staff in line?"

"Intimidation is. You scare the bejeezus out of your staff and then they work more efficiently."

She laughed, just like he hoped she would. "I'm not very intimidating."

"Have you ever tried to be?" he asked. He

doubted she had. There was an innate goodness that surrounded Bella. He suspected that was part of what had originally drawn him to her. Despite the fact that she'd been down on her luck, she'd still been looking out for those around her instead of just focusing on herself.

"Well, no. That's not my style, really. Even when Dare was rebelling and I knew I should be tough on him, I couldn't." In her voice he heard the echoes of what he'd heard that night three years ago when they'd struck their deal. Her doubts in herself and her abilities to pull her brother back from the edge.

He let go of her hand, sliding his arm around her waist and drawing her into his side. She held her body stiff until he stroked his free hand down her spine. Then she relaxed against him.

"He respects you," she said quietly.

"He admires you," Jeremy said. He didn't know how he'd become a father-confessor to Dare McNamara, but somehow he had. The young man e-mailed him a couple times a week and called every few days to check in.

Jeremy knew part of it was that Dare expected him to keep an eye on Isabella. Her brother wanted to make sure she was looked after. And as Dare said, he wasn't man enough to do it yet.

Since taking care of Bella played into his plans, that was an easy enough promise to give Dare. Sometimes he had a few qualms about how Dare would feel if he knew the nature of the relationship between him and Bella, but that was no one else's business.

"I really don't have time to be talking about my brother or leaning on you."

"What do we need to do?"

"The florist dumped the arrangements in the kitchen and I need someone to place one on each round table."

"Um…"

"Come on, Jeremy. It'll be good for you. It'll build character and earn you my gratitude."

"That's all well and good but I want more than gratitude."

"Help me out and I'll give you whatever you ask for."

"Deal," he said, holding open the door to the convention space and entering Bella's world. He watched her direct her staff and realized he respected the way she worked. She didn't micromanage anyone—just expected them to do the job they'd been assigned. And he noticed that everyone worked harder when she was around them. Not because they were afraid of her, he suspected, but to bask in the glow of her smile and the praise that accompanied it.

He told himself he wasn't the same as these workers. That he was here to collect the woman who was contractually bound to him. But when she glanced at the finished tables and smiled at him, he felt something stir inside him.

Something that had nothing to do with lust. Something that wasn't bound by a contract. Something he hoped like hell was going to go away when his time with Bella was up.

"I'm so glad you're here," she said.

He walked away without saying a word because he wasn't too sure that *he* was happy. He'd wanted Bella and gone after her with the single-minded determination he went after anything he wanted, and was only now realizing that getting her might not be his smartest business decision.

She'd expected Jeremy to whisk her out of the museum and to a private place where they'd be intimate. But when the bar association members started to arrive, some acquaintances of his were in the group. He signaled her to join him but she shook her head and motioned that she'd be a few minutes.

Every time she was in his presence he knocked her a little further off-kilter. She pulled her cell phone from her pocket to check the time and pretend she was busy instead of going to his side. She wasn't ready to be at his side. Not now. She needed a reality check. The kind that focusing on the details of her job could deliver.

"There you are," Shelley said, coming up behind her. She had a clipboard in one hand and a radio in the other. She looked like a staffer, unlike Bella, who was dressed for her date with Jeremy. She realized that she was right where she'd never wanted to be. Right on the cusp of two worlds. Her two worlds.

Her two lives. The one she'd once had and dreamed of getting back. And this one, the one she'd built from the wreckage.

"Please don't give me bad news," she said when Shelley reached her side.

The blonde had her hair pulled back in a ponytail and her button-down, oxford shirt open at the collar. She looked young but competent. "Geez. Is that my rep now?"

"Well you did keep coming to find me with another challenge to report."

"Challenge…I like that. I'm going to use it the next time my boyfriend says I'm too much work."

Shelley was a dear, sweet person who didn't have a mean bone in her body. And her boyfriend took advantage of that. "Did you need something?"

"Yes. I'm playing delivery girl again." She reached into her pocket and pulled out a small envelope. One that the florist had inadvertently put in the arrangements. That had been one of the first challenges of the day—removing all those picks with the blank cards in them.

Her name was written across the back of the cream-colored envelope. "Thanks, Shelley."

"No problem. He's very romantic."

Bella had no idea how to respond to that. "We need to double-check the jackets on the waitstaff. I don't want anyone going out there with stains."

"I'll double-check. You need to leave."

"Are you sure?" she asked. Her duty manager had been involved in a car accident, so there was no senior person at the event. Bella had toyed with canceling on Jeremy, but Shelley had made a bid to be in charge, wanting to use this event to prove herself.

Shelley rolled her eyes. "Yes."

"You've got my cell number, right?"

Shelley shook her head, reached over and took the museum radio from her hand. "You're being challenging."

Bella laughed. "You're right. Sorry about that. I'll see you in the morning."

"Have fun tonight," Shelley said as she walked away.

Bella left the theater and went in the back to collect her purse. She'd left her car at the office since Jeremy had said he'd pick her up.

She lifted the back flap and stared down at the card inside. She pulled it out. It was a cheap generic one, the kind that florists used for bulk arrangements.

On it was simply a phone number. This was what Shelley had thought was romantic?

What had she expected? Some kind of love note?

She was his mistress, not a woman he was seducing. She was a sure thing. And she was beginning to realize she had absolutely no idea how to convince him she should be more than a mistress.

She dialed it, a little disappointed. And mad at herself for being upset. She had no claims to Jeremy other than those he'd laid out in writing. Why had she forgotten that?

"Harper."

"It's Bella," she said, moving away from the convention food and beverage staff, who were making a lot of noise as they readied all the dishes to go out to the tables at one time.

"Are you free now?" he asked.

"Yes. I'm all yours."

"Mine? Not quite."

"What do you mean?"

"Why didn't you join me earlier?"

"I had some stuff to finish up."

"Stuff? That sounds like an excuse. You're my mistress, Bella. That means that when we are together—"

"I'm working tonight, Jeremy. That's my first priority."

"Why?"

"Why what?" she asked, stalling. She really had to figure out how to filter every thought that came into her head so that they didn't all end up coming out of her mouth.

"Are we going to play this kind of game?"

"You started it," she said.

She hated that he'd called her on avoiding him. She was nervous again, and that was beginning to bother her. Why hadn't she figured him out yet? Normally it took her maybe two meetings with a person to decide how to deal with them. But with him...

She sighed. "I'm sorry. I was being sarcastic and it was uncalled for."

"Bella, what am I going to do with you?"

"Anything your contract gives you the right to."

He said nothing for a long moment and she heard the head of the Palm Beach Bar Association get up and start talking.

"I'll meet you in the Tsai atrium and we can start our night."

"Okay."

She hung up before he had a chance to say anything else. No more nerves. She'd promised herself that this morning. She wanted more from Jeremy than six months and she wasn't going to get that by hiding.

Seeing her tonight with her staff and the way she'd treated him when they were with other people showed him that she was still nervous about any intimacy between them. And he knew the quickest way to push past it was through seduction.

He had been to many events at the Norton during his lifetime and knew the museum like the back of his hand. He'd attended most of the events with one of his parents. Never the two of them together. They were happier apart, something his father had explained to Jeremy when he'd turned nine.

That talk about marriage and relationships had been diverted by a few innocent questions about sex. Because nine-year-old Jeremy hadn't been too sure that Kell had known what he was talking about when he said that a boy's penis had to get hard before he could have sex.

The sex part…well, his dad had firm opinions about it. He'd said that women saw sex as more than just a physical release. That a gentleman didn't marry for sex, he had mistresses for sex. And that when a man found the right woman, sex was an incredible thing.

Bella stood in the center of the now empty atrium on the cracked ice terrazzo floor. Remembering his father's advice about women and sex made him realize that he wanted Bella to be different. To somehow be the kind of woman that Lucinda must be for Daniel to still be so into her.

But he was afraid to take the risk of caring for her. He would likely only confirm that he was essentially his father's son. After all, he was definitely his father's progeny in the business world. Making money and turning a profit was something that came easily to him. As did the women…and there had never been anyone he wanted to marry.

And now, there Bella stood, her dress so close to the same deep blue as the tiles that she looked like part of the decor. An ethereal woman that he could only glimpse. He hated that. For most of his life he'd struggled with trying to hold on to people in his life. He didn't have a lot of lasting relationships.

The heels of his Italian loafers made a soft sound as he approached and she pivoted to face him. He hesitated there, unable to move toward her. Feeling once again that punch in the gut. She was more beautiful than any woman he'd ever seen.

He walked up to her and had to fight the urge to put his arms around her. She was a mistress. His mistress. *His.*

That word resonated inside him. He knew it wasn't politically correct but it suited him to claim her even if only in his own mind. There was something soothing about knowing exactly what to expect from another person.

She turned to look at him. "I love this place. It's so soothing and quiet at night."

"Then you're going to love the surprise I have planned for you."

"Love it?"

There was skepticism in her voice, but he wasn't daunted. Now that he had a plan, he was back on his game. Seduction was the key to wooing her and having her.

"Wait and see."

He took her hand in his and led her to a small, wedge-shaped room off the atrium. The J. Ira and Nick Harris Family Pavilion. There was a small table set in the middle of the room in front of the glass doors that led to the Italian gardens outside.

But it was the ceiling that made the room. The Chihuly glass was spectacular and Jeremy knew he'd made the right decision when he heard her breath catch.

Her hand fell away from his and she walked farther into the room. The lighting behind the Chihuly ceiling painted the room in hues of aquatic blues and greens.

"Jeremy…this is lovely. Are we having dinner here?"

"Yes," he said, crossing to the freestanding ice-bucket to pour them both a glass of champagne.

"This is…okay, I do love it."

"What did I tell you?"

"You're doing the arrogance thing again."

"In this case I think I've earned the right."

"Okay, I'll give you that."

He handed her the champagne flute and then tipped his glass to hers. "To the next six months."

She nodded and took a delicate sip of her drink, keeping eye contact with him the entire time. But he saw her hand tremble as she lifted the glass to her lips.

She put her glass on the table and walked slowly around the room, observing the ceiling from every angle. When she came back to the table, he signaled to the waitstaff to begin serving their meal.

He held her chair, seating her. When he pulled his own chair out he saw the small gift box he'd asked to be put there.

He picked it up and placed it on the table.

She glanced at the gift box and then back up at him. He couldn't read the expression in her usually expressive eyes.

"You don't have to seduce me," she said carefully.

"That's my privilege."

"Oh."

"Yes, oh." He handed her the package and watched as she held it carefully between her fingers.

"I'd rather you make a donation to charity than keep giving me gifts."

He shook his head. "Mistresses should take as many gifts from their lovers as possible."

He'd hurt her. He could see it in the way she subtly flinched and sank back in her chair. She let the small present fall to the table.

He felt like an ass. He'd been on his game just a few moments earlier. Why had he said that? It shouldn't matter to him if she didn't want his gifts—and yet it did. She was already blurring the lines between mistress and…girlfriend.

"Just open the present, Bella."

She removed the ribbon and the wrapping and then opened the box. Inside was a small placard that showed a Chihuly sculpture he'd ordered for her. It would be delivered in three weeks time.

"Thank you, Jeremy."

He shrugged like it meant nothing to him, but it was too late to pretend with himself. His gut-deep confirmation earlier that she was his made that impossible. He could only fall back on the contract they had between them. Hope that six months of holding her would be enough.

After they ate, he took her on a moonlit stroll through the Renaissance-inspired gardens and then led the way back to his car.

She'd relaxed during the walk but his tension had increased. He wanted her. And that seemed more dangerous now then it had at the beginning of the evening when he'd felt safe and protected by his contract. He could have everything he wanted from her. But now he knew that their arrangement wasn't going to protect him from the emotions that she brought swirling to the surface.

Six

Bella had no idea where they were going as they flew down the highway. The top was down on Jeremy's convertible and the breeze made it impossible to talk, which was something of a relief.

Tonight had made her feel every inch the pampered woman of a wealthy man. There was something very attractive to her about being Jeremy's mistress. The problem was that the glimpses she'd seen of the possessive man Jeremy was made her want him for more than a temporary affair.

She hoped they weren't headed for the town house he'd leased. Suddenly, she thought of it as a test for him. If he took her to the townhome, then she'd know she hadn't made any progress in getting him to see her as more than a mistress. But it wouldn't make it any easier for her to remember that this was an arrangement and not a real love affair.

But damn it all, it was starting to feel that way. He should have just taken her to dinner instead of going out of his way to have a meal catered for them. And she knew the Norton's convention policy—they had minimums like everyone else. He must have spent a fortune on dinner.

Money wasn't an issue for Jeremy. She should have remembered that. Maybe the evening was nothing more than a convenience. Maybe what she'd interpreted as a romantic gesture was just the way he operated.

She didn't think so. The Chihuly glass sculpture was breathtaking, even in a picture. She wanted to take the card out of her purse and look at it again. But she didn't.

As they neared town, she glanced over at him. His attention stayed focused on the road and she noticed that he handled the car with ease. Not surprising. He did everything with ease.

He slowed even further and pulled into the parking lot of the Palm Beach hotel. The hotel was old and refined, a grande dame in the area. It was known for luxury and quality.

Please don't let this be where he is taking me, she

thought. She didn't want the first time they made love to be in a hotel. She wanted it to be in a place that meant something to one of them.

As he neared the valet parking station, she reached over and put her hand on his thigh. "What are we doing here?"

"Meeting some business associates for a drink."

More time spent waiting. The tension that had been riding her for the last two days—heck, to be honest, the last three years—tightened painfully inside her. She knew that Daniel Posner was his business partner. And Lucinda Cannon was Daniel's wife. She wasn't ready for another meeting with either of them.

She didn't want to add another nerve-inducing element to the evening, and talking to his business associates wasn't going to relax her. But she'd never say that to him. She owed him. He'd spent an insane amount of money on her already and she hadn't done anything other than kiss him.

"Is that okay?" he asked, looking pointedly down at his leg.

She was digging her nails into his thigh. "Of course."

She hastily removed her hand, putting it back in her lap. Oh, my God, this was getting out of control. Why had she ever thought she could do this? Because she'd been desperate. And desperation was the creator of opportunity.

It didn't feel like opportunity right now, as she looked at the beautiful hotel entrance. A place where she'd once attended cotillion dances and afternoon teas with her mother's circle of friends. She'd taken tennis lessons from a Wimbledon champion at this hotel. And played golf with her father a lifetime ago.

"Who are we meeting?"

"My partner and his wife, plus a very important client, and his wife."

"Daniel?"

"Yes. Is that a problem?" he asked.

She shrugged, determined to play it cool this evening. She refused to give Lucinda the power of unnerving her, though her sweaty palms said the other woman already had done so.

"Not at all. Who's the client?" she asked. This might be the perfect opportunity for her to show him that she'd make a better wife than mistress. The kind of woman he'd want by his side in business and pleasure.

"Frederick Merriweather. We've been trying to convince him to merge with our company."

"And tonight is another attempt?"

Jeremy pulled the car to the side of the driveway and stopped. "Yes, it is. I'm glad to see that you're so interested in this meeting."

"Why?"

He shrugged.

She waited. But he didn't say anything else. She started to feel small and insignificant. And very much, she realized, like a mistress.

She turned her head away from him. She didn't want to play games. Games were their own form of lying. And she had played enough of them when her mom was alive.

Let's pretend we don't see the Cannons or the Fell-Murrays or anyone else we used to know.

"Just tell me why, Jeremy."

He reached across the space in the car, fingers on her cheek. "Because it's the first interest you've shown in something for me."

Didn't he realize she paid attention to every detail that was his life? It was probably a good thing that he didn't, at least not yet. But she took as a good sign that he wanted her attention. "Then tell me what you need me to do. I'm pretty good at putting people at ease."

"Just be yourself," he said.

He cupped his fingers around the back of her head and drew her steadily toward him. In his eyes she saw the light of something more than desire.

It made her want to trust him, she thought. But then his head bent toward hers and everything in her body tensed in awareness and need. Her blood flowed heavier in her veins. Her breasts felt fuller and her lips tingled. She started to close her eyes but then kept them open.

She wanted to know how he felt when he kissed her. Did he reveal anything? She noticed the tiny gold flecks in his light green-gray eyes. She noticed the way his pupils had dilated and his nostrils flared right before she felt his mouth on hers.

She closed her eyes then. It was impossible to think of anything other than Jeremy when his mouth touched hers. The details of their deal dropped away as she created new memories of this man.

Of the way his hands moved over her skin like he was trying to learn her by feel. The way his tongue conquered her mouth with languid thrusts as if he had all night to learn the taste of it. The way he rubbed his thumb over her moist lips and then held her hand as he drove to the entrance of the hotel.

When he put his hand low on her back and escorted her into the hotel, she no longer felt like an outsider.

The bar was crowded, but Jeremy found Daniel and Frederick with no trouble. He wanted this meeting to go smoothly and quickly so he could hustle Bella home. And then take her to bed. He'd set up the meeting to put Bella more at ease in his world, part of his deal with her.

But his body was tight and his mind was only on the woman at his side, not the upcoming meeting. He'd been a little rattled when she'd asked him what he needed of her. He didn't want to analyze it, yet the words kept circling around in his head. He needed her there because the other men would have their wives and it would keep the party even.

There was a sense of rightness in having her by his side. But he knew that it was a mistake to feel possessive about her. He wasn't a man who kept things. He prided himself on looking to the future. On moving through life unencumbered.

Bella was just one more pleasure to be enjoyed as he moved forward. Once he had her silky body under his and he claimed her, had her, he could move on.

That elusive thing about her would be realized and she'd become like every other woman he'd had a relationship with. Just another mistress.

Frederick was an older man in his late forties with a leonine mane of blond hair that made him look like an aging hippie. He wore a Brooks Brothers suit and a pinky ring. Frederick was a self-made man who didn't care what anyone thought about the way he and his wife dressed.

"Evening, Frederick. Where's Mary?"

"She saw something in the window of the boutique that she had to have. Who is this?"

"Bella McNamara. Bella, this is Frederick Merriweather."

"It's nice to meet you, Frederick," Bella said.

Jeremy nodded toward Daniel. "And I'm sure you remember my partner, Daniel Posner."

"Yes. Good to see you again, Daniel."

They shook hands and then Jeremy seated Bella at the table.

"You'll have to go to the bar if you want a drink," Daniel said.

"What would you like?" he asked Bella.

"Drambuie, please," she said.

He made his way to the bar to get their drinks.

"She doesn't look the way she used to."

Jeremy glanced over to see Lucinda standing next to him. Lucinda was one of the most beautiful women he'd ever met. She had classically good looks and she'd been raised in a moneyed world that showed in every graceful movement she made.

His family had socialized with hers, but he'd never noticed her as a child or teenager. In fact, until Daniel had started dating her, he'd never paid much attention to her.

"What did she look like?"

"At fourteen?"

He nodded. God, he hadn't realized how young she'd been when her world had fallen apart.

"More like me. Manicured, pedicured and hair chemically perfect."

He smiled at the faint mocking tone in Lucinda's voice. "Circumstances change."

"Yes, they do," Lucinda said.

"What are you trying to tell me?"

"I'm not sure. Her family and mine were once very close…"

Jeremy had done some Internet research on Bella and had read the AP newswire accounts of her father's fall and consequent suicide. And then just a tiny article when her mother died a few short years later. But there were details of her life that he couldn't fill in. How did a girl who was a princess turn into the single-mother type she'd been when he met her? True, it was her brother she'd been raising, but…

"When did you lose touch?" he asked, prying the way he would if this were a business deal. He'd never expected to glean information from Lucinda, whom he thought of usually as someone to be avoided since she was always trying to foist her single friends on him.

She shrugged and bit her lower lip. "When she stopped moving in our circle. She's not like us anymore, Jeremy."

He wasn't sure where she was going with this conversation, but had an inkling of why Bella had been so upset when she'd seen Lucinda the other night.

"Just spit it out. I'm not good at guessing games."

"No, you're not. That's why you need Daniel."

"In business I do need him and the subtle way he has of smoothing over my rough edges, but that still doesn't tell me about Bella and you."

"When she lost everything, she became a different person. She wasn't the girl she used to be, and to be honest I'm not sure that she isn't dating you for some kind of revenge."

"I don't understand."

"She means I wasn't suitable to speak to any longer."

He hadn't heard Bella come up to them. Lucinda shrugged delicately and stepped away from them. She stopped a few steps away to look back at Bella, and there was tension between the women that went beyond not talking to one another.

"Well, you and I both know that we don't socialize with the staff."

Bella froze. He wrapped his arm around her shoulder and pulled her solidly against him. She put her hand on his lapel and he felt the fine tremors in her body.

"Bella's not the staff any longer, Lucinda."

"Of course she isn't. She's your…what exactly is she, Jeremy?"

Bella cleared her throat and he saw a flash of her temper. That same temper that she always tried to hide. "None of your business, Lucinda. We're not friends any longer."

"And whose fault is that?"

"Assigning blame is a juvenile thing to do," Bella said in a small voice.

He had the feeling that there was much more between the two women than a change in Bella's financial circumstances. And though he was curious, he knew it was past time to put an end to this.

"We need to get back to the table. We're here for a business meeting."

"Of course," Lucinda said and made her way to Daniel's side.

He handed Bella her Drambuie. "Want to talk about it?"

She shook her head.

He couldn't stand the hurt in her eyes and wanted to do whatever he could to soothe it—to soothe her. "Bella—"

"Leave it, Jeremy. I'm not your girlfriend. I'm your mistress."

Her words struck him like a barb. And this was why he didn't want to allow her any closer than he had to.

"That's right. You are."

They didn't talk much on the car ride back to his place and Bella was glad of it. She had no idea how to make amends for her stupid comments. Once again she'd allowed Lucinda to get the better of her and to threaten a relationship that was coming to mean a lot to her.

She needed to apologize to Jeremy. Wanted to get the tension between them out of the way before they were intimate. And she knew without a shadow of a doubt that Jeremy was going to take her to his bed tonight. If for no other reason than to prove to them both that she was nothing more than his mistress.

She swallowed hard, searching for some words. Any words. *I'm sorry* wouldn't do, because then she'd have to admit that she realized she'd hurt his feelings earlier.

But once they entered his house, she was nervous about more than the apology, which was so silly because she wanted Jeremy. Her lips still tingled from his kiss in the car earlier.

Maybe that had played a part in her remarks to him. She had a history of shooting herself in the foot socially when she was…

"Jeremy?"

"Yes." He tossed his keys on the table in the hallway leading from the garage to the house. Standing on the threshold of the media room, he didn't turn to look at her.

"I…" She just couldn't say it. Didn't want to have to talk about Lucinda and the bad blood between them. Lucinda hadn't been particularly nice to her, but Bella knew she hadn't been all that good to Lucinda, either.

"You?" He pivoted on his heel.

She took a deep breath. "You know I've said that you're arrogant."

He nodded.

"Well, I'm not. When I'm unsure of myself—

and it happens more than I like to admit—I lash out. It's my way of protecting myself."

He leaned against the wall, crossing his arms over his chest.

"When did you start doing that?" he asked.

She took a deep breath. "Probably the summer I was fifteen and my mother started working for the Cannons as their upstairs maid. I helped her sometimes. It was awkward. I...I've never been able to just be quiet and pretend nothing bothers me."

"So you attack?"

"Yes."

He nodded. "Was there anything else?"

She shook her head.

"Then let's go have another drink before we head upstairs."

"Jeremy."

"What?"

"I don't like this tension between us. Despite everything, we've always been friendly. Let me do something to make it up to you."

He rubbed the back of his neck, and she realized that tonight might really be a sexual encounter. And she'd have to renege on her word.

She didn't give herself easily and had slept with only one other man. An event which was singularly unmemorable. She wanted earth-shattering passion with Jeremy, but a big part of her believed that was just the stuff of romantic stories—that in real life, sex was just sweaty and somewhat enjoyable.

"Come inside and we can discuss this," he said.

She followed him into the media room. He shrugged out of his jacket, tossing it over the back of the couch.

"I really enjoyed meeting Frederick and Mary," she said. As soon as they'd returned to the group, she'd realized her faux pas with Jeremy and had tried to make up for it by charming his would-be business associate.

She didn't know why she was talking about the business meeting he'd had. She certainly didn't want to open up the conversation to Lucinda. God knows she didn't want to think about the way she'd felt when she saw the two of them talking at the bar. A part of her knew that there was nothing Lucinda could say that Jeremy didn't already know. He'd seen her at rock-bottom.

"They liked you, too. I'm having a party on my yacht for them on Saturday."

She was grateful for the subject change.

"Do you want to use my caterer?" she asked, trying to ignore the fact that he'd removed his tie and loosened the top two buttons of his shirt.

"No. I want you by my side and not thinking about business."

"Oh," she said, feeling a little hurt. "I'm really the best event planner in the area."

"I don't doubt that."

"Then why don't you want me to take care of the details? It's short notice but I can—"

"Bella."

"Yes?"

"I have a personal chef who'll attend to the details, and if it's really so important to you, you can make the menu choices."

"Okay. I can hire servers for you, too."

"Forget about business. You have only one thing to think about right now."

"And that is?"

"Being my mistress," he said, and took her in his arms.

He tipped her head back and she met his gaze. He was serious now. And she realized she was seeing the real man. The trappings of society were stripped away as he watched her.

He wanted her.

She shivered. No man had ever wanted her this much. She was acutely aware of her femininity and the primitive power that she carried with it.

She caressed his back, felt the power in his shoulders. His arms shifted around her. One around her waist, the other low on her hips.

He didn't speak, didn't have to. At this moment words would be superfluous and neither of them needed to talk about anything.

His hair was cool and silky under her fingers.

She cupped his head in both of her hands, standing on her tiptoes as she drew his head down to hers.

She pressed her lips to his and traced the seam between them with her tongue. He tasted faintly of the scotch he'd consumed at the hotel and something else that she associated only with Jeremy.

He groaned deep in his throat, shifting her in his arms, lifting her off her feet. His mouth never left hers as he carried her up the stairs to his bedroom.

Seven

He set her on her feet next to his bed. The bedroom had one wall that was all windows. Framed in glass Bella saw the stars and the subtle lighting around the pool.

At this moment she was so very afraid that Jeremy would think she was only here because of the contract. And yet, at the same time, it would make things so much easier if that's what he believed.

Liar.

She grimaced. No matter how many times she said the words, they weren't true. She was here with Jeremy because she wanted the man and he'd…he'd gone to a lot of trouble for her. She was touched in a way that she didn't want to be.

He looked at her through half-lidded eyes, making her hyperaware of him and at the same time of her own body. She felt his gaze moving over her. She shifted her legs and let her arms drop to her sides.

She didn't need to protect herself from the past tonight. She was here with Jeremy. The man she'd been thinking about too much of the time. And damned if she wasn't going to enjoy him.

"Still want to talk about my party on Saturday?"

She bit her lip to keep from laughing. He was too confident, too sure of himself and with plenty of cause. He reached for her and pulled her into his arms. He lowered his head and she held her breath.

Brushing his lips over her cheek, he held her close but with a tenderness no man had shown her before. His long fingers caressed her neck, slow sweeps up and down until she shivered in his arms. She needed more from him. She grabbed his shoulders, tipped her head and opened her mouth under his.

He sighed her name as she thrust her tongue into his mouth. Sliding his arms down her back, he edged her toward the bed. It hit the backs of her legs and she sat down. He followed her, never breaking their kiss.

His tongue moved on hers with ease, tempting her further, tasting her deeper and making her long for him. Her skin felt too tight. Her breasts were heavy, craving his touch. Between her legs she was moistening for him, ready for him.

Squirming, she shifted around until she was on his lap, her legs straddling him. She lifted her head to look down at him. His skin was flushed, his lips wet from her kisses. She flexed her fingers against his shoulders.

God, he really was solid muscle.

"Take your shirt off," she said. She'd been longing to touch his chest since that long-ago summer day when she'd served him at the yacht club.

He reached between them, the backs of his fingers brushing her breasts as he unbuttoned his shirt. She shook from the brief contact and bit her lip to keep from asking for more.

He unbuttoned the small pearl buttons that held the bodice of her dress. Ran his finger down the center of her body, over her sternum and between her ribs. Lingered on her belly button and then stopped at the waistband of her high-cut thong panties.

He slowly traced the same path upward again. This time his fingers feathered under the demi-cups of her ice-blue bra, barely touching her nipples. Both beaded, and a shaft of desire pierced Bella, shaking her.

She needed more. She wanted more. Her heart beat so swiftly and loudly she was sure he could hear it. She scraped her fingernails lightly down his chest. He groaned, the sound rumbling up from his chest. He leaned back, bracing himself on his elbows.

And let her explore. This was so different from the hurried couplings she'd had with that one boyfriend in the past. Encounters that had happened in the dark and were over almost before they'd begun.

His muscles jumped under her touch. She circled his nipple but didn't touch it. Scraped her nail down the center line of his body, following the fine dusting of hair that narrowed and disappeared into the waistband of his pants.

His stomach was rock-hard and rippled when he sat up. He reached around her back and unhooked her bra and then pushed the cups up out of his way. He pulled her closer until the tips of her breasts brushed his chest.

"Bella." He said her name like a prayer.

His hard-on nudged her center and she shifted on him, trying to find a better touch, but it was impossible with the layers of cloth between them. Her dress was hiked up but it wasn't enough.

He kissed his way down her neck and bit lightly at her nape. She shuddered, clutching at his shoulders, grinding her body harder against him.

He pulled the fabric of her dress up to her waist, slipping his hands under the cloth. Those big hands burned hot on her skin as he cupped her butt and urged her to ride him faster, guiding her motions against him. He bent his head and his tongue stroked her nipple.

Everything in her body clenched. She clutched at Jeremy's shoulders as her climax washed over her. She collapsed against his chest, and he held her close. Bella hugged him to her and closed her eyes, reminding herself that to Jeremy this was just an agreement. But it didn't change the fact that she felt like she'd just found the man she'd been secretly dreaming of.

Jeremy had never seen anything more beautiful than the woman in his arms. She was so responsive to his touch and he wanted more. It fed his obsession in a way he hadn't expected. If he didn't take her soon he was going to self-combust.

The word *mine* swirled around in his head.

She pushed his shirt off his shoulders and he tugged it off, tossing it away. She shrugged out of her dress and bra. She was exquisitely built, soft, feminine. Her breasts were full and her skin flushed from her recent orgasm.

He ran his hands slowly over her torso, almost afraid to believe that after all these years, after all his negotiating, she was really here. Finally, in his bed, where he'd been fantasizing about her for so long.

Her nipples were tight little buds beckoning his mouth. He'd barely explored her before and he needed to now. He needed to find out how she reacted to his every touch.

He fingered her nipples carefully and she shifted her shoulders, trying to increase the pressure of his touch. "Tell me what you want."

"Don't you know?" she asked, her hands coming to his wrists, trying to control his movements.

He shook his head. "I want the words, Bella."

"I want…" she blurted.

He realized then that there was something very fragile inside this ultracompetent and professional woman. He pulled her more fully into his arms. Cradled her to his chest. She closed her eyes and buried her face in his neck. Each exhale went through him. God, he wanted her.

He was so hard and hot for her that he could come in his pants. But he was going to wait. He felt the minute touches of her tongue against his neck. Her hand slid down his chest and opened his belt, unfastening the button at his waistband and then lowering his zipper.

Hot damn.

Her hand slid inside his pants and his boxers. Smoothly her touch traveled up and down his length. He tightened his hands on her back. He glanced down his body to watch her working him with such tender care and he had to grit his teeth not to end it all right then. But he wanted to be inside her the next time one of them climaxed.

She smiled up at him. *Little minx.*

"I want you, Jeremy. All of you, deep inside me."

"You're going to have me," he said, his voice raspy.

She pushed the rest of her clothing away. His breath caught in his throat. She was exactly as he'd dreamed she'd be. Nipped-in waist, long slender legs and full breasts. He nudged her over on her back.

He leaned down, capturing her mouth with his as he shoved his pants farther down his legs. She opened her legs and he settled between her thighs.

The humid warmth of her center scorched his already aroused flesh. He thrust against her without thought. Damn, she felt good.

He wanted to enter her totally naked. At least this first time. But that was a huge risk and one he knew better than to take.

He pushed away from her, fumbled with his pants, taking them all the way off along with his boxers, then found the condom he'd put in the pocket earlier today.

He glanced over at her and saw that she was watching him. The fire in her eyes made his entire body tighten with anticipation. He put the condom on one-handed and turned back to her.

"Hurry."

"Not a chance. I'm going to savor you."

"Betcha can't," she said.

"You really want—"

"I really want you, Jeremy. Come to me now." She opened her arms and her legs, inviting him into her body. He lowered himself over her and rubbed against her. Shifted until he'd caressed every part of her.

She reached between his legs and cupped him in her hands, and he shuddered. "Not now. Or I won't last."

She smiled up at him. "Really?"

He wanted to hug her close at the look of wonder on her face. "Hell, yes."

He needed to be inside her *now*. He lifted her thighs, wrapping her legs around his waist. Her hands fluttered between them and their eyes met.

He held her hips steady and entered her slowly until he was fully seated. Her eyes widened with each inch he gave her. She clutched at his hips as he started to move.

He leaned down and caught one of her nipples in his teeth, scraping very gently. She started to tighten around him. Her hips moving faster, demanding more, but he kept the pace slow, steady, wanting to feel her climax again before he did.

He suckled her nipple and rotated his hips to catch her pleasure point with each thrust. Her hands clenched in his hair and she threw her head back as her climax ripped through her.

He leaned back on his haunches and tipped her hips up to give him deeper access. Her body was still clenching around his when he felt that tightening at the base of his spine seconds before his body erupted into hers. He pounded into her two, three more times then collapsed against her, careful to keep his weight from crushing her. He rolled to his side, taking her with him.

He kept his head at her breast and smoothed his hands down her back, realizing he'd just made a colossal mistake.

Having sex with Bella hadn't lessened his obsession with her. It had deepened it.

Jeremy got out of the bed and padded into the bathroom. Bella stared up at the ceiling, her entire body tingling from his lovemaking. She'd never expected it to be like this. *This* was beyond anything she'd experienced. She was pulsing.

He came back into the room and climbed back in the bed, then propped the pillows up at the head and drew her into his arms, not saying anything.

She had no idea what to do now.

"What are you thinking?" He finally broke the silence.

"That you are incredible."

"Incredible, eh? I like the sound of that."

"Great, just what you need. Another reason to be arrogant."

He tipped her head back and lowered his mouth to hers. His kisses overwhelmed her. They should both be sated and not interested in making love again. Yet as his tongue played in her mouth, she felt the rekindling of her own desire. She wanted him again. She tried to angle her head to reciprocate, but he held her still.

This was his embrace and she felt the fierce need in him to dominate her. To remind her that she was his. She'd found the proof she was searching for that Jeremy was different from every other man she'd ever met.

His biceps flexed as he shifted her in his arms, rolling her under him and then running his hands over her body.

His mouth moved down the column of her neck, nibbling and biting softly. He lingered at the base of her neck, where her pulse beat frantically. Then he sucked on her skin. Everything in her body clenched. Not enough to push her over the edge, just enough to make her frantic for more of him.

She scored his shoulders with her fingernails before skimming them down his chest, caressing his flat male nipples as he held himself above her on his strong arms. She liked the way she was surrounded by him, feeling very feminine as she lay there under him. His skin was hot to the touch and she wrapped her arms around his body, pulling him closer.

He pulled back, staring down at her. Then he traced one finger over the full globes of her breasts. She shifted her shoulders, inviting his caress. He took one of her nipples between his thumb and forefinger, pinching lightly.

She shook with need. Couldn't wait for him.

She reached between their bodies, but he shifted his hips out of her reach. His mouth fastened on her left nipple, suckling her strongly. She undulated against him, her hips lifting toward him. He drew his other hand down her body, his fingers tangling in the hair at her center.

He caressed her between her legs until she was frantically holding his head to her breasts, trying to find a release that remained just out of reach. She skimmed her hands down his body.

His breath hissed out as she reached between his legs to cup him and caress his length.

"There's a condom in the nightstand."

"Hmm…mmm," she said, too busy exploring him to really pay attention to what he said.

"Bella, baby, you're killing me."

She liked the sound of that. The way his breath caught whenever she gently scored him with her nails. He shifted over her, opening the nightstand drawer and pulling out a condom.

"Put it on me."

"With pleasure."

She opened the package before she remembered she hadn't done this before. But it wasn't that hard to figure out. He groaned as she covered him, and she thought maybe she'd done it right.

She started to reach lower again but he caught her hand and stretched it over her head. He lifted her leg up around his hip, shifted his body. She felt him hot, hard and ready at her entrance. But he made no move to take her. She looked up at him.

"You're mine."

She couldn't respond to that. "I…"

"Watch me take you, Bella, and know that this means that you belong to me."

He thrust inside her then. Lifted her up, holding her with his big hands as he repeatedly drove into her. He went deeper than he had earlier. She felt too full, stretched and surrounded by him.

He bit her neck carefully and sucked against her skin and everything tightened inside her until she felt another climax spread through her body. Her skin was pulsing, her body tightening around him. A moment later he came, crying her name and holding her tightly to his chest.

She rested her head against his shoulder and held him. Wrapped completely around his body, she realized the truth of what he'd said. She was his.

Eight

The phone rang just after lunch and Bella hesitated to answer it. Shelley had been in her office twice trying to pump her for more information on her date. And Bella didn't want to share those details with anyone. She wanted to hold them close.

Plus, despite their synchronicity in bed, there was still tension between her and Jeremy.

She struggled to keep that romantic dinner under the Chihuly glass in her mental scrapbook as one of the best meals of her entire life. There were so few in that category. And most of them had happened a long time ago, when both of her parents were still alive.

The phone stopped ringing and then the intercom buzzed.

"Yes, Shelley."

"Dare's on the line. Why didn't you pick up?"

"I'm working on a proposal," she said, which was partially true. She'd spoken to Jeremy's personal chef, Andy Conti, earlier and she was in the process of planning the details of his yacht party as a surprise to him. He'd given her so many gifts and she thought this would be a nice way to give back to him.

Andy said it was a casual event. But from their discussion, she knew it wasn't her idea of a casual event, where she offered to grill chicken and her friends brought over side dishes and bottles of wine.

She wanted every detail of Jeremy's party to be perfect. She knew Lucinda would be there. Bella figured this was her chance to show how well she fit in Jeremy's world.

"Hey, sis." She heard old-school Beastie Boys playing in the background. "No Sleep Till Brooklyn." She loved that song and had introduced her brother to the group when he'd come home with a Tupac CD.

"What's up? And can you turn the radio down?"

The volume immediately was lowered. "I'm coming home this weekend with a few friends and I'm planning to crash at your place. Is that okay?"

"Dare, it's your place, too." She liked that he

asked, but he didn't need to. She still missed him around the house. Even though he'd only lived with her off and on since she'd moved to her current place, she was still used to thinking of it as their home.

"Not anymore. I'm subleasing a place in Manhattan."

"Can you afford it?" she asked, but she knew he could. He had matured so much in the last few years. She didn't like the thought of him living so far away. She'd always had Dare close by. And New York wasn't close.

She was alone. Really alone, she thought.

"Yes, sis, I can. I'm going to be making big bucks at my new job."

"Don't spend it before you've earned it," she warned him. She'd taken several money management classes after her mom had declared bankruptcy. She hated that feeling of having nothing. Of watching strangers come in and take everything they'd owned and sell it to pay their debts.

"I'm not. We both learned that lesson the hard way, didn't we?"

She took a deep breath and smiled to herself. She still thought of him as a rebellious boy even though he'd straightened up his act. "Yes, we did."

"I want you to plan a trip to the city to visit me this fall after I've settled in."

"I will."

Dare really had turned out okay. There had been

a time—well, three and a half years ago—when he was running wild and getting arrested, that she'd thought she was going to end up visiting him in jail.

"I've got something on Saturday. Do you still have your key?"

"Yes. What are you doing?"

For some reason she didn't want to mention Jeremy's name. "A yacht party."

"One of your wealthy clients again?"

"Um…not exactly."

"A date? Bella, who are you dating?" He was teasing her and she wanted to laugh with him but wasn't sure how he'd react.

"Jeremy."

"Mr. Harper?"

"Do we know any other Jeremy?" she asked a little sarcastically, because she was nervous.

"No. Are you sure you know what you're doing?"

No, she had absolutely no idea what she was doing. But at this point she wasn't going to back out. And after last night, she'd confirmed that she wanted a lot longer with Jeremy than a mere six months.

"Sis?"

"What?"

"Be careful."

"I've been taking care of us for a long time."

"Yes, you have, and now that I'm older it's time I stepped up and watched out for you."

"Jeremy's not a bad guy."

"I'm not saying that. But he is a smooth operator and you're not his normal type of woman."

"What's that supposed to mean?" she asked, not exactly sure where her brother was going with this.

"Just that you've been busy taking care of me and haven't done a lot of dating. He's a pretty experienced man, remember that."

"I will."

"I like him. He's done a lot of good things for us, but that doesn't mean he's family."

"I know that, Dare. I don't think he understands how to let anyone close."

"And you don't know how to keep anyone at arm's length once you get to know them."

"What time will you be here on Saturday?" she asked, forcibly changing the subject.

"Sometime after lunch. Don't forget what I said."

"I won't."

She couldn't believe Dare was giving her advice. But it warmed her heart in ways she'd never be able to articulate. For so long they'd struggled and now…now she felt that they were both going to make it. And she knew they both had one man to thank…Jeremy Harper.

Jeremy wasn't sure what to expect when he arrived at Bella's house. She'd sent him a text message earlier saying that she had a weekly dinner she couldn't cancel. Since they'd spent the last two nights making love, he figured they were due for more socializing.

And it would do him good to be around other people. His focus on her was becoming too narrow. He kept feeling like he was never going to get enough of her, which wasn't helping his obsession at all. No matter how often he made love to her, he still wanted her. No matter how many hours he held her in his arms, he still felt like six months wasn't going to be long enough.

She'd told him to bring a bottle of wine and to dress casually. He heard the sound of voices and music coming from the backyard when he arrived. He recognized Kenny Chesney's song, "No Shoes, No Shirt, No Problems."

He walked around back carrying the wine he'd picked up in France when he'd been there on business two weeks ago. As soon as he came around the corner he saw a group of ten or so people sitting around the pool.

He hesitated, remembering Kell and Lucinda's reactions toward Bella. His friends hadn't been exactly welcoming. How would her friends react to him? Did he want to know her outside of their agreement? He was a step away from turning around when she stepped out of the house onto the patio and saw him.

She smiled and it lit up her entire face. He wasn't

leaving, no matter how much he might want to. This was definitely crossing the line beyond what he'd outlined in their contract. But when she waved at him, he simply walked toward her.

Everyone stopped talking and he felt like he was on display, but that was nothing new. He ignored it as best he could.

"I'm so glad you made it," Bella said, wrapping one arm around his waist and leaning up to give him a kiss on his cheek. He turned his head and captured her lips.

Then stepped away. "Where do you want the wine?"

"Over there. Charlie is manning the bar. Let me put this down and I'll introduce you to everyone."

He handed the bottle of wine to Charlie, who shook his hand. She introduced him to the rest of her friends and he found them to be an inviting and eclectic group, ranging from business professionals such as an accountant and a stockbroker to a romance novelist and her animator husband to a couple who ran a tourist sailing operation.

Jeremy was comfortable with the group and found himself falling easily into the role of host by the time the evening ended and everyone left. But despite the fact that he was enjoying himself, he didn't like the fact that he and Bella were clearly a couple here.

Bella smiled and held his arm as the last couple walked to their car. "That was fun. Next week we're supposed to go to Charlie's house. Will you be available?"

"Ah, I don't know. I'll have to check my schedule," he said. He didn't want to isolate her from her life and her friends, but he was struggling to keep her in the box labeled *mistress,* and hanging out with her friends wasn't going to help.

"Okay. Just let me know if you can make it."

"It seems like an odd group."

"Kind of. We've been meeting for about two years now. It started out being just a few of us, hanging out at Chili's, but then we decided we could hear each other better at home."

"You're not much for going out, are you?" he asked, realizing that she always suggested something in.

"No."

"Why not?"

She shrugged and turned aside to gather up some empty wineglasses.

"Tell me, Bella."

"For a long time people used to stare at us. Dad's death was front-page news."

He couldn't imagine what that had been like. "I read some articles about him."

"He wasn't like they said in those articles. He really loved our family and he was such a dreamer. He just had no head for business. Eventually he lost all he'd inherited."

"What do you remember most about him?"

"He hated to be away from us. When he'd come home, the first thing he'd do was give Mom and me a big hug and then we'd all sit around the table and talk."

"Was he gone a lot?"

"Yes…more and more that last year."

"I'm sorry."

"It's been a long time."

"But it doesn't go away, does it?"

"No, it doesn't. And people don't stare anymore. I just got used to staying home."

He looked around her house. It was smaller than his, and not decorated with designer furniture, but it was warm and cozy. He liked the looks of the overstuffed sofa and could easily imagine sitting there with her.

"I think the Heat are playing tonight. You can probably catch the end of the game if you want to."

"Do you want to watch it?"

"After I'm done cleaning up. Dare and I try to watch all the games. He e-mails with his highlights and asks for mine."

"I'll help you," he said.

"You don't have to help. You're my guest."

He didn't say anything to that, just started gathering plates to clear the table. "Have you been to a Heat game?"

"Yes, a few. But my business is unpredictable, so I don't have season tickets."

"I have tickets with Kell and Daniel. The next home game, we'll go."

"I'd like that."

He gathered up the plates from the table on the patio and loaded them into the dishwasher. She didn't say anything as they worked and soon they had the place clean. They put on the game and finished the bottle of wine he'd brought. He wrapped one arm around her and held her close to him.

She fell asleep before the game ended and he shifted her into his arms and carried her down the hall to her bedroom. He didn't want to think about tonight or the feelings she evoked in him. So instead he took off her clothes, waking her up. He took off his own and joined her on the bed, making love to her.

She fell asleep in his arms and he stared at the wall for most of the night, wondering how his carefully crafted plan had gone so wrong.

The next few weeks flew by and Bella felt that each step she took toward making Jeremy view her as more than a temporary mistress was countered by an obstacle either from her past or his friends. She carefully avoided Lucinda at any events where she and Daniel were in attendance. And Jeremy's cousin Kell spent a lot of time talking to her about prenups and the advantages on both sides.

Which made her sad, because it was clear that he thought she was only after Jeremy for his money. If he knew how well Jeremy had protected himself against that, she suspected Kell would back off. And that made her more emotional, because she sensed that Jeremy cared enough about her to keep quiet about the mistress contract.

Yet he didn't care enough to say that they didn't need a contract between them any longer. Honestly, that was what she really wanted. She reminded herself of the contract to keep a certain distance between them. To protect herself from allowing her emotions to get the better of it. But it wasn't working.

She glanced around the elegant ballroom, no longer feeling out of place. Lucinda had cornered her once and Jeremy had rescued her. It was one of the most heroic things he'd done for her. But now she was alone again, in a beautiful Oscar de la Renta gown that Jeremy had given her.

"Somehow I didn't expect to find you hiding out on the terrace."

Kell walked over to her. He looked very elegant and sophisticated in his tuxedo. Handsome, but not as attractive to her as Jeremy was.

"Jeremy asked me to wait here." She was situated behind large potted trees that had been filled with twinkling lights. From her vantage point she had a view of the entire room, but no one else could really see her.

"Now it all makes sense," Kell said. "This is one of our favorite spots."

"Favorite spots for what?" she asked.

"Hiding out," he said with a wry grin. Kell could be charming when he tried.

She opened her small handbag and took out an article on prenups she'd clipped from the *Wall Street Journal* a few days ago. "I saw this and thought of you."

He took the article, glanced down at it. A brief smile touched his lips. "You're not what I expected."

She still hoped that her relationship would outlast the three months remaining on the mistress contract. And if it was going to have a chance to survive, she knew she needed to make more of an effort with Jeremy's friends. He didn't do a lot with them but she knew they were important to him—especially Kell.

"Well, I think all of us gold diggers are a little bit different."

He arched one eyebrow at her. "Jeremy doesn't see you that way."

"Then why do you?" she asked.

"Let's just say I've been there."

She finally saw more than a good-looking, successful man in Kell and it was more than a little disheartening to realize she'd been so shallow. "I'm sorry. I care about Jeremy."

"I've noticed that."

"Why did you think I was a gold digger?" she asked.

He shrugged.

She knew that she should stop this line of questioning, but she had to know. What had he heard about her? Please don't let it about the mistress contract, she thought. She'd absolutely die of embarrassment if all of his friends knew that they weren't in a real relationship.

"Tell me. It can't be anything I haven't heard before."

"It wasn't anything about you," he said. "Jeremy would kick my butt if he heard me talking to you about this."

"Well, he's not here," she said carefully. She was almost a hundred-percent positive that whatever Kell had heard he'd mentioned to Jeremy. So he already knew whatever damaging gossip Kell had told him about her. And it had to be gossip, because she hadn't done anything for money that she regretted.

"You'd keep secrets from him?" he asked. Immediately he lost his charm and she saw the barracuda look in his eyes. She'd heard he was a corporate attorney who never lost a case and she could see why. There was an utter ruthlessness in his gaze.

She sighed. "No, I wouldn't."

"Of course she wouldn't, Kell. What are you two talking about?"

She accepted the Bellini from Jeremy and

took a sip of the smooth peach-and-champagne drink. Jeremy wrapped an arm around her waist and pulled her firmly to his side.

"Um…"

"Gold diggers."

"Not that again," Jeremy said under his breath.

"I wanted to know what he'd heard about me to make him believe I'd be after your money."

"It was old news about your family," Jeremy said.

From Lucinda. She was the only one who would have known all the sordid details. The papers had reported that a business deal had gone wrong and her father, distraught from it, had killed himself. But the truth was a little darker. Her father had somehow gotten involved with the mob in a shady deal that she didn't know all the details of. She could only imagine how desperate he must have been. The day after her father's suicide, the DEA had arrived at the door to seize all of their property in connection with her father's business dealings.

Even the papers hadn't gotten all the details. But her dear friend Lucinda had, because Bella had told her.

Tears burned in the back of her eyes. She didn't think she could still feel betrayed from that long-ago friendship. But of course she could. At one time, Lucinda had been like a sister to her.

"Thanks for telling me. Does anyone else know?"

"Just Daniel, and he won't repeat it," Kell said. "Neither would I. It's not anything personal—"

"I know," she said, putting her hand on his arm to stop him. "You were just looking out for Jeremy."

"I can look out for myself," Jeremy said wryly.

Kell didn't say anything, just kept watching her with that stare of his. Finally she sighed and said, "I can't blame you there."

Kell nodded at her and then left. Jeremy drew her back against his solid frame, not saying another word. She let the strength in his body surround her and soothe the wounds left over from Lucinda.

Nine

Jeremy watched Kell walk away. He'd known that Kell didn't trust Bella, but he had no idea that the two of them had spent so much time chatting alone. He knew that Bella could handle herself, but he should have paid closer attention to Kell.

"Sorry if he was being a pain."

She took another sip of her drink and glanced sideways at him. Her hair slid along the sleeve of his tuxedo jacket and he wished they were home alone so he could feel her hair on his skin. She had the softest hair.

"He wasn't. It's sweet the way he tries to take care of you."

"*Sweet?* I don't think anyone would describe Kell that way."

They watched as Kell stopped to speak with his sister, Lorraine, and her group. Her women friends all moved subtly, trying to attract his attention. One woman tossed her hair, another touched his arm.

"He does have that barracuda smile—you know, all teeth—that makes you feel like you're about to be eaten, but underneath that…he watches out for you. Why is that?" she asked.

His relationship with Kell was deep and complex. He doubted that either of them would know how to explain it. But they'd been alone a lot with the same lazy nanny and they'd spent a lot of their time escaping her. "He's six months older than I am. And his mom used to make him promise to watch me."

Almost absently he remembered the long days of summer when their mothers would spend afternoons on the beach drinking fruity concoctions and gossiping while he and Kell ran free like wild boys.

"I remember you mentioning that his side of the family was goofy."

He grimaced at his old joke. He shouldn't have said that. Most people were unaware that Kell's mother was a recluse, prone to depression. For as much as he had happy memories of his childhood, it was also tinged with memories of Aunt Mary's "sadness," as his mother called it. They'd often rushed to her house so that his mom could cheer her up.

He suspected his mother used Aunt Mary's illness to ignore the fact that Jeremy's dad spent more time with his mistress than with them.

It didn't always work. His childhood memories were clouded with the secrets of his aunt Mary's depression and Kell coming to live with them for months at a time. He wouldn't share that with Bella. Some secrets weren't his to tell.

Just as Lucinda should have kept quiet about Bella's family. He'd said as much to Daniel.

"That's because my branch of the family isn't crazy," he said.

She looked steadily at him. "I think there's more to it than what you just said."

Jeremy shrugged, not really comfortable talking about Kell or his relationship with him. But there were some things he wanted to share with Bella. She quietly accepted everything about him. Even his flaws.

Whenever he was with her, he felt…complete. Which made no sense to him. He'd been happy with his life before they'd become lovers. Now he didn't like to think about what going back to life without Bella would be like.

"Tell me," she said. She wrapped one arm around his waist and glanced up at him expectantly.

"He saved my life one time."

"Literally?"

"Yes." A sailing accident that had surprised Jeremy. He'd always been at home on the water. But he'd been hit by the boom as they'd changed direction and been knocked overboard. One minute he'd been on the yacht, and the next thing he remembered was Kell's hand on his wrist, pulling him to the surface.

She cupped his jaw, bringing him back to the present. He glanced down into her honey-brown eyes. There was such a well of caring there that he felt like he'd taken a punch to the gut.

"I'm so glad he saved you," she said, raising up on tiptoe and kissing him. It was a soft and sweet kiss. The kind that made him glad to be alive and holding this woman in his arms.

"Me, too," he said. Never more so than this moment.

From the first time he'd met Bella, he'd sensed she was different from other women. At first he'd thought it was because she was no longer part of the moneyed set he ran in. But the more time he spent with her, the more he realized that she had an innate innocence that drew him to her.

He knew she wasn't innocent, that her life had been carved out of emotionally tough events. But she'd retained a certain sweetness that she showered on those around her. And he thanked God that he'd been fortunate enough to bind her to him when he had.

They only had three months left on their contract. His gut tightened at the thought of her leaving him. He needed to start planning for the next phase of their relationship, but he had no idea what that would entail.

"You ready to get out of here?"

"You did promise me a dance."

And he realized, as he deposited their drinks on a tray and led her to the dance floor, that he never wanted to break a promise he made to her.

She and Jeremy stayed for another half hour before they left the party. Twice Lucinda had made eye contact with her and indicated she wanted to talk. But Bella's evening had been perfect and she hadn't wanted to ruin it, so she'd ignored her onetime friend.

Jeremy put the top down on the convertible and drove them to the beach. It was a Saturday night and luckily she didn't have to work tomorrow. He held her hand loosely on his thigh.

Everything felt just about perfect, and that worried her. Because whenever she got too comfortable, something bad happened. And she was depending a lot on Jeremy—more than she wanted.

When she'd signed the contract with Jeremy she hadn't been too sure what she expected. Maybe a chance to reclaim something that had been stolen from her as a young woman. But she'd found so much more.

Did he feel the same? Sometimes she sensed he did, though it was true that he kept part of himself from her. He didn't speak of emotions or longevity—but neither did she.

Part of her was afraid to rock the boat. She was used to her life being constantly in flux, never taking anything for granted, but there was something very solid and reassuring about Jeremy and his presence in her life. And she wanted to believe that he was going to be a permanent addition to it.

She'd never been in love before, but she was falling for Jeremy.

"Deep thoughts?" he asked.

She shook her head, frantically trying to think of something to say that wouldn't leave her vulnerable to him. "Just enjoying the night and the wind in my hair."

He lifted her hand to his mouth, brushing a kiss along her knuckles. She liked that he was accepting of the limits she placed, that he didn't push her past them. Of course, it was different when they were in bed. There he would stand no barriers between them.

He'd pushed her further than she'd ever expected to go with any man. He made her give him everything she had, and never let her hide behind her own inhibitions.

"Then you're going to love what I have planned for us."

"What is it?" she asked. This was yet another instance that gave her hope. He was being very romantic and not at all businesslike about their relationship. After he'd offered her the town house, she expected him to focus on just the sexual side of things. Instead, he was always romancing her, planning evenings that fulfilled secret dreams she'd scarcely realized she had.

"A surprise," he said, slowing the car as they turned into the yacht club.

"I don't like surprises." But she did like going out on his yacht. She'd realized fairly early in her relationship with Jeremy that he was most at peace at sea. He liked to entertain on his boat, sleep on his boat, hold her on his boat. He never said much about it, but she could see a difference in him as soon as they motored out to sea.

"Or gifts," he said.

"I like your gifts. It's just that they're so extravagant." He'd overwhelmed her with the gifts he'd given her during the last three months. Some of the gifts were jewelry, which she half expected, but others were sentimental. Such as her mother's classic '69 Mustang, which had been sold to a collector to pay off some of their debts years ago. The collector had put it in storage and left it intact; their mom had been the last one to drive it.

She had so many memories of that car. Sometimes she just sat in the backseat and felt a little closer to her mom. Even Dare had been rendered speechless by the car.

He rubbed the diamond tennis bracelet that he'd given her earlier this evening. "I like you in diamonds."

"Is that why you insisted I wear the choker tonight?" she asked, lifting her free hand to touch the band of diamonds around her neck.

"Yes," he said, parking the car in his assigned spot. "Now, tell me what you were really thinking about."

She sighed. They were getting too close to each other. He saw parts of her that she normally hid away.

"You know me too well."

"Not yet. But soon I'll have all your secrets figured out."

"I'm not sure I like the sound of that."

"Why not? Don't you trust me?"

She did trust him on one level. She knew that, unlike Lucinda, Jeremy would never reveal anything personal about her to the world. But that didn't mean that he was planning to stick around for the long haul. And if he still left after three months, she was going to have to deal with the fact that her trust in him had been misplaced.

"Ah, that's a telling silence," he said. It was impossible to tell what he was thinking from his tone. He was a master at hiding his emotions. She wished she had that same ability. Everything she felt seemed to be broadcast like a twenty-four-hour news channel.

"It's not so much that I don't trust you."

"Then what is it?"

She took a deep breath. How could she say that every day they spent together made her wish time could stand still? "I'm afraid of what will happen when you're gone."

"Your secrets will always be safe with me."

"Yes, but I won't always be with you and I'm not sure I'm ready to think about that."

He pulled his hand free and got out of the car without another word. She watched him walk away from her. His stride was angry and she couldn't blame him, but they both had to acknowledge that there was a clock ticking as far as their relationship was concerned.

And so far he hadn't made any overt indication that he was interested in keeping her around any longer, despite their growing closeness. She wasn't going to pretend that her life was one thing when she knew it was something else.

Jeremy heard her footsteps behind him and turned to make sure her heels didn't get caught in the tiny cracks between the boards on the dock. He shouldn't have left her alone in the car. The flash of anger had surprised him.

Even as a child he'd always been even-keeled.

But with Bella so many reactions were unexpected. Even their lovemaking, though satisfying, always made him yearn for her again.

"Jeremy…"

There was a sadness in her voice that he couldn't stand hearing. He knew that she'd only given him the truth he'd asked her for. He had the same fears. Sharing so much of himself with her was bound to leave them both hurting when the relationship ended.

"No more talking tonight."

"I didn't mean to ruin the evening."

He was being an ass and he knew it. "You didn't. I'm just not ready to talk about our relationship being over."

"Me neither," she said softly.

He walked back to her. "Wait here."

He went back to his car and grabbed their overnight bags from the trunk, then locked it. Bella stood on the dock looking out to sea. She was good at keeping her true feelings and thoughts to herself. Too good.

The only time he felt her guard drop was when he made love to her.

He didn't say anything, just walked with her to his slip and lifted her aboard his boat. He untied the lines that held the boat in place and then climbed aboard. She took their bags to the stateroom as he prepared to leave the marina.

"Do you want a drink?" she called from below deck.

"No," he said. What he wanted he doubted he could ever have. He wanted everything she had to give. He wanted it from the safety of the relationship they had.

He knew that wasn't fair. But he'd designed this relationship so he'd have all the advantages. He was only now realizing he'd forgotten a few things.

"Are you going to stay mad at me all night?" she asked from right behind him. Her hair blew around her face and shoulders in the light breeze. The skirt of her dress swirled around her legs.

"I don't know," he said honestly, because watching her standing there brought home to him how far out of reach she really was. He could hold her and make love to her, but it was temporary.

"I'd rather go home than spend the night with you acting like this."

Screw that. He wasn't going to waste one night of the three months they had left together. He wanted her by his side for all of them. "I don't want you to go home."

She smiled at him, that fey little grin that he never could read, and took a few steps closer to him. "I don't want you to be sulky."

"I sound like an eight-year-old when you put it that way."

"Well…" She stopped in front of him, placing her hands around his neck. She rested her body against his and spoke softly against his skin. He felt each word the instant she said it. "You don't resemble an eight-year-old."

He wrapped his arms around her, lowering his head to the top of hers and just breathing her in. He rested his hands at the small of her back, nestling them together until not an inch of space separated them.

"I'm acting like one?" he asked, brushing his lips along the column of her neck. He traced the line of the choker with his tongue. God, she was beautiful. If she ever had an inkling of how he felt toward her…fear gripped him. He didn't want to let her go. Not tonight. Not in three months. Not ever.

"I guess I was being pretty childish, too, keeping secrets," she said, tipping her head back so that their eyes met.

But she hadn't been. He knew how hard it was for her to let anyone close to her, despite the fact that she had a large circle of friends. There were very few people that she actually let know the real woman.

And he wanted to be one of those few.

She trailed her fingers over his jaw, then down his chest. She laid her head there, right over his heart. He tightened his arms around her. Held her as close as he could without saying a word.

He didn't want to talk anymore. Why had he started a conversation that went where he didn't want it to go?

"In the car, I was thinking about this."

"Making love?" he asked, leaning down to kiss her. Sex was on his mind most of the time when they were together. Hell, even when they were apart he was thinking about how it felt to have her in his arms. The soft sounds she made when he thrust into her body and how she wrapped herself around him when they finished.

He lifted his head, brushing his lips along the curve of her cheek down to her neck. He suckled at the smooth, soft skin, wanting to leave his mark there. Wanting in some way to brand her as his so that everyone she met knew she was taken.

Taken by him. His, he thought. Really his, and not just for a few months.

She smiled up at him. "In a way."

She took a step away from him, wrapping her arms around her waist and staring out at sea. He hated how she could isolate herself from him in one movement. He stepped up behind her, pulling her back against him.

"What way?"

"I was thinking about how quickly the last three months have gone by, and wishing that the next three months never had to end."

Jeremy smiled at her, but words stuck in his throat. Could he risk being that honest and open about wanting her?

Ten

Jeremy woke the next morning, scrubbing a hand over his face and staring at the woman lying curled so close to him. Her confession last night had set a fire in him he hadn't been able to put out. Something had started winding its way unexpectedly into his life.

She'd organized a couple of parties for him, acting as his hostess. He knew she did some business at the parties, drumming up new clientele, but mainly she acted the way his mother always had at his father's business functions. And that unnerved him.

He wasn't ready for their relationship to end, yet at the same time those three months couldn't come fast enough. He felt like this relationship was unraveling, and he had no idea how to get it back on the track he'd planned.

He pushed himself out of bed—because he wanted to linger.

"Jeremy?"

"Right here," he said, sinking back down next to her. If he wasn't careful they'd spend the rest of the weekend together on the boat, in bed.

"Is it morning already?" she asked, leaning over to kiss his chest. He shifted so that he lay next to her, his morning hard-on pressing against her hip. He shouldn't want her again so soon. He'd had her three times last night.

"Yes." He took her mouth with his, letting his hands wander over her body.

Her stomach growled and he laughed. "Hungry?"

She buried her red face against his chest. "Yes. I didn't eat at the party last night."

"Maybe that's because you kept trying to avoid Lucinda." He pulled the sheet back from the bed and reached for one of the silk bindings he'd used to tie her to the bed the night before, trailing it over her torso and breasts.

She shivered with awareness and her nipples tightened. He arranged the silk binding over her breasts. "I wish you hadn't noticed that."

He leaned down to lick each nipple. Then he blew gently on the tips. She raked her nails down his back.

"Are you listening to me?" she asked.

"To your body," he said.

He knelt between her thighs and looked down at her. "Open yourself for me," he said.

Her legs moved but he took her hands in his, brought them to her mound.

"Lift your hips, honey."

He leaned down, blowing lightly on her. She lifted her hips toward his mouth.

He drew her flesh into his mouth, sucking carefully on her. He pushed his finger into her body and lifted his head to look up at her.

Her eyes were closed, her head tipped back. Her shoulders arched, throwing her breasts forward with their hard tips, begging for more attention. Her entire body was a creamy delight.

He lowered his head again, hungry for more of her, using his teeth, tongue and fingers to bring her to the brink of climax, but held her there, wanting to draw out the moment of completion until she was begging him for it.

"Jeremy, please."

He slid deep into her. She arched her back, reaching up to entwine her arms around his shoulders. He thrust harder and felt every nerve in his body tensing. Reaching between their bodies, he touched her between her legs until he felt her body tighten around him.

He came in a rush, continuing to thrust into her

until his body was drained. He then collapsed on top of her, laying his head between her breasts.

He turned his face away from her, afraid to admit that something had changed between them overnight, but knowing that he wasn't going to let her go. He was going to find a way to keep her at his side.

The next few months flew by. Jeremy became a part of her life in a way she hadn't predicted. After their intense night together, neither of them had mentioned the contract or the fact that they didn't want to end their relationship after six months.

But that didn't bother her. Jeremy was everything she'd always wanted in a man and more. She didn't know when her dreams for the future had been reborn. But she found herself thinking of long-term plans instead of dwelling on what had been taken from her.

This afternoon was a perfect example. It was Jeremy's birthday and she'd planned a surprise party for him. Kell, despite his initial misgivings about her, had warmed considerably in the last few weeks and had helped her with the guest list. The party was going to be at her home.

She'd never have been able to do this with his circle of friends even a month ago. But it had felt right for this event. Jeremy seemed to like her house, and catering a party for him at his place felt too presumptuous. She really wanted this to be a special day.

He was turning thirty-five, a milestone that he'd mentioned to her one time and then let drop. His parents were flying home early from Europe to come to the party. They had been surprised when she'd called. Apparently Jeremy hadn't mentioned her to them.

She was a little nervous about that. She'd never met his parents, and she knew she and Jeremy weren't really dating.

"This place looks great."

She glanced at Dare. She was always a little startled to see him looking like a man. For so long he'd been that half-wild boy with eyes that broke her heart. Now she saw wisdom and maturity in him. "Yes, it does. Did you get those extra bags of ice?"

"Yes. And I made another run to the liquor store, so the bar is overstocked. Quit worrying, sis. You've thrown thousands of parties." He put his arm around her shoulder and they stood together in the living room of her home.

"But this one is different," she said. She'd never really hid anything from Dare. Not this Dare any-way. The teenage rebel he'd been hadn't been inter-ested in anyone except himself.

Dare looked at her like she was crazy. "You really like Mr. Harper?"

"Yes, I do."

He hugged her close and then went over to the mantel to adjust a framed picture of the two of them from last summer. "I'm glad, Bella. I'm really glad."

"Why?" she asked. It wasn't like Dare to adjust anything.

"It makes it easier to take that job in New York."

She had an inkling of where Dare was going with this conversation. "Why would it?"

"Because you won't be alone."

She shook her head at him. "I'm never alone. I have a very busy life."

"Yes, you do. But you didn't have anyone to take care of while I was gone, and now you do."

His words gave her pause. Was that the main attraction she felt toward Jeremy? The fact that he let her take care of him, and she'd been searching for a long time for someone who would? "He's good to me, too."

"Glad to hear it."

The doorbell rang and soon the party guests started arriving. Daniel and Lucinda arrived in the midst of her friends from her weekly dinner. She didn't have to greet them individually, but Bella was tired of avoiding her childhood friend. Tired of running from the lies and the hateful things they'd both said.

Lucinda was standing in a mixed group of some

of her friends and Jeremy's business partners. Bella started over toward the crowd. Lucinda glanced up at her and excused herself from the others to meet her halfway.

"Bella, thank you for inviting me."

"You're welcome. I…well, I'm sure you noticed I've been avoiding you."

Lucinda laughed, and it was a kind sound. It reminded Bella of their childhood and how much fun they'd once had together.

"Yes, I have. I think I had something to do with that. I'm sorry for telling Kell and Daniel the details about your dad."

"I wish you hadn't," she said. But Bella was surprised that she didn't feel that knot in the bottom of her stomach that she always had when she thought of someone finding out about her past.

"Well, I did. It was in bad taste and I have no excuse except that I was so shocked to see you. Last time I saw you, you and your mother were cleaning my house."

There was something in Lucinda's voice that Bella had never noticed before. It sounded almost like anger. "Why does that bother you?"

She shrugged. "I hate what your dad did. He stole my best friend from me. And I'm still mad at myself for not being a better friend to you."

"I don't think I could have handled it then. I felt so destroyed and unsure of myself."

"I'm sorry. I'm really sorry for how I acted back then and for bringing it up again."

Bella forgave her friend, knowing that a portion of the blame sat on her own shoulders. "Don't worry about mentioning it to Kell. He researched me on the Internet anyway."

Lucinda started laughing and Bella noticed Daniel glancing over at them. "He did the same thing when Daniel and I started dating."

"I guess we can't fault him for caring about the men we like."

Lucinda took her hand and drew her into a corner away from everyone else. "I'm glad you're with Jeremy, but…"

"What?" she asked, almost afraid to hear what Lucinda might say.

"Be careful with your heart, Bella. Jeremy always moves on."

"I know that. But I think maybe I'm changing his way of thinking."

"I hope so. I'm looking forward to having my old friend back in my life. Even if things don't work out with Jeremy," Lucinda said.

Bella was, too. She'd renewed many acquaintances from her childhood these past few months and it had felt right to be back in that circle. Some of the people she had nothing in common with, but others were turning into good friends. It had made her realize how much she'd missed the social part of her old life.

The door opened before she could respond and
Jeremy walked in. She saw the surprise on his face
as everyone broke out into a chorus of the birthday
song. He didn't greet his parents or his friends first
but made a beeline to her side, pulling her into his
arms and kissing her.

Everyone broke into applause and Bella felt like
she'd found something that she'd spent a lifetime
searching for. And she was certain that Jeremy
realized it, too.

The party lasted until after midnight. Kell's and
Jeremy's mothers were the last to leave. His dad had
left early for a meeting, which Jeremy knew meant
he was going to see his mistress. His mom really
liked Bella and had taken him aside three separate
times to tell him so. Finally the last guest left and
he and Bella were alone.

"Thank you," he said when they'd finished
cleaning up and were sharing a glass of wine on her
patio. He pulled her down on the glider next to him,
keeping her tucked close to his side.

"Were you surprised?"

"Yes," he said.

"Good. I know how much you like surprises."

"I like surprising you," he said quietly.

"I think I know why. It was so much fun planning
this and waiting to see how you would react to it."

He didn't say anything else, realizing he didn't

want to talk. He tipped her head back against his shoulder and leaned down to kiss her. She tasted of the sweet wine they were drinking and of something unique to her. He loved that taste. Couldn't ever get enough of it. He shifted around until he could place the wineglass on the floor and then maneuvered her sideways on his lap so he could caress her while they were kissing.

He'd never let anyone be a part of his life the way he had with Bella. Tonight had brought that home in many ways. His mother liked her. Even Kell, who was leery of all women and treated most of them with disdain, was starting to soften toward her, though he still seemed wary of Jeremy getting suckered in.

He lifted his head, rubbing his thumb over her lower lip. It was moist and swollen from his kisses. "What were you and Lucinda talking about?"

She shrugged, laying her head on his shoulder. Her fingers traced a random pattern on his arm. "Nothing really. Just making peace."

"Everything cool between you two now?" he asked. His instinct had been to go over and pull Bella away from Lucinda.

"Yes. This is going to sound kind of silly, but I think a lot of the blame was mine. I felt so…naked when it happened that I didn't really give Lucinda or my other friends a chance to reject me. I just shut down. And then my mother ended up working for some of them, which was very awkward."

He held her closer, rubbing his hand up and down her back. He loved how fragile she felt in his arms. It made him feel that he could protect her. And he wanted to do that, he realized, not just physically but also emotionally. He didn't want anyone to snub her or make her feel less than worthy.

"I can understand that. What changed now?"

"You changed me," she said softly. Her fingers moved from his arm to the buttons of his shirt. She toyed with the open button at his collar and then opened a second one, slipping her hand under the fabric to caress his chest.

He arched one eyebrow at her. "How did I do that?"

He was trying to keep his mind on the conversation, but his blood seemed to be flowing heavier in his veins.

"I think it was the way you accepted me and Dare. The way you were never condescending to us." She circled his nipple with her fingertip, scratching her nail around it. He groaned deep in his throat.

"Money doesn't mean everything," he said, but a part of him knew that wasn't what he really believed. Their entire relationship was based on finances. He'd given her his contacts and entrée back into the world she wanted to belong to.

She shifted on his lap.

"It does to some people," she said.

He didn't want to talk any longer. He wanted her naked, he wanted to open the birthday present he'd been planning on savoring all day long.

He tugged at the hem of her camisole top, but she caught his wrists in her hands. "Not yet."

She hopped off his lap. When he moved to stand she pushed him back to the glider.

"Wait here. I have a present for you."

"You don't need to give me anything else. I'll be happy to undress you and count that as the best present I've received."

She smiled at him with her heart in her eyes and he had trouble swallowing. "You can do that after you open my other gift."

She left him alone on the porch while she went inside. A few minutes later he heard the sound of a Jimmy Buffett ballad—"Stars Fell on Alabama"— and then she reappeared. She held a small box in her hands.

He took it, recognizing the blue box with the white ribbon. He knew she was on a budget and worried that she might have given him something too extravagant.

"Open it," she said.

He did, and saw a pair of silver fish cuff links. Masculine, understated. He looked up at her. Perfect.

"I know how you love the sea and being out on your boat," she said.

He realized then that he'd fallen for her. And he didn't like it. Didn't like the power she had over him. The intense vulnerability that feeling brought with it.

He suddenly felt unworthy of her. Everything he had in his life had been given to him due to the lucky circumstances of his birth. Bella had lost everything, then carved a life and a place for herself in the world through sheer determination.

If he'd learned anything tonight, it was that he couldn't let her go. And watching his parents had strengthened his resolve to never ruin his relationship with Bella by marrying her.

Eleven

Bella's day wasn't going according to plan. Tomorrow was the official last day on her contract with Jeremy and she wanted to put the finishing touches on the private event she'd been working on for the two of them.

But instead of focusing on Jeremy, she had to turn her attention to her business. And for the first time, she really resented it.

Her business had always been the center of her life, the thing she used to keep herself on track and balanced.

But now Jeremy filled that need.

They'd had brunch with his mother and aunt

Mary on Sunday, merging their lives even more closely together, and she'd found that she liked that. She'd arrived at work today feeling hopeful.

Now Shelley had been in a minor fender bender and was late for work. One of Shelley's clients had shown up early, while the client Bella was supposed to be meeting with was late.

She smiled at Huntley Donovan of the Art Council Guild as she showed her to the conference room and left to get her something to drink.

Randall, one of her event managers, walked in the door. Bella pounced on him. "Thank God you're here. Shelley was in an accident. She's fine, but she was supposed to be doing a precontract bid for the Art Guild this morning."

"I know. That's why I'm here. She called me before she called her insurance agent."

Randall was one of her best employees. He'd joined her staff only three months earlier and had proven himself invaluable. He was a tall African-American man with an easy smile and affable charm as well as a sense of calmness that put even the most temperamental clients at ease.

"I think it's time I gave her a raise," Bella said with a smile.

"Where is Ms. Donovan?"

"In the conference room. She'd like a cup of Earl Grey tea, and the file is somewhere on Shelley's desk," she said, gesturing toward the messy stack of paper.

Randall walked over to the desk and started going through the piles there. "I've got it."

"Thanks, Randall. I'm expecting a new client any minute."

Her phone was ringing when she entered her office and she was almost afraid to answer it and have one more thing go wrong.

"Good morning, this is Isabella."

"Hey, honey. Got a few minutes?" Her pulse sped up just at the sound of his voice. Oh, man, she had it bad for him. She propped her hip on the edge of her desk so she could keep an eye on the front door for her client.

"Yes. My client is running a few minutes late," she said, trying to reach her coffee cup while they were talking. It was too far away. With anyone else she'd put the phone down and grab her coffee but she didn't want to miss anything that Jeremy said.

"I want you to clear your calendar for tonight and tomorrow."

That arrogance of his was going to get him in trouble someday, but not today. She did like the way he was so confident in everything he said and did with her.

"I'll try," she said, adding that task to the growing to-do list in her head. Frankly, after this morning, she wanted to take a few weeks off and just hide away.

"Don't try. I need you to do it."

"Is this more than mere bossiness?" she asked.

There was a tone in his voice that she'd never heard before. Something she couldn't place.

"Yes."

"What's up?" she asked. "Is everything okay with your family?"

"Yes. I have something special planned for tonight and I think we're going to want to spend the day together tomorrow."

"What do you have planned?" she asked. She should have realized that he'd be as aware as she was that they were nearing the end of their contracted time together.

"Something special that's just for you," he said. There was an odd huskiness to his voice.

"Another surprise? I think I'm beginning to like them." And she was. Before Jeremy, she'd liked to know every detail of her day and any variation would immediately send her into crisis mode. But she'd learned that not every upheaval was a bad one. Not every surprise was to be dreaded. In fact, most of the ones he'd sprung on her were to be embraced.

"You'll like this one."

"Promise?" she asked, knowing that was just her knee-jerk reaction. Her conditioned response to anything unexpected.

"Guarantee it, honey."

"I'm going to hold you to that."

"You do that. I'll pick you up around six tonight."

"Where are we going?"

"Out on my yacht."

They hadn't been out on his yacht since the night they'd had that argument and he'd said that he didn't want their time together to end. She told herself not to get her hopes up, not to expect more than he'd promised her. But she felt a tinge of excitement.

"What are we going to be doing?"

"Having dinner and discussing the future."

A surge of joy went through her and she could hardly speak as he said goodbye. She hung up the phone, her mind alive with the possibilities of what the future held for her and Jeremy.

Jeremy checked every inch of the yacht before leaving to pick up Bella. Andy had prepared Bella's favorite meal and left him explicit instructions for heating it up. He'd had the housekeeping staff ensure that the dining room was set to Jeremy's exact instructions.

The bed was made up with the new Egyptian cotton sheets he'd ordered that would just match Bella's honey-brown eyes.

He had her favorite white wine chilling in the fridge, her favorite songs queued up on his Bose stereo. In fact, everything was as perfect as he could make it. He adjusted one of the blooms in the vase of purple tulips before he climbed the stairs two at a time and vaulted from the boat to the dock. He could probably run all the way to her house and not get rid of the excess energy that was dogging him tonight.

Seldom was he nervous about anything, but he was about tonight. He had played the scenario in his head a million times during the last few days. He'd gone over every possible answer she could give him and had a contingency plan worked out for each one.

He forced himself to stand still and calm the nervous energy. This was the same as closing a big deal at the office. Except a big deal never affected him this way. He had a lot invested in the outcome of this evening. He'd done everything he could to ensure he got the outcome he wanted.

Then why the hell was he so nervous?

He shook his head at his own stupidity and walked to his car. Once he had Bella on his boat out at sea, everything would fall into place.

He knew she wanted to be with him. She'd said as much the last time they were here. And he knew she needed some kind of stability, so his plan was absolutely perfect.

He drove to her home and parked out front, waiting for a few minutes before getting out. He refused to give in to the urge to get to her sooner. He had to manage his emotional response to her and so far, tonight, he was doing a piss-poor job of it.

He rang the bell instead of letting himself in with

the key she'd given him. He liked her quiet neighborhood more than he'd expected to. One of her neighbors waved at him as she backed out of her driveway. It seemed like a good sign. A sign that things were meant to be between him and Bella.

The door opened with a rush of cold air. He glanced at Bella, his words dying on his lips. She was breathtaking in her simple silk sundress. The halter top dipped down in the front between her breasts.

"Aren't you going to say anything?" she asked, looking like a femme fatale.

"Uh-huh," he said, but he couldn't get his brain to work. Her hair was pulled up on top of her head and a few tendrils fell around her face.

She had on some kind of dewy lip gloss that made him ache to lick her lips. To taste them. He skimmed his gaze higher and saw the amusement in her eyes. He knew he was a goner.

He stepped forward, put his hand on the back of her head and tilted her head up to his. He leaned down and licked at her lips. They tasted sweet but when he thrust his tongue into her mouth, he realized he liked the way she tasted more. Craved her on his tongue.

His body stirred. He thrust her away from him, turning his back to her before he did something crazy like make love to her on the front-hall table.

"Jeremy?"

"Bella…dammit, woman, I have plans for this evening."

"Ah, sorry?"

He shook his head and cleared his throat and then turned around again. "Good evening. You look gorgeous tonight."

"Thanks. You look very nice as well," she said. There was a lightness about her tonight that he'd never seen before and as soon as he recognized it, he was at ease. She wasn't on her guard around him.

"I hope this is okay," she said.

"I have no idea what you're talking about," he said.

"My clothes. You said it was going to be a special evening, so I thought I'd dress up."

"I like you dressed up," he said. The only thing he liked more was her naked. But her clothing tonight was perfect for what he had in mind. He was glad she'd picked up on the vibe he'd sent her. Glad to see that she, too, was ready for a special night.

When he'd asked her to be his mistress he had no idea how important she'd become to his life.

"I thought you would. Do we have time for a drink before we leave?" she asked.

"We're going out on the boat so we have all the time we'd like."

"So, do you want a drink?" she asked.

"I want this evening to be perfect for you, Bella."

"I think it will be," she said, pushing the door all the way open. "Come on in."

He followed her into her home and saw she'd taken the time to prepare for this drink. She had all the ingredients for his favorite cocktail on her bar. She mixed him a Grey Goose martini and poured it neatly into a glass, then garnished it with a cocktail onion instead of an olive. Then she poured herself one as well.

"To the future," she said with a faint smile.

"The future," he said, tapping their glasses together.

He watched her take a sip of the cool drink and tip her head to the side to watch him. He knew there was no such thing as a sure thing, but he felt very sure of Bella.

Very sure that he'd made the right decision as far as tonight went.

The sun was setting as they left the marina behind. Bella relaxed against the padded bench at the back of the yacht while Jeremy piloted the boat. Her entire body was buzzing from the way he'd kissed her when he'd shown up at her door.

They'd talked on the way to the yacht club, but not about anything important. Just the day's events. And it was nice to be able to share that with someone. She'd never really had that before Jeremy. Dare asked how she was, but he didn't really listen unless something was wrong that she needed him to attend to.

It was so different with Jeremy. She had given up cautioning herself about expecting too much from him. She was filled with the love she felt for him. It made her nerves tingle.

She wanted him. Needed him. Needed to be by his side.

Kicking off her high-heeled sandals, she walked across the deck to him. The breeze tugged at her hair and a few more strands escaped her clip. She felt them curling over her bare shoulders. Finally she reached him and she wrapped her arms around his back, resting her head between his shoulder blades.

He turned in her arms, lowering his head to hers. She lifted her face, meeting him halfway. The kiss was everything she wanted, yet left her wanting more.

She framed his face with her hands as he moved his mouth over hers, skimming his tongue along the seam of her lips and then pushing inside. He tasted wild and untamed, like the sea surrounding them. He groaned and angled his head for a deeper penetration of her mouth.

He pulled her body more tightly against his. She felt the weight of her breasts against his chest and his big hands wrapped around her waist. She stroked his face and neck with her hands. He lifted her more fully into him.

His kiss left room for nothing but thoughts of

Jeremy. His hands slid down her back, pulling her closer. He nibbled on her mouth and she felt like she was completely at his mercy.

Exactly where she wanted to be. She dug her nails into his shoulders as she leaned up, brushing against his chest.

She glanced down and saw her nipples pressing against the thin bodice of her dress. Jeremy skimmed his thumbs over her breasts before he slid his hands beneath the fabric.

"Baby, you are playing hell with my plans."

"Should I go sit back down?"

"Oh, hell, no," he said, caressing her back and spine.

She had a feeling she was going to remember this night for the rest of her life.

Jeremy dropped anchor when they were in the middle of nowhere. They were out of shipping lanes and away from other boats. The moon had risen and the sky stretched forever, enveloping them both in the night.

His body still pulsed from making love to Bella, and he wanted her again. He wanted to take her down to his bed and have her again and again until she forgot every name except his.

But first he wanted to ask her to stay with him.

She'd gone down to the master stateroom a few minutes earlier to touch up her makeup. He hoped she reapplied that slick lip gloss. He was looking forward to kissing it off again.

He went into the galley and readied their meal, then took out the presents he'd purchased for her, setting them in the different areas where he needed them.

He took a deep breath. He was a little nervous about her reaction no matter how well he thought he'd planned for it. He wanted her in his life for a long time. This was what he needed. What they both needed.

He opened the bottle of wine and left it to breathe and then checked the drawer where he'd left the paperwork he'd need later if she agreed to his proposition.

"What's that?"

He shut the drawer and turned to look at her. She'd taken her hair down and it hung in waves over her shoulders. She had reapplied her lip gloss and her dress was refastened. In the center of the V-neck he noticed a mark he'd left on her.

He took a box off the counter. "This is for you."

She glanced again at the drawer but took the gift and let the other matter drop. He poured her a glass of wine, then leaned one hip against the counter and just watched her.

"You're making me nervous."

He shrugged, taking a sip of his wine. "I like looking at you."

"I like having you look at me," she said, a hint of shyness in her voice.

"How can you be shy with me after all we've done together?" he asked, coming over to stand next to her.

"I don't know. It's different when we're together. I forget about everything else."

"Good. Now open your present so we can have dinner."

She opened it. He heard the gasp of surprise in her voice and he was pleased. He took the diamond and sapphire pendant necklace from the box.

"Hold your hair up," he said.

She lifted her hair and he fastened the necklace. Keeping his hands on her neck, he leaned down and kissed her. He wanted to find a way to tell her everything that was inside him even though he knew he couldn't.

He lifted his head slowly and took her arm, escorting her to the dining area. He picked up the gift-wrapped box by her seat.

"Open this one while I'm getting our dinner."

"Jeremy, you spoil me."

"It's about time someone did," he said. He ached for her past and her childhood. The way it had been torn away from her. He wanted to make sure that she had a safe cocoon for the rest of her life. That she never again had to face financial insecurity or worry about being left alone.

That's why his plan would work for both of them. It was a safe way for them to be together and not have to worry about the unexpected things that life sometimes threw at them.

He dished up their food and brought the plates over to the table. She'd opened the second present, a bracelet that matched the necklace he'd just given her.

She fastened it around her wrist and glanced up at him. There was so much hope in her eyes that it was almost painful to glimpse it.

He knew he had to do this right. He couldn't screw this up for her. Her trust was a precious gift and he didn't want to abuse it.

"Thank you for the bracelet, Jeremy. I wish I had something to give you."

"You already did."

"Sex?"

"No, Bella. So much more than that. Ralph Waldo Emerson once said that 'the only true gift is a portion of yourself.' You've given me a gift that I can never reciprocate. Bringing me into the circle of your friends. Welcoming me into your life and into your bed."

Tears glittered in her eyes and he thought, yes, this was right. For once he was doing what he needed to do. He wasn't betting on charm to get him through, but speaking straight from his gut.

"That is the sweetest thing anyone has ever said to me."

"It's only the truth."

The conversation ranged over many topics as they ate, and soon Jeremy was clearing the dishes away. He brought out a fruit-and-cheese tray with a small box nestled on it.

He handed her the box after he seated himself.

"I have something I want to ask you, Bella. But first please open this last present."

Bella held her breath as she opened the box. She could hardly concentrate on the gift, wanting instead to know what he was going to ask her. Would it be to marry him?

After brunch last Sunday with his family, she suspected he had something permanent in mind for the two of them. And she wanted that. She'd already made up her mind to ask him to move in with her after their contract was up.

"Bella, open the box," he said.

She did and found a pair of teardrop earrings that matched the necklace and bracelet he'd already given her. Jeremy was at his most romantic tonight. And she couldn't help falling more deeply in love with him.

He was everything she'd ever wanted in a man. Caring, attentive, supportive and the kind of lover every woman dreamed of having. She glanced up to find him watching her. She removed the silver hoop earrings she had on and put on the ones that matched her necklace and bracelet.

Was a matching ring soon to follow?

"Thank you."

"You're welcome, honey."

She didn't want to rush him but he didn't say anything else, and finally she couldn't stand it any longer. "You said you had a question."

"I do. I'm not sure how to ask it."

"Whatever it is, just ask."

He leaned forward. "Do you remember when we met?"

How could she forget? Her secret crush noticing her at a party where she was working, taking the time to talk to her and flirt with her and then offering her something that could never be repaid. "Yes."

"From that moment, you've been like an obsession for me. The last three and a half years I've been consumed with thoughts of you."

"Oh, Jeremy," she said, unable to keep her emotions from her voice. It was like he had glimpsed inside her heart and knew what she felt for him. "Me, too."

He smiled at her then. It was a sweet expression and not one she'd ever seen before on his fierce face.

"Obsessions aren't healthy things because they are all or nothing. Our relationship was nothing at first, just a piece of paper that was kept in a file. But then it became…well, I think you'll agree it became more than either of us ever anticipated."

She'd never been a man's obsession before and

was flattered he'd thought about her so much. It made her feel a lot less vulnerable. It reminded her that Jeremy was invested in this relationship, too.

"I'd definitely agree to that," she said. She'd never expected to fall so completely in love with Jeremy. In the beginning she might have even intended to use him to get back into the crowd that had once been her own, but that had quickly faded. She wanted *him*, and it didn't matter if he was part of her old social set or not.

"I was hoping that you'd feel this way, Jeremy. For the last few weeks I've been dreading this day. Knowing that it would mean an end to our contracted time together."

He reached across the space between them and took her hands in his. She liked the way his big hands enfolded hers.

"Me, too. I've been thinking our situation over. Trying to come up with a new relationship that would suit us both."

"Anything where we can be together will work with me. I don't think I can take living apart now. You really have become so much a part of my life."

"I hoped you would say that."

He tugged her to her feet, drawing her to him. He led her upstairs. He hit a button and low-level lighting illuminated the deck. She saw that there were a bunch of pillows on the bench where they'd made love earlier.

"What are we doing up here?"

"I wanted to hold you in my arms," he said. He pushed a button and music came from the speakers. Not pop music, but Ella Fitzgerald, her evocative voice singing about love and heartbreak in a way that made Bella believe that the woman had experienced them. She rested her head on Jeremy's shoulder as he danced them around the deck.

In this moment everything felt perfect. The anticipation of his question hung between them, sweetening the moment. For the last few months she'd been so aware of the contract and the expiration date of their relationship, and now she felt something so magical she could scarcely comprehend that this moment was here.

When the song ended he pushed a button and the music stopped. He led her toward the railing of the boat and turned her in his arms so they both faced the distant horizon. He wrapped his arms around her and pulled her back into the cradle of his body. He surrounded her completely.

She took it all in—the moonlight on the water, the softly blowing salt-scented breeze. The rocking motion of the boat and the heat of the man standing behind her.

He took a deep breath. "This is so much harder than I thought it would be."

Suddenly she was afraid. But she took a deep breath and turned in his arms. "Whatever it is,

Jeremy, if it involves the two of us staying together, then my answer is going to be yes."

He crushed her to him in a hug that made her feel like he'd never let her go. "I'm so glad to hear that. I've had a new contract drawn up and it is more generous than our last agreement."

She pulled back to look at him. "What kind of contract? I thought we'd moved beyond needing some legal paperwork between us."

"Honey, I want to make sure that you're protected. That you have everything you've ever wanted."

That sounded so nice that she cautioned herself from letting her temper get the better of her. Maybe it was some kind of prenuptial agreement. The kind that Kell had been talking about these last few months. "Do you have the contract with you?"

"Yes, I do."

"Let me see it."

Bella heard Jeremy talking and knew he was saying something important, but for the life of her she couldn't understand what the heck it was. She followed him down the gangplank back to the dining room where the remains of their dessert still sat on the table.

The last five minutes had been so bizarre she was sure she'd entered some kind of twilight zone. He seemed normal, but maybe there'd been some kind of break in the time-space continuum that had put her in an alternate universe where the man she loved would offer her a contract to stay with him.

"Here's the contract," he said, handing her a folder with a thick sheaf of papers inside.

She took the folder from him and drifted over to the table. Sitting down, she opened it up and saw the words at the top that stopped her. This was the same shell agreement as the original mistress contract she'd signed three years ago.

Anger began a slow churning deep inside her and she used that anger to help stem the tears that wanted to flow. How could he have completely missed the point?

"I think you'll agree that the new contract is more generous than the first one was. I've recently started doing business with an international firm that I think will net you a lot of new contacts. I've offered that as well as an exclusive arrangement with my company to be our only party planner."

"Please don't say anything else," she said, forcing the words out in a reasonable tone. But inside she was screaming and she didn't think she was going to stop for a long time. This evening that had been picture-perfect had shattered into a million little pieces. Pieces that cut deeper than she would have thought they could. And hurt so badly she didn't feel like she was going to recover.

But she'd deal with that later. She just wanted to

keep it together until she could get away and be by herself so she could lick her wounds in private.

Once again she'd fallen for an illusion. Something she knew didn't exist for her. She wasn't one of those women who was meant to have a stable, happy future. She was meant to live one day at time.

"Bella? What's the matter, honey?"

She glanced up at him and realized that he meant this to be in both of their best interests.

She took a deep breath and fought to find the words she needed. "Why do you still want a contract?"

"It's the only way to make sure we're both protected. I know that you need financial security and I need…"

"What do you need?"

He shrugged and looked away from her.

"Jeremy, I don't want to be your mistress anymore."

"Is it that you doubt the business I can generate for you? I can add an addendum that guarantees at least a million dollars a year in new business for the length of the contract."

She shook her head and got to her feet. "I think you should take me home."

"Not yet. Talk to me, Bella. I'm willing to sweeten the deal."

Was he really? Was he just afraid to admit he cared for her without knowing where she stood? For a minute she stood there, undecided, afraid to take a chance. But then she remembered that life was precarious and changed on a dime. And this might really be her only chance at love.

"I don't want you for your contacts or the amount of business you can generate. I want you for you."

He frowned at her and rubbed the back of his neck. Crossing to the bar he poured himself a shot of whiskey and downed it in one gulp.

"Jeremy, don't you feel anything for me?"

"Obsession," he said, the one word bit out between drinks as he refilled his glass again.

His earlier words circled in her mind. She'd thought he was joking, but saw now that he viewed her as something unhealthy for him and his life. Less than worthy, she thought. Still not worthy of someone in that social set.

"You're an obsession for me, Bella. This is the only way I know how to control our relationship. I have to know the parameters."

"Why would you want that? We could have a really great relationship. The kind that most people only dream of. Why can't you see that?"

"These last six months haven't been realistic," he said. "We have the illusion of a relationship. Because we both know that it can't end until the contract runs out."

She couldn't believe what she was hearing. "Do you really think that what I feel for you is some by-product of the contract?"

He shrugged. "I don't want to analyze it too closely. Whatever you feel for me...whatever you tell yourself, that's all immaterial to the contract. I think we've both proven that we're trustworthy."

She felt tears stinging her eyes and this time had no anger to assuage them. She tried to say something else, but her mouth trembled and she couldn't make herself talk.

She'd thought she'd been hurt in all the ways a person could be. That her heart had been thoroughly broken. But until this minute, when she stood in front of the man she'd given her heart to and heard him describe her as contractually trustworthy, she realized she hadn't known how deeply love could hurt.

"I can't believe I fell in love with you."

"You aren't really in love with me," he said. "It's obsession, honey."

"I think I know the difference between love and obsession, Jeremy."

He didn't say anything else and finally she couldn't stand the silence between them for another second. "Please take me back to shore. I want to go home."

Twelve

Bella ignored the phone and her friends and concentrated only on business. But at the end of two weeks, even though she was utterly exhausted, she still couldn't sleep through the night. She'd gotten used to Jeremy's presence in her bed and in her life, and she missed him.

Even though he was a huge jackass with some stupid ideas about her and their relationship, she still missed him. That really ticked her off because it made her feel like an idiot. But in the middle of the night, when she stared out her window at the waning moon, she couldn't help but remember their last night together and how perfect it had been. Until he'd brought out the contract.

Her lack of sleep made her cranky at the office. Randall and Shelley had insisted she go home early. So here she was in the middle of the afternoon, sitting on her porch on the glider, Jack Johnson playing on her iPod and a cup of blueberry tea at her side.

She was putting together a bid for another event at the Norton and wanted to double-check the images from the last event. She absolutely refused to think of Chihuly glass ceilings or the exquisite sculpture that was now in her backyard.

She uploaded a batch of pictures from her digital camera, forgetting that she'd used it the night of Jeremy's thirty-fifth birthday until the images starting popping up on her computer screen.

She stared at them. At him. At the picture she'd snapped of him with Kell, both men looking intense and serious just standing in a corner talking.

"Jeremy," she said, hearing the heartache in her own voice.

She cropped the picture down so that it was just him. Soon his face filled her screen and she traced his eyebrows and the sun lines around his eyes. God, she missed him.

Maybe she should go back to him. Swallow her pride and say yes to his contract. Except she knew she could never be happy as his mistress. She wanted to be his wife. That was the truth of it.

She wished she'd had a friend who could have

offered her a bit of advice at the beginning of the
original mistress contract—*don't fall in love*.

"Too late."

Lucinda had called her twice. Each time the
messages had been short and to the point, just saying that she was there for Bella.

Her doorbell rang and she minimized the screen
she'd been working on, setting her computer on the
glider seat before going to answer the door.

She checked the peephole first and scowled as
she recognized Kell. She opened the door and he
frowned at her and then cursed under his breath.

"You look like hell."

"Uh, thanks." She pulled the jacket of her sweat
suit closer together before crossing her arms over her
chest. Randall and Shelley had pretty much said the
same thing when they'd sent her home this afternoon.

"Damn, this is a mess. I thought I had everything figured out but I think I'm missing something here," Kell said, running his hand through his
thick blond hair.

"What are you talking about? It's really too early
in the day for you to be drunk."

"I don't drink. Listen, can I come in?" he asked,
taking a step toward her before she could even move.

"Sure."

She wanted to pretend he was the last person she
wanted to talk to but the truth was she was starved
for news on how Jeremy was doing. She had even

tried to delicately pump her brother for information, but Dare hadn't heard from Jeremy, either.

She led the way into her house, stopping in the middle of the living room. "What's up?"

He paced around the room like a caged tiger. There was a grim set to his mouth. "That's what I want to know."

"What did Jeremy tell you?" she asked, knowing that no one was going to be able to help them. Over the sleepless nights she'd spent alone in her bed, she'd rehashed everything a million times. She knew she couldn't force Jeremy to love her, and she didn't want to be with him without love.

"Nothing. He hasn't said a word about you in two weeks. All he does is work."

She shook her head. She wished he was getting on with his life, but by the same token a part of her was happy to hear she wasn't the only one suffering. It made her believe that maybe he had cared for her. "I'm sorry to hear that. I don't think it has anything to do with me."

"It has everything to do with you. It's clear to me that you two have had a fight. Whatever it was about, you need to go to him and fix it."

"It's not that easy."

"Yes, it is. No problems are that insurmountable."

"Some of them are, Kell. This isn't just a fight or a difference of opinion. We want different things from life."

Kell sighed. "I pushed him to offer you a prenup. Don't hold that against him."

"It wasn't that. I would sign one if he asked me to."

"Then what is it? He's so into you."

"He's not into me. At least not the way you mean. I'm an obsession that he's trying to exorcise from his soul."

"He said that?"

"Yes, he did. And I don't know how to convince him otherwise. I'm not sure what you want from me, but I can't just go back to him and pretend to be whatever he wants until he gets tired of me."

Kell stared at her for a long time. "Because you love him."

She nodded.

Kell paced over to the front door and opened it. Glancing back at her, he said, "Just think about talking to him."

She nodded and watched him leave, knowing that she'd think of little else other than Jeremy.

Jeremy watched the sunset from his multimillion-dollar home. He glanced around at the luxury furnishings and the life that was full of the best things money could buy. But it felt empty. It felt the way it had before he'd met Isabella McNamara and his life had changed.

Obsessions had a way of doing that.

But the thing was, he no longer believed she was only an obsession. Her words that last night on his boat haunted him. A million times he replayed them. Heard her say she loved him and then quietly ask to go home.

He'd broken her heart and he had no idea how to fix it. For a while he hadn't even contemplated fixing it. He'd wanted to find another woman and prove to Bella exactly how desirable he was to other females. But he'd been disinterested in any other woman.

Then this last week he'd realized how much she'd brought to his life. Not just her presence in his bed, but the way she'd brought his circle of friends together with hers. The effortless way she had of making connections between people and ensuring no one felt inferior.

The way she had long ago. And he'd offered her a contract to stay in his life. In retrospect, he understood perfectly where he'd gone wrong.

His gut said to go back to her and make another offer. One where she set the terms and he'd do whatever she wanted. Be her love slave or whatever else she'd have from him.

But another part, a bigger part, was truly afraid of what she made him feel. He'd hurt this past week in a way that he'd never felt before. His life had been a gilded one of privilege where no one denied him anything.

Until Isabella. His Bella. He wanted her back. He wanted her happy.

There was a knock on his study door before it opened. He glanced over his shoulder to see his butler standing in the doorway. "Are you receiving, sir?"

"Who is it, Thomas?" he asked, hoping against hope that it would be Bella. If she came to him, he'd take her back and throw out the contract.

"Kell, sir."

The last thing he wanted to do was talk to Kell, who kept trying to take the blame for his breakup by pointing out that some women found prenups offensive. If only he'd offered her a prenup, he had the feeling she would have signed it with no qualms. God, he'd been a total ass.

And Bella wasn't going to come back. She deserved a man who loved her the way she loved him.

She loved *him*. That's what she said. What if she'd been mistaken?

"Sir?"

He rubbed the back of his neck and glanced around the study. His desk was littered with files and he'd closed more deals this week than he had in the previous three months. He'd been working nonstop, jacked up on coffee and adrenaline. Afraid to close his eyes because he dreamed of her in his bed and woke aching and hungry for her.

"Yes, send him back."

Jeremy logged on to his e-mail while he was

waiting for Kell and saw that he had a message from Bella. Before he could open it, Kell came into the room and headed straight to the bar, grabbing a bottle of Perrier. "What the hell did you say to Bella?"

"Why?" he asked, distracted from her message for a moment by his cousin. Damn, he should have refused to see Kell—then he could have read her message in private.

"Because I went to see her to apologize for putting you up to asking for the prenup and…"

"And what?" He was surprised by Kell's actions, but he shouldn't have been. Kell had spent the last week telling him that just because he'd screwed up by trusting the wrong woman, Jeremy shouldn't screw up by not trusting the right woman.

"She looked like hell. I don't think she's slept in a week."

Dammit, he thought. He'd wanted to be her hero and to protect her. Instead he'd left her and she was worse off for having known him. "Leave it alone, Kell. I told you to stay away from her."

Kell didn't respond to that, just scooped some ice from the ice bucket and poured his Perrier into a glass. "You're miserable, too."

"And your point is?" he asked, trying not to look at his Outlook inbox, but failing. Why had she e-mailed him?

"You've never been stupid about anything. Not women, not business. Don't let her be the first."

"Why is this so important to you?"

"I want to believe that you and I can be happy."

"I'll take that under consideration," he said, glancing at his computer screen again.

"What's so important on your computer?"

"Bella sent me a message."

"Did you open it?"

"No, I'm waiting for you to leave."

"Are you sure you don't need me?"

He nodded. Kell walked toward the door. "I'll call you tomorrow."

Jeremy watched him go before finally clicking on the icon to open the e-mail message. It was brief and to the point. No smiley face after her name. Just a listing of JPEG file names.

Pictures from his birthday party. He opened them up one by one and felt like he'd been punched in the gut. In front of him in full color was the life he'd been afraid to imagine for himself and Bella. A life that was full of friends and family. One that they shared together.

And he knew then that there was a small chance that she still loved him. A woman who'd go through all this effort for her lover wasn't someone who could walk away easily. And he remembered other things she'd said that last night. Remembered that she, too, wanted a life together. Just not as his mistress.

Finally he got it.

He pushed away from his desk, grabbed his keys and walked out of his house. He didn't realize he was running until he reached his car.

The knock on her door just after dinner startled her. But a part of her had been hoping, ever since she'd e-mailed the pictures, that Jeremy would come. She was almost afraid to look in the peephole and see someone other than him.

But there he was. Wearing a pair of faded jeans and a faded college T-shirt. His hair was unkempt and he scarcely resembled the fashionable man she knew him to be.

She opened the door and stared at him. He didn't say anything to her, either. He shifted from one foot to the other.

"I got your e-mail."

"Oh. Did you like the pictures?"

"Yes. They turned out really nice," he said.

God, had he really come over here just to thank her for the pictures?

"I don't have any other ones."

"That's okay. Thanks for the ones you sent."

"You're welcome," she said, waiting for him to say something else, but minutes dragged by and he said nothing. Finally she realized that he wasn't going to say anything and a part of her was ready to beg him to take her back. But then she remembered how hard she'd struggled to rebuild her life. And she knew she couldn't. He had to meet her halfway.

"Goodbye, Jeremy," she said, starting to close the door.

His hand shot out and he blocked the door from closing. "Can I come in?"

"Why? To talk more about the photos?"

"No," he said, thrusting his hands through his hair. "I didn't come over here because of the pictures. I'm here because I'm an idiot."

"No, you're not."

"Yes, I am," he said, stepping over the threshold and closing the door behind him. "I want you in my life. I can't live without you."

"I want those things, too, but I don't want to be your mistress."

"I don't want that, either, not anymore. I was afraid to admit how much I need you, but that doesn't change the fact that I do need you, Bella. I'm asking you to take me back on your terms. I don't have a contract or gifts. I don't have anything except myself."

"Someone once told me that the best gift was one of yourself."

"A wise man."

She was almost afraid to hope that he meant what he said. "What if I said my terms were marriage and a family?"

"That offer would be more than I deserve," he said, drawing her into his arms and holding her so tightly she knew he'd never let go. "But I'd say yes before you changed your mind."

"I'm not going to change my mind."

"That's good." He buried his face against her neck. "I love you, Bella."

"I love you, too."

He lifted her in his arms and carried her into her bedroom. He made love to her and then cradled her to his chest. They talked about the future and made plans. Permanent plans. Plans for their life together.

* * * * *

*Be sure to read the next sensual romance
in Katherine Garbera's*
THE MISTRESSES!
High-Society Mistress *will be available
in August 2008.*

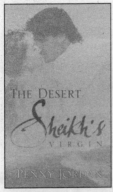

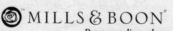

Celebrate 100 years of pure reading pleasure with Mills & Boon®

To mark our centenary, each month we're publishing a special 100th Birthday Edition. These celebratory editions are packed with extra features and include a FREE bonus story.

Plus, you have the chance to enter a fabulous monthly prize draw. See 100th Birthday Edition books for details.

Now that's worth celebrating!

July 2008

The Man Who Had Everything
by Christine Rimmer
Includes FREE bonus story *Marrying Molly*

August 2008

Their Miracle Baby by Caroline Anderson
Includes FREE bonus story *Making Memories*

September 2008

Crazy About Her Spanish Boss by Rebecca Winters
Includes FREE bonus story
Rafael's Convenient Proposal

Look for Mills & Boon® 100th Birthday Editions at your favourite bookseller or visit www.millsandboon.co.uk

2 FREE

BOOKS AND A SURPRISE GIFT!

We would like to take this opportunity to thank you for reading this Mills & Boon® book by offering you the chance to take TWO more specially selected titles from the Desire™ series absolutely FREE! We're also making this offer to introduce you to the benefits of the Mills & Boon® Reader Service™—

- ★ **FREE home delivery**
- ★ **FREE gifts and competitions**
- ★ **FREE monthly Newsletter**
- ★ **Exclusive Reader Service offers**
- ★ **Books available before they're in the shops**

Accepting these FREE books and gift places you under no obligation to buy, you may cancel at any time, even after receiving your free shipment. Simply complete your details below and return the entire page to the address below. You don't even need a stamp!

YES! Please send me 2 free Desire volumes and a surprise gift. I understand that unless you hear from me, I will receive 3 superb new titles every month for just £4.99 each, postage and packing free. I am under no obligation to purchase any books and may cancel my subscription at any time. The free books and gift will be mine to keep in any case.

D8ZED

Ms/Mrs/Miss/Mr ....Initials ....
BLOCK CAPITALS PLEASE

Surname ....

Address ....

....

....Postcode..

Send this whole page to:
UK: FREEPOST CN81, Croydon, CR9 3WZ